'TIS THE

Season for Secrets

'Tis The Season For Secrets
KATE CALLAGHAN

Edited By: Emma O' Connell
Cover By: Pru Schuyler

ISBN: 9781916684058
ISBN:9781916684041

www.katecallaghanauthor.com

KATE CALLAGHAN

Tis the Season for Secrets

Gifted an old family chest, aspiring editor Juliet Frost stumbles upon closely guarded family secrets... and her tranquil holiday season transforms into a whimsical circus of revelations. For starters, how is she supposed to process the fact that she is the outcome of a forbidden love affair – let alone that she has connections to some kind of magical Christmas village called Yule?

To complicate matters, the mysterious Will Duncan, whom she never thought she'd see again after a night of passion, reappears with the answers she seeks about her past. It swiftly becomes clear that he has plenty of secrets of his own. Is their chance meeting fate, or the result of a carefully laid plot? Juliet will have to battle her heart and her head to discover who she is... and where she truly belongs.

Read Me

Other Books By The Author

Young Adult Dark Fantasy | A Hellish Fairytale Series
Crowned A Traitor I
Where Traitors Fall II
When Traitors Rise III

Towerwood | Novella
Stepmother | Novella

Village of Yule | Stand-Alone Series
The Naughty Or Nice Clause
Tis The Season For Secrets
How My Ex Stole New Years

Village of FoxFord | Stand-Alone Series
Potions & Proposals
Don't Go Baking My Heart

Romantic Suspense | Stand-Alone Series
Ms Perfectly Fine
Not Another Rockstar
The Situation Ship

Juliet & Will's Playlist

The Night We Met |Lord Huron
Red Dress | Nova Miller
Singularity | BTS
Treacherous | Taylor Swift
Shameless | Camila Cabello
Kissin' In The Cold | Julia Michaels
Gold Rush | Taylor Swift
Under The Tree | Sam Palladio

Scan Me

Glossary

Technically, you don't have to read The Naughty or Nice Clause to enjoy Juliet & Will's story. However, here's a cheat sheet for the few bits you missed or need to be reminded of since we last ventured to Yule.

Yule/North Pole: A magical village set in a protected area of the North Pole.

Gold Bells: Ringing the bell causes the ringer to be magically transported to Yule. Only those who believe in Christmas will be able to use it.

Guardians of Yule: Those who help citizens of Yule live away from the village and adjust to the outside world, should they wish to leave Yule. They also make sure the secrecy of Yule is protected and maintained at all costs.

Council of Yule: The oldest families of Yule help run the village. The Klaus family are the most powerful, as the eldest son, Mason Klaus, is the current Santa Klaus.

KATE CALLAGHAN

For those who've had their heart broken by those who were meant to protect it most.

KNOCK! KNOCK! KNOCK!

"A moment of peace! Is that too much to ask for?" Juliet groaned, placing a rather lacking manuscript on her mint couch. Ms Baum, her boss, was expecting a full report by Monday on whether it was worthy of the slush pile or publishing. Not that what Juliet wrote in her reports mattered, because Ms Baum always insisted on double-checking herself.

KNOCK! KNOCK! KNOCK!

"Coming!" Juliet figured that Margot, her roommate, must have forgotten her keys. Just in case, she pulled her favourite Supernatural hoodie over her grey sweatpants. Not that she'd worked out today, or intended to; reading in jeans in the comfort of her small apartment just felt like a sin.

Across the small lilac living room, she caught her reflection in the long mirror by the door. She winced at the sight of her frizzed-out hair and the dark circles beneath her brown eyes. At least her hair looked somewhat deliberately styled, twisted up in a claw clip. The messy look drew attention to the honey and copper highlights in her dark brown hair that she was impatiently waiting to grow out.

Looking through the peephole, Juliet released the door

chain when she saw the courier waiting in the hallway. *Baum must have messengered over more manuscripts.*

It wouldn't be the first time she'd sent someone after eight pm, or on a Saturday. Ms Baum wanted to get through as many books as possible before Harley & Rowe Publishing House went on Christmas break. Juliet also suspected her boss was punishing her for applying for the new junior editor position in the Young Adult department.

"Miss Frost?" the courier asked, revealing a wide toothy grin.

"That's me." Juliet smiled politely, reaching out for the box, but paused when she saw there was no Harley & Rowe stamp. "There must be some mistake. I didn't order anything?" She tried to recall if she was guilty of any late-night book orders, but she'd imposed a book-buying ban on herself until she read the ones stacked on either side of her bed. Between Margot's obsession with clothes and Juliet's books, they'd be accused of hoarding soon.

"Juliet Frost, Apt 13, Willow Drive?" The courier frowned, pulling out an invoice. He handed her the carbon copy. Under 'specific instruction', it read:

> To be delivered directly to Juliet Frost on the 2nd of December, following the death of my husband, Mr Reginald Frost.

A water stain on the paper had dulled the ink, but Juliet still recognised her nana's handwriting and signature. *This can't be right... unless Nana is sending me parcels from beyond the grave? Why wouldn't she give this to me before she died, and why did it have to be sent after Grandfather's death?* Still, to receive anything from her, especially around the holidays, felt like a gift from heaven.

"Can you sign?"

The courier's impatient tone snapped her back to reality. Juliet initialled the delivery slip, noting the company name on the man's uniform in case she needed any further information. *Stanley Couriers?* Frost Industries, the mining company her family had run for generations, had its own couriers and safety deposit boxes.

Why would Nana Rose use a private company? she wondered, taking the box from his arms. She nearly dropped it – she hadn't expected it to be so heavy.

"Do you have any more information about this? Did Mrs Frost leave any other instructions?"

"I'm sorry, but I only go where the packages take me. The only clause was that it was to be delivered on this exact date, and not to be signed over to anyone but you."

The courier headed for the stairs – the elevator in their building hadn't been operational for years – before Juliet had a chance to ask any more questions. She closed the door with her foot and placed the heavy package on the round white coffee table in the middle of their tiny kitchen.

She couldn't stop staring at the box. After she'd been left on her father's doorstep at the Frost estate twenty-six years ago by a mother she'd never known, Nana Rose had been the only member of the family to show her any kindness, while her Grandfather Reginald had done everything in his power to avoid her.

Adding that she didn't want me to receive the parcel until after Grandfather's death means Nana really wanted to make sure he didn't find out. He'd died during the summer, so she couldn't exactly ask him what his wife had been up to before she'd passed. *Even if he was alive, he wouldn't give me any answers. He was furious when Nana secretly paid for my college tuition, so I doubt he'd be pleased that she's sent me some sort of secret package.*

The mystery baffled her as she warmed her hands with a cup of black coffee. *Maybe this is some sort of secret inheritance that she didn't want to include in her will?*

Gathering her courage, Juliet grabbed a knife from the drawer to slice through the thick tape. The sweet smells of wood and cinnamon filled her senses as she opened the box. Beneath the many packaging peanuts, she found a small wooden chest.

She ran her fingertips over the F carved into the lid. Carefully lifting out the antique chest, she marvelled at the delicately carved snowflakes decorating the lid and the clasp – a golden snowflake.

Could this have been Nana's? Once Juliet had left the estate to study English Lit, she'd only returned a handful of times to visit her younger half-sister, Beth, and for Nana's funeral in July. Grandfather Reginald had died the following August, and Juliet was still haunted by her stepmother's comments when she'd failed to return home for *his* funeral. How she'd humiliated the family who'd taken her in, blah, blah, shame and disgrace. Juliet had argued that her absence was her parting gift to Reginald – something he'd longed for when he was alive. Her decision not to attend had been proved right when dear ol' Reginald excluded her entirely from his will, while Beth received money, property and shares in Frost Industries. Juliet hadn't wanted anything from him, but the lack of recognition as a member of the Frost family stung.

Juliet shivered, wondering if it was the cold winter's night or the memories chilling her to the bone. Either way, she turned up the heating as she noticed the frost gathering on the window looking over the bright lights of New York. She didn't want Margot to get home and complain about the chill. Juliet didn't feel the cold much, whereas Margot liked to keep the apartment at tropical temperatures.

Glancing at the cloud-shaped kitchen clock, she realised Margot would be back soon from her client dinner. She'd better open it quickly if she wanted to get any answers to all her questions.

Popping open the clasp, she found a gold necklace with a golden bell charm sitting atop some letters wrapped in red ribbon. Picking up the thin gold chain, she examined it. She'd never seen anything so dainty and ornate; on the clasp, their family name, Frost, was engraved. *An old heirloom?* Her heart ached, remembering how much Nana Rose had loved the holidays, but she couldn't recall her nana ever wearing such a necklace.

She shook the bell. There was no chime, but the tiny golden swirls etched into the metal caught the light, shining like new. Gently, she set the necklace down on the table, noticing an inscription on the inside of the chest's lid.

To Find Your Way Home

Juliet thought all the family heirlooms had been left to her father or the Frost estate in her grandparents' will. She pulled out a chair, needing to sit. *Maybe this is a secret inheritance Nana put together without the rest of the family's knowledge?* It wouldn't be the first time her nana had gone out of her way to make her feel like she was a part of the family – unlike her grandfather, who'd simply wished for Juliet, the stain on the Frost name and evidence of their son's youthful mistake, to disappear. Her father had been attentive, but only to mould her into the perfect eldest daughter of the Frost family. A darling of society – a society which she'd fled as soon as she turned eighteen.

Juliet chewed her lower lip, nervous, as she picked up the bundle of letters. She couldn't undo the knot in her stomach, so she decided to unknot the ribbon instead and do what she did best: read.

Dear Juliet,

My darling granddaughter, I'm sorry I couldn't give this to you in person and explain its contents. This chest was entrusted to me by your mother, to be passed on to you only after the passing of your grandfather. I'm afraid that in keeping my promise to your mother, I've had to keep you in the dark. There are many elements of our family's past and your own story that have been kept from you, for both your own safety and that of others. However, the time has come for you to learn the truth.

Having watched you grow into such a thoughtful, kind and honest woman that I'm proud to call my granddaughter, I feel you should be allowed to make your own decision and find where you truly belong. I hope you can forgive me – us – for what we've kept from you over the years. Please keep your mind and your heart open, and I promise you'll find the home you've always deserved. One I'm afraid that we failed to give you—

At the sound of a key turning in the lock, Juliet scrambled to put the pages back inside the chest and bundle it to her bedroom. She'd only just managed to shove the chest under her bed, amongst the many books, when she heard the clang of Margot dropping her keys in the bowl in the hallway that separated their rooms.

"Have you moved since I left?" Margot stood by her bedroom door, so wrapped up in a chunky pink scarf and hat that Juliet could hardly see her face as she kicked off her mini woolly boots.

"Yes. I went from the couch to my bed. Baum wants me to go through what remains of the slush pile before the holidays." Juliet hated lying, but she wasn't ready to tell her friend about the chest until she discovered what Nana Rose wanted to confess.

"This was in our post box." Margot reached into her coat pocket. "You should switch everything to email."

"Some of us like post. Not everyone is as obsessed with computers as you are." Juliet was always intimidated by the complicated-looking code Margot was always tapping out on her desktop that took up most of their sitting room. Plus, she'd seen Margot hack her way into one too many computers to ever feel safe online.

"Nice deflection." Margot handed her a red envelope and shrugged off her coat.

On reflex, Juliet tossed the red envelope into the bright orange bin by her bed.

"You aren't going to read it?" Margot frowned, running her hands through her bleached white-blond hair, which the hat had stuck to her head.

"Don't need to. It's another invitation from socialite hell to attend some festive event or another. Dad loves giving out my address, hoping I'll give in and attend. If I don't read the invitation, then I've got plausible deniability." Juliet wanted to spend this festive season in the city with their tiny Christmas tree, safely tucked away from her father's schemes.

Margot's sad smile told her she understood the logic. As Juliet's roommate throughout college, she'd witnessed many late-night screaming matches as her father tried to control her life. When Juliet had stopped answering the calls, her stepmother, Gillian, had turned up on their doorstep with crocodile tears about how she was 'hurting the family'.

"I'm in awe of your avoidance skills, but you could always use the connections to your own advantage." Margot headed into her bedroom, where Juliet could hear her rifling through her wardrobe. "Speaking of which, the client meeting went well, and I got an invite of my own for the evening!" Margot had mastered working a crowd in college, while Juliet preferred the library.

"What I need is a killer manuscript to give Baum to secure my promotion! Would this be a date? Because I thought you didn't date your clients."

Margot reappeared in her doorway in a purple sequinned midi dress and matching heels, which made her long legs look never-ending. Her tall stature fit her personality to a T: she never let anyone look down on her.

"Not a date! I don't mix money and pleasure," she insisted, touching up her make-up at Juliet's dresser.

"If it's not a date, then where is this Saturday night taking you?" Juliet asked, wanting to move the conversation away from her life.

"Taking *us*." Margot beamed. "My new client – a sleazy high-profile banker who, by the way, thinks deleting his browser history will protect him from his wife's prying eyes – invited me, us, to an exclusive Christmas party at the Bryce Hotel. Champagne, city lights, and plenty of clients for me to sign. Grab your jacket, I need a wingwoman." Margot danced around the room, hips swaying as she grabbed a short red dress from Juliet's wardrobe and threw it at her.

"Did you not see the stack of manuscripts on the couch in the sitting room? I can't go out tonight!" Juliet looked outside her frosted window, refusing to give up her cozy blankets for frostbite.

"Please, please, please! I need some new and less morally

repugnant clients to take on staff in the new year." Margot gave Juliet her biggest puppy-dog eyes.

"And I've got to finish this pile by Monday, or Baum will refuse to promote me," Juliet argued half-heartedly. An evening out *was* long overdue.

"You work harder than anyone. That promotion is yours." Margot grabbed her arms and hauled her off the bed.

"That's not true. I'm taking an extra week off this Christmas!"

Before she could protest further, the strappy red mini dress was thrust into her arms.

"That's only because you had mandatory vacation days left over. You even took Baum's dog to the groomers last weekend. Is the promotion worth all this?"

"Yes. I've put in *five years* as her assistant. You don't understand, because you own your own company – you can promote yourself." Juliet loved her job; spending all day every day with books was her dream. Nearly all her happiest memories involved books. The only part that made it feel like a job was Ms Baum breathing down her neck. Margot, on the other hand, had set up her own tech-based private investigator firm. Juliet liked to tease her that she made her money working off the books for some secret government agency. Margot always rolled her eyes and told her not to read so many spy novels.

"How about I promote you to bestest best friend if you come with me? You can consider it an early Christmas present to me."

Juliet caved, knowing Margot wouldn't take no for an answer. "Okay, I'll come with you! But I can't stay out too late."

Margot squeezed her tightly, before leaving to let her get ready. The red dress was either a little shorter or her butt was a little bigger since she'd worn it to last year's Christmas work party, but it hugged her figure to perfection. Juliet waved her poker-straight hair and prayed the hairspray would stop it from turning into a frizzy mess once they stepped outside into the sleet and snow.

Margot reappeared, changing her studs for some gold hoops from Juliet's dresser. They shared everything. Juliet dreaded the day one of them moved out; at this point there was no way of telling what belonged to whom. "Also, please remember that you've already found two bestselling authors for Ms Baum. If that doesn't convince her to promote you, nothing will. I'm sure other publishing houses would love to hire you."

"I've put in too much work to go somewhere else. I must believe that good things come to those who wait. One more week, and that position is mine." Juliet finished her makeup with winged liner and a red lip to match her dress. Heading to the kitchen, she put her debit card in her clutch. "Once I find my heels, we can go." She darted down the hall to their overflowing shoe cupboard and fished out some chunky black satin heels. "Found them!"

"The taxi is downstairs," Margot muttered, taking a careful bite out of some toast so she wouldn't smudge her lipstick. "I've put your keys in your clutch." Margot confirmed, pulling on her thigh high boots.

Meeting Margot by the door, Juliet felt a moment of regret as she saw the manuscripts on the couch. *I've got all of tomorrow to finish them. A few hours of fun can't hurt,* she reasoned. Locking the door behind them, she tried to get into the party spirit, deciding to forget about work and the mystery chest under her bed.

The taxi's dashboard read 10:45pm as they pulled up to Bryce Hotel. After paying, Juliet and Margot darted out of the sleet and into the plush, five-star hotel's glittering lobby. A few guests at reception looked them over questioningly; they were wearing much less than anyone else, even with coats.

"We should've had a drink before we left to warm up," Juliet said, breathing into her cold hands as they passed a cosy yet crowded bar just off the lobby. What she really wanted was something to settle her nerves. Social anxiety had been Juliet's lifelong companion: a side-effect of being the illegitimate daughter of the Frost family, and the years of gossip and judgement that came with it. Margot had been her saving grace – *she* didn't care about Juliet's last name. Margot liked to use society to her advantage, but let very few people into her life. A trait they shared.

"I know, my fingertips are blue. I can't wait for summer," Margot groaned. "Bikinis and the beach are much more to my liking."

In the elevator, Juliet's heart started to pound as Margot started listing off all the important people who'd be attending. However, there was no turning back as the reflective copper doors opened onto the top floor with a loud ping.

They were walking down the carpet-to-ceiling cream corridor when Juliet's phone vibrated in her tiny purse. The two suited security guards posted outside the party shot her a warning glance. Clearly, phones weren't welcome at this exclusive event. The Bryce Hotel's golden stag logo embroidered on their jackets told her they were hotel security, not just hired by those throwing the party.

"Oh no you don't." Margot peered over her shoulder at the phone. "You can't bail out now."

"I'm not going anywhere. I'm just going to read the message to make sure it's nothing important." Juliet moved down the hall and away from the guards' heavy stares.

> Baum: URGENT MANUSCRIPT
> COLLECTION. Hugo didn't send in his draft
> last night as promised, and it's already a
> week past his deadline. If we're to publish his
> biography by next Christmas, we need that
> draft NOW! Have it on my desk by tomorrow
> morning, so I can prep for the editor meeting
> Monday. If successful, we can discuss your
> promotion. He's hosting a Christmas party
> tonight before he heads to London, and we
> CAN'T miss this opportunity. Bryce Hotel,
> Suite 4.

Juliet stared at the text in disbelief. *Baum knows dangling my promotion at the end of an impossible task would lure me into the office on a Sunday. There's no way I can turn down this chance to get out of the non-fiction department,* she thought, trying to figure out how the hell she was going to pull this off. Harley & Rowe had been trying to get Hugo's book deal secured for the last two years. Another reformed rockstar (just Hugo, no last name required) telling his trainwreck-to-sober journey to repair his tattered reputation. *Hopefully, being in the Christmas spirit will inspire Hugo to hand over his pages. That's assuming he even has them. Of course, Baum assumes I don't have plans... not that I wouldn't have dropped everything for a chance to get an inch closer to my dream job.* Well, now she had to find some other swanky Christmas party to attend. Luckily, she was all dressed up already.

Then it hit her. Her head snapped to the number on the hotel door behind her. It read **Suite 4.**

What are the chances?! At least I don't have to bail on Margot. She glanced at her friend, who was busy charming the security guards into letting them keep their phones, as they'd been invited on business and couldn't possibly work without them. Juliet quickly tapped out a reply to Ms Baum while Margot negotiated. Not that it was proving difficult; the guard with a questionable eyebrow piercing and tattooed hands was looking at Margot like he would give her a kidney if she asked.

Juliet: Consider it done.

"All done, and as promised, I'm staying," she said, snapping her clutch closed with her phone tucked safely inside.

"Are you serious? I thought if Baum was texting you this late it would be an emergency?" Margot asked quietly.

"An emergency of sorts," Juliet agreed. "Baum wants me to pick up a manuscript from Hugo – who just so happens to be throwing this party."

"Whaat?! No way! You totally owe me for dragging you out here, then. In that dress, Hugo won't be able to say no to you." Margot whispered.

"Ew," Juliet shuddered, "don't even joke. He is over twice my age."

The men, who hadn't smiled once, opened the door for them. The night had only just begun, yet the party was in full swing. An oversized flatscreen played Hugo's music videos on repeat at a volume that made conversation a struggle. She wasn't surprised, given his legendary ego.

"Funny how you don't seem surprised. Did you arrange this somehow?" Juliet asked quietly as they walked to the champagne bar, receiving welcoming nods and a few stares. "It's quite the coincidence that you received an invitation to such an exclusive party the same night I'd have to find my way in."

Margot suddenly seemed far more interested in the décor of the suite. Every expensively designed corner was littered with ashtrays overflowing with cigarette stubs and lipstick-stained champagne flutes.

"How could I? I can't read Baum's mind, and I'd never want to," she scoffed, still looking away.

Juliet grabbed two full flutes from the bar and handed her one so she'd be forced to meet her gaze.

"Stop staring at me! You're making me nervous." Margot sipped her champagne, scanning the room for potential clients. Her evasion told Juliet exactly what she needed to know.

"You hacked Baum's email again! After the interview incident, I told you not to do that again," Juliet gasped. She'd be fired if they were caught.

"It was only her work email." Margot rolled her eyes. "I didn't see anything personal. Anyway, that time was an emergency. You wouldn't leave the apartment or change out of your pyjamas because she was making you sweat about whether you got the assistant position." Margot sipped her champagne.

"I haven't been reduced to staying in my pyjamas this time. Why now?"

"I should've told you before I did it," Margot admitted,

"but Baum's been overworking you for months, using this promotion as an excuse. I got pissed off when it seemed like she kept moving the goalposts, so I thought I'd just… check in. One small line of code, and I saw that the uppers at Harley & Rowe were giving her a hard time about failing to get Hugo's manuscript, when they'd already paid his insane advance. What I didn't expect to find was that Baum told her boss she'd entrusted the collection to you, as a test of whether you were up to muster! I wasn't going to let her throw you under the bus. I figured if you turned up on Monday with the manuscript then she'd *have* to promote you, and then you could get away from her once and for all." Margot's cheeks flushed angrily, and she hugged her friend.

"Thank you for looking out for me," Juliet said. "If you hadn't, I'd be at home, blindsided." She wasn't surprised Ms Baum had passed the buck to her. She would've welcomed the challenge, had she been given the task in time, but the last-minute text confirmed that her mentor didn't want her to succeed.

"You're welcome," Margot sighed.

"But please don't break the law for my sake. I can't afford our apartment by myself if you get arrested – again!" Juliet teased.

Margot nudged her off. "I was only arrested once, and you don't have to worry. My brothers will always bail me out." She clinked their glasses, never afraid of getting into trouble.

"And I didn't do it entirely for you. I figured if I could get us into one of the most exclusive Christmas parties of the year, then you could secure your promotion and I could sign a client or two. A win-win for both of us."

Their conversation was interrupted by a hulking man in a too-tight suit, who turned out to be the client Juliet owed a thanks to for inviting Margot. Leaving Juliet, they disappeared to the balcony to discuss private business.

"Here so soon?" The speaker was shrouded in a puff of vapour.

Juliet frowned, fanning strawberry-scented clouds away from her face. Hugo's excessively white smile greeted her through the mist. She'd only met him once at the office, when he'd first signed on with Harley & Rowe. She was surprised he recognised her.

"I should've known Baum would send someone to do her dirty work, but I won't allow any business tonight." He placed a sickly warm hand on her shoulder.

Juliet shrugged away, never wanting to get too close to clients, especially not when there were so many eyes on them. "I won't say a word about business." She smiled, finishing her champagne. "If you simply hand over your pages, you won't have to think any more of it, and you can spend the rest of the holidays without being hounded by us."

Hugo considered her words for a moment, and she hoped his desire to be left alone would win her some points.

"The manuscript is in my office upstairs. I insisted on having a suite with an office since I've always found New York so inspiring. I've been working on the final pages religiously since I got into town but to leave such a party even for a moment would be a travesty," he told her, rocking back and forth on the short heels of his crocodile-skin boots. She didn't need to guess where he was headed next. "Unless you came up with me." His hazy, bloodshot eyes leered at her through his long, greasy hair, and he reeked of alcohol.

So much for sobriety, she thought as his face lit up at the possibility of her being his next conquest. She glanced around the room and spotted Margot standing with two women she recognised from their ads; they ran the largest non-profit shelters for women and children in the city. She didn't want to interrupt her friend, but she needed some back-up.

"I don't think leaving together would be very appropriate," she hedged, not wanting to go anywhere alone with him. "I wouldn't want to take you away from your guests."

"I'm sure we wouldn't be missed." Hugo rested his hand on her lower back. Juliet made a mental note to burn the dress once she got home.

"Lead the way," she sighed, managing to catch Margot's concerned gaze as she followed the slimy man up the glass staircase to the second floor of the suite. "Watch your step!" she added as Hugo stumbled on the carpet and caught her arm. She steadied him before separating herself. He wasn't the first letch she'd ever dealt with.

"Can't I have your arm for support?" He mocked a sad frown.

"I'm afraid I'm not as strong as I look. In heels I can barely support myself," she joked, but that only seemed to brighten his eyes.

"Afraid I might take you down with me?"

"Why risk it?" Juliet said, clenching her jaw as she tried to put her repulsion aside. Thankfully, he walked ahead, taking the not-so-subtle hint.

They reached the office and Hugo unlocked the door, Juliet wishing she wasn't so far from the party. She felt some relief when she saw there was no way to lock the door from the inside. Hugo's satisfied groan as he collapsed into the desk chair brought her attention back to him.

"What a great space to write in," she said politely, admiring the small office. "Ms Baum is very excited to read your new pages."

"All work," Hugo sighed. "How about we have a drink and

talk about the book? I'd love to hear your thoughts before I hand it over." He licked his lips, making it clear that talking was the last thing on his mind.

"Oh, my opinion hardly matters. I'm only an assistant, and I think an editor would be much more equipped to offer a man with your success and reputation any suggestions," she told him, remaining on the far side of the desk and out of his reach.

"You shouldn't put yourself down." His eyes wandered over her body, and she wished her dress wasn't so short. "Baum wouldn't send a nobody to my door. I've got an eye for talent, and I think you're far too beautiful to be some assistant." Hugo opened a drawer and produced a bound stack of papers. "With those legs and waist, those big brown eyes – my God, it's a waste to have you stuck behind a desk."

Juliet resisted the urge to roll her eyes; what did her body or her appearance have to do with her work? She was beginning to question what she wanted more – her promotion, or to slap this pathetic excuse of a man. But when his manuscript landed with a thud on the desk, she could almost taste the promotion.

"I'm happy at Harley & Rowe." She reached for the manuscript, but he placed his hand over hers on the front page.

"How happy?" Hugo got up to walk around the desk, putting himself between her and the manuscript. "What if you left that stuffy office and wrote for me? I've got several ideas to put on paper, and I don't think one book is enough to tell the story of my life. I'd double your current salary… it never hurts to have a pretty face around to spark my creativity."

Juliet gritted her teeth, but forced a small smile. "I'm flattered, but Harley & Rowe have a number of ghost writers with far more experience who would happily work with you."

He hesitated for a moment, and she didn't dare guess what he was contemplating.

"Suit yourself," he said eventually, sliding the manuscript towards her. It felt too easy, but she reached for it, wanting to retch as his hot breath lingered on her neck. "Now that you've got your pages, how about you do something for me?"

Juliet ripped his hand away as it settled on her waist. His smile was replaced with a scowl, but the door flying open distracted them both.

"How could you do this to me?!" Margot stumbled in, acting drunk off her ass. Juliet resisted the urge to laugh as her friend grabbed Hugo's shoulders and shook him like a ragdoll. "You cheating asshole! I've been looking for you everywhere, and I find you with *her*."

Juliet used the opportunity to get away from Hugo, manuscript tucked safely under her arm.

"Who the fuck are you?" Hugo sneered, removing Margot's hand. Gone was his false charm. "Get out of my office, or I'll call security."

"Pretending you don't know who I am? You heartless pig." Margot feigned tears and reached for him, but he recoiled in disgust.

"You're fucking crazy!"

Juliet was suddenly grateful for the loud music hiding the commotion.

"Never call a woman crazy," Margot snapped, and Hugo gave a gurgle as she planted her knee in his groin. He sank to the ground, curling into a pathetic moaning ball. Juliet was amazed he even felt the blow, considering the amount of alcohol in his system.

"I thought you'd never show," Juliet whispered to Margot,

patting the manuscript pages to tell Margot she'd got what she needed before putting on false concern. "How dare you hurt him? Hugo, are you alright?"

"Call security!" he cried.

Juliet looked between them; Hugo's wide pupils pleaded with her. "I don't think you want to do that. Wouldn't this be terribly bad for your recovered reputation?" she sighed.

"She assaulted me! If you don't help me, I'll make sure you're fired!" The washed-up rockstar tried to regain his feet, but only got as far as his knees.

Juliet nodded. "You *could* have me fired, but then I'd go to the press and explain how you were trying to get into my pants by abusing your power while drunk off your ass. Harley & Rowe have a strict sexual harassment policy, and you'd be forced to pay back that sizeable advance – which I don't think you have anymore."

"I don't know what you're talking about," he lied. "No one will believe an assistant over me."

"That's true. Who am I compared to you? So, how about I go get the hotel security posted outside the suite? I must warn you that they'll call the cops. With any report of assault you'll be sent to the hospital, where you'll have to explain all the drugs and alcohol in your system." She watched the colour drain from his face as reality sobered him up. "With all the drama, I'm sure the tabloids will get wind of your relapse – and again, you can kiss goodbye to your advance."

Margot crouched down beside him. "How about we do you a favour instead? We'll leave, and this never happened?"

"Seems fair," Juliet added, her hand on the office door handle.

"Get out!" Hugo barked, too embarrassed to look at them.

"Absolutely. I'll be sure to send Ms Baum your best." Juliet closed the door behind them, hoping this incident would make him think twice about trying the same stunt on the next assistant sent his way. Her hand shook as she gripped the manuscript tightly, and she followed Margot through the crowd of guests to the door. Hopefully Margot had had enough time to make a few contacts, because she needed to leave.

Leaving the suite, Juliet bumped into a guest heading in. The smell of aftershave filled her senses, and an embarrassed chuckle escaped her. She'd been distracted, glancing over her shoulder to make sure that Hugo wasn't following them.

"Sorry," she muttered, before being utterly frozen by a set of dark eyes staring down at her.

The man's scowl softened, and for a moment he stared at her as though he recognised her. "I—" he started, only to shake his head. His eyes narrowed, as though he was studying every inch of her face. Juliet chewed her lip, waiting for him to speak or let her pass, since his broad stature was blocking her path.

"Juliet?" Margot called from the elevator.

"Excuse me." Juliet blushed, sure her cheeks matched the shade of her dress.

Thankfully, her friend's words seemed to break the man from his trance. He offered her a small smile, though the crease in his forehead made her think something was bothering him. The guest, whom she guessed to be in his early thirties, moved aside to let her pass, and she felt his eyes on her back as she did so. Glancing over her shoulder, she noted that security let him in without question.

How strange. Maybe he mistook me for someone else. She didn't recognise him. If they'd met before, she'd remember such a nice jawline. Still, no matter how handsome he was, nothing would drag her back inside the party.

"What was that about? Do you know each other?" Margot asked, once Juliet joined her in the elevator.

"I don't know. He didn't say anything. I probably just surprised him." Juliet shrugged, hitting the button for the lobby.

"He looked like he knew you. If a man looked at me the way he was looking at you, I'd have swooned!" Margot swayed dramatically.

"What is it about tall, dark and handsome men that turns us all to jelly?" Juliet tried to hide the heat in her cheeks, still unsettled by his gaze.

"Is that a serious question? Don't act all unbothered – I saw you eyeing him up. I mean, that man was giving you serious bedroom eyes. I could feel the tension halfway down the hall. I should have just left you to it."

Juliet glared at her, but once the doors closed, they erupted into laughter.

"There was no way I was going back to that party with Hugo probably still licking his wounds. I can't believe you hit him!" Juliet giggled, trying to forget about the mystery man.

"He deserved worse! When I saw you going upstairs, I knew there was no way he would let you go easily," Margot said, drying her laughter-induced tears.

"Thank you for coming up. If you'd arrived a second later, I'd have slapped him with the manuscript," Juliet told her, hoping Hugo would take her threat seriously and keep his mouth shut.

"If I remember correctly, the hotel bar looked rather inviting on the way in," Margot said with a long sigh. "We both deserve a drink to celebrate."

"And what are we celebrating?" Juliet clutched the manuscript as though her life depended on it. For getting her the invitation to the party and saving her from the washed-up perv, she reminded herself to get Margot a very big Christmas present.

"I've booked three clients for the New Year, and *you're* about to be promoted." Margot beamed, eyeing the manuscript.

"I'm so proud of you," Juliet said, squeezing her friend.

"Of us!" Margot amended as the elevator doors opened.

"Now I've got to make sure his pages are somewhat decent. If it's terrible, Baum might use it as an excuse not to give me that promotion!" Juliet hooked her arm through her friend's as they walked past the gleaming Christmas tree and into the bar.

"Celebration first," Margot countered, waving down the penguin-suited bartender across the brass bar. "First round's on me."

After an hour or two of much-needed gossiping, Juliet and Margot were joined in the bar by Margot's new potential clients, who'd been smart enough to leave Hugo's party early. They were promptly invited to go dancing, which Margot eagerly accepted. It was a little past midnight, and though Juliet didn't want to go home, she didn't feel like going to a club. Her personal space had been invaded enough for one evening, and she was far too comfortable with the bar's oversized armchairs, Christmas tree glittering with red and gold ornaments, limitless snacks, and a cosy fire to be tempted out into the snow.

Left alone, Juliet enjoyed the quiet ambience. Only a few stragglers remained at the long bar behind her, and she couldn't have been more content with her hot whiskey and the unattainable manuscript. Unfortunately, it didn't take long for her sense of victory to drain away. Settling in, she slipped off her heels and slid them under the low, mirrored coffee table in front of her, since no one was paying her any mind.

"How could he write this crap?" she groaned after struggling through the first twenty pages. Burying her face in the pages, she prayed for it to get better, but after reading two more pages of Hugo prattling on about his many conquests, she couldn't help but laugh. *There's no way Baum, or anyone, could publish this.* "I'm never going to get promoted!"

After going through so much trouble to get the damn book, it wasn't even worth the effort it would take to burn it. It was so sad, all she could do was chuckle; if she didn't laugh, she was sure she would cry.

The waiter distracted her from her sorrows by placing a drink next to her already empty glass.

Her brows pulled together in confusion. "Sorry – I didn't order this?"

The waiter, who was clearly no stranger to self-tanner, smiled at her politely. "It's from the gentleman at the far end. He said you looked like you needed it," he said, motioning over his shoulder to the bar.

Slowly, Juliet turned round to find the staggeringly hand-some stranger from the earlier collision in the hallway, staring unashamedly at her. Swiftly turning away, she wondered if he would take her acknowledgment as a sign to come over. Clearly, he hadn't stayed long at Hugo's party either. *Is he at least going to ask for my number? My name? What's the point in sending over a drink if he's not going to ask me out?* The questions were killing her.

"Thank him for me," she said quickly, though she had no intention of drinking anything from a stranger, no matter how handsome he was. *Maybe this is his way of making up for not saying anything outside the suite?* The kind gesture might be his apology.

The waiter nodded in acknowledgment and went back to the bar. Juliet cursed herself for not inviting the guy over – or maybe she should've gone over to apologise again for bumping into him. Taking a deep breath, she turned to wave him over, but it was too late. He was gone.

Sinking into her chair, she rationalised her disappointment. He was a stranger. A three-second encounter shouldn't have melted her brain, but it had.

"You're welcome." The stranger's sudden appearance by her side shocked her from her thoughts. Was this guy some sort of magician? A cute, British magician, judging from his accent.

"Sorry, I didn't mean to startle you."

"You didn't. I was just distracted," she finally said, wondering what shade of red she was. She guessed from his pale blue shirt and the tie tucked into his black trousers that he was here on business. Despite her dress riding up her thighs, exposing her smooth, pale skin, his eyes remained fixed on hers. Suddenly feeling self-conscious, she tucked her bare feet under her.

"Then I'm sorry I distracted you. I don't normally approach beautiful woman in bars in the middle of the night." He shifted back on his heels, and she wasn't sure whether he was actually nervous or just acting so. She couldn't help but stare at his prominent cheekbones and the dark eyebrows that highlighted his dark grey eyes.

"I find that hard to believe." Juliet couldn't believe she'd just spoken her thoughts aloud. She gripped the manuscript on her lap tightly, wishing the chair would engulf her. He smiled, and went to reply, but he was cut off by his ringing phone.

"Forgive me," he said, answering his phone. Much to her disappointment, he left the bar without so much as a second glance. It happened so quickly, she thought she'd imagined the interaction.

How weird was that? Juliet shook off the encounter and decided to punish herself with more of Hugo's attempt at charm.

"The bar is closing for cleaning," the bartender called out, and Juliet jumped like she'd been caught doing something she shouldn't.

"I'd better get home," she muttered to herself, strapping on her heels and grabbing the manuscript and her clutch. It was amazing how fast time flew by when you were reading page after horrendous page.

Walking through the lobby, she saw the doorman was still on duty.

"I need a taxi, please?" Juliet asked him, only to notice that the path outside was coated in a thick layer of snow.

"I'm sorry, ma'am, but the snow is coming down something terrible. We haven't been able to call any taxis." The white-haired man with the large top hat smiled at her sadly. She winced, not fancying a freezing trek, but she had to get home.

"Do you think I could catch one on Douglas Street? It's only a five-minute walk up the block." She'd never considered the snow.

"I wouldn't risk it." He shook his head. "They can arrange a car first thing in the morning at Reception. It's 3am right now, and the earliest we're expecting to have the road's clear is seven. There might be a room or two left if you check at Reception." Given how the information rolled off his tongue, she wasn't the first person he'd given the spiel to. She wasn't in any position to argue; she wouldn't get far in heels.

"Thanks. I'll ask at the desk."

It turned out that Juliet wasn't the only one stranded and in need of a room. She waited in a small queue, surprised when she spotted the stranger from earlier talking to someone by the elevator. He glanced in her direction, and she snapped her gaze forward, wondering why he hadn't come back to the bar after his phone call. Not that she cared. Okay, maybe she did a little.

Luckily, a receptionist with bright red lipstick waved her over.

She stepped forward, then came to an abrupt halt when the stranger from the bar walked in front of her.

"Excuse me, but I believe I was next," she protested. Even if he'd bought her a drink, she wasn't going to let him cut the queue.

"Oh, I'm so sorry, I didn't realise," he said, glancing at her over his shoulder with an apologetic smile. "I just needed to get a keycard – of course you can go first." He motioned for her to go ahead. She did so quickly, embarrassed that she'd snapped.

"I'm sorry, Miss Frost, but there are no rooms left," the receptionist informed her.

Juliet sighed, feeling the stranger's eyes on her. He was probably amused by her being turned away.

"I can ask one of the other ladies with emergency accommodation if they wouldn't mind sharing for the night, but I'm afraid it'll be at their discretion." The receptionist's smile didn't falter as she delivered the rest of the bad news: all the cars in their service were booked until the afternoon.

Juliet really didn't like the idea of sharing with a stranger. "I'll wait in the lobby. Hopefully the taxis will start running again soon." She cursed herself for not leaving earlier with Margot. There was no way to know when the snow was going to stop or when taxi service would resume, and she had to get across the city by 8am to give Ms Baum the manuscript.

The receptionist moved on without a second glance. Juliet moved to the end of the counter as the stranger winked at her. She was beginning to think he was a curse. He seemed to turn up whenever something went wrong.

"Mr Duncan, is there anything I can assist you with?" the

receptionist asked him. Juliet guessed he was a regular from the warmth of the greeting.

"Will, please," he corrected her, and the receptionist blushed. "I've stupidly locked myself out of my suite. There's a party happening beside me, and when I went to ask them to keep it down, I forgot to bring my keycard with me."

Juliet rolled her eyes. The receptionist had lingered on every word and looked to be about a second away from salivating.

"I'm very sorry for the disruption. Please allow us to comp the night for you." The receptionist's wide smile told him she was eager to please.

"Thank you, but that won't be necessary. Someone is handling it as we speak." Will's eyes drifted to Juliet as she pretended to look at her phone. She assumed the man he'd been speaking to by the elevator worked at the hotel. Looked like Hugo was in for an even rougher night.

"Could we talk for a moment?" Will said from beside her. She hadn't noticed him approach; she kept trying to text Margot, but her messages weren't going through.

"I'm not going to apologise for asking you to wait your turn," she said defensively, putting her phone in her clutch.

To her surprise, he rested his hand on her lower back. Normally she'd have scolded a guy for uninvited physical contact, but he was merely guiding her away from the onlooking guests.

"I heard about your dilemma, and I wanted to ask if you'd like to stay with me?" he asked, placing his hands in his pockets.

Juliet stared at him, confused.

Reading her hesitation, he explained, "I've got a suite, and I promise to be a perfect gentleman. You can't wait in the lobby all night."

"Thank you, but I can't impose. We don't even know each other," she hedged, searching his eyes for any hidden agenda. All she saw was kindness.

"I'm Will." He extended his hand, and that cheeky grin threatened to break down her walls. "And if you're worried about imposing, don't. Consider it a Christmas miracle that you don't have to stay in a draughty lobby for hours. At least, consider it my way of apologising for bumping into you earlier, then rudely leaving you in the bar, and then jumping the queue. I believe I've made a terrible first impression."

The thought of staying in his suite made her heart flutter, while her better judgement tried to bypass her desire and remind her that he was a perfect stranger. *Perfect being the operative word.* However, as a cold breeze cut through the lobby and her bare legs, her desire won.

"Juliet," she told him, taking his hand.

"A pleasure to meet you. Now, can we get out of this lobby?"

His kindness did something to her. She was far from drunk, but felt utterly intoxicated by his sheer presence. They walked to the elevator, her feet guiding her more than sense. She didn't know what the hell she was doing, but she didn't care.

"I was watching you earlier in the bar before I summoned up the courage to come over to you. You seemed like you were struggling. Nothing worse than a bad book," Will said as the elevator doors closed behind them.

Why is there nothing sexier than a man who reads?

She didn't think courage was something he was lacking. He had an air of ease about him.

"Watching me? I think serial killers use the same line." She wanted to see if there was a sense of humour in those dark eyes.

"Watching you might not have been the best way to put it." His deep laughter radiated low from his chest; the hearty sound only added to his charm. "I should've said it was your laugh that caught my attention. I couldn't help but wonder what had you both so perplexed and entertained."

Maybe it was the hot whiskeys making him so alluring, but his bashful explanation made her insides giddy. *Sense of humour? Check.*

"Just a manuscript that should never see the light of day." Juliet hadn't meant to draw attention to herself, but she didn't mind attracting his.

"You work in publishing?" He eyed the manuscript, and she turned over the title page, afraid of bad-mouthing a client. *Is he really asking me about work?* Was he flirting or not?

"Trying to," she said, letting out a sigh. "However, this book might kill my chances."

"Good things come to those who put in the work. I'm sure you'll get all your heart's desires."

"Are you in the business?" she asked, trying not to be distracted by what her heart desired right now as his hand brushed hers.

"No, just a keen reader. I'm in recruitment. Helping people find where they belong." Given his evident ease with people, that made sense. *Please don't be a serial killer.* Stealing subtle glances, Juliet established that there was no ring on his left hand. Not married, then.

"Genre of choice?" she asked, still ignoring the way his fingers were brushing hers playfully. With his easy charm and disarming smile, she wondered how many women he had loved and left haunted.

"True crime." His gaze didn't waver, but there was a teasing glint in his eye.

"Very funny." Juliet nudged him gently, but her heel

caught in the carpet as she moved. He caught her as her ankle gave way. "Sorry – carpet and heels aren't a great combination." She blushed as he held her flush against him.

She had planned to pull away, but the way his attention settled on her lips made her still. One night of absolute freedom with the most insanely handsome man she'd ever seen might be the best Christmas present she'd got to date. *Maybe I should take a page out of Margot's book and live a little!* Taking a chance, she dropped her clutch and the manuscript and wrapped her arms around his neck.

The small smile on the corner of his mouth was all she needed. She rose on her tiptoes and brought her lips to his, gentle, seeking permission. In response, his hand travelled from her waist and into her hair, his lips demanding and possessive as he pinned her against the wall of the elevator.

"Sorry," he panted, breaking away for a moment. She could feel the heat of his hand through her thin dress. "I promised to be a perfect gentleman."

"What if I don't want you to be a perfect gentleman?" she asked before she lost her courage. Being so bold felt rather refreshing and terrifying all at once. She had one or two brief relationships, though her last name tended to get in the way, but a one-night stand? Never.

"If?" Will asked, and she forced herself to meet his heavy gaze.

Her heart pounded. "I. Want. You."

"Your wish is my command." He kissed the back of her hand tenderly and brought it to his chest. She blushed as she felt his heart hammering beneath her palm. Seconds later, his lips crushed hers urgently once more.

She didn't need air any more, only his lips. His hand grazed her thigh as he pressed her against the elevator wall. He took every inch she offered, and it was a heady sensation.

No man had ever made her feel so desired in a matter of moments. She moaned into his lips as his fingertips brushed the edge of her short dress – but the *bing* of the elevator doors opening thrust them apart.

Juliet hurried to collect the manuscript, and when Will crouched to pick up her clutch, they couldn't help but laugh as their eyes met. He seemed as surprised as she was by how carried away they'd got.

"This is just a one-night thing," she clarified as they stepped out of the elevator, not wanting him to think she expected more.

"One might not be enough, but if that's your wish, my night is yours." It didn't take them long to reach his suite; outside the door, he brushed a strand of hair behind her ear. "Before we go any further, I want you to know that we can stop at any time. I'll take the couch, and even give you first dibs on the shower in the morning. You can change your mind at any point, and I'll happily make sure you get home safe," he promised, his gaze drifting from her eyes to her lips.

"I should be the one giving you the choice. I practically threw myself at you in the elevator." Juliet blushed again, her lips already feeling puffy from his kisses.

"I was an idiot for letting you walk away in the first place," he said, brushing his lips against hers. A taste of what was to come.

He opened the door. She stepped inside, turning on the light by the couch in the centre of the suite and hyperaware of his presence at her back. He slipped his arm around her waist, and butterflies swirled under his touch.

"Sit down," she rasped, regretting his absence as he did as he was told.

Reaching for the zip at the back of her dress, she hesitated, but his unashamed gaze reminded her of what he'd said: it was her night to do whatever she wanted. No space for embarrassment, shame, or overthinking about her imperfections. Standing between his legs, she unzipped her dress and let it fall down her body until she was completely exposed to him.

"I could spend the rest of my life watching you do just that." He reached for her, but she rested her hand on his chest and pushed him back gently so that he settled on the cushions.

"I've got some other things in mind." She smiled wickedly as she sank to her knees between his strong legs. He caressed her cheek as she undid his belt and unzipped his trousers. He was already hard, and the size of him startled her for just a moment before lust pooled in her belly and her fear turned to need.

Will groaned as she mercilessly tasted every inch of him. She smiled, proud of herself for bringing him so close to the edge, but she wasn't done with him yet. His hand dropped from her hair as she stood, and he watched hungrily as she removed her heels and walked to the edge of the bed.

Getting up, he stood over her, his thumb brushing her rosy lips. "This mouth, these lips, could kill a man."

She gasped in surprise as he lifted her and then stepped backwards so she ended up straddling him on the bed. She pulled the shirt from his shoulders, her tongue trailing over the tattoo that snaked over his shoulder and down his arm. Who the hell was this man? Actually, she didn't care, too lost in the sensation of his hand on her waist. He tangled his hand into her hair, forcing her to look at him.

His kiss felt like punishment for her teasing as he palmed her breast. Her nipples hardened into sensitive peaks. Taking one in his mouth, he sucked relentlessly as she felt herself dripping down her thighs. The ache at her core begged for him.

"You're so wet," he breathed against her ear. She shivered as his fingers teased her clit.

"I've been ready for you since the lift," she said breathlessly as he slipped his finger inside her. Desperate for release, she groaned when he took his hand away. His chuckle as she glared at him made her stomach clench.

Will stripped off his trousers and removed a condom from his wallet. A giggle escaped her, but his fierce gaze told her he was serious. He pinned her wrists above her head, nipping her neck as she wrapped her legs around his waist, desperately trying to pull him closer.

"Keep looking at me like that, and I can't promise I'll be gentle." He ripped the condom free from the foil and slipped it over his length, and she licked her lips, remembering how he tasted.

"I thought I was meant to be in control," she protested, feeling his impressive length press against her centre.

"I don't think I can take much more. Let me take it from here?" His kisses grew gentle, which was all the more cruel as her heightened senses amplified every light touch.

She nodded breathlessly.

"Trust me?" he asked – no, demanded, eyes piercing her. She didn't know how or why, but she did.

"Yes," she rasped. "My body is yours." The words escaped her before she could stop them, but he only smiled wickedly.

"That mouth." He pulled at her lower lip and claimed it once again before easing inside her.

The care he took almost made her tearful; no man had worshipped her body this way. She was afraid he would ruin her for anyone else. Grinding her hips against him, desperate to relieve the pressure building between her legs, she took him deeper. A growl escaped him that nearly shattered her.

"That's it, take all of me," he praised as he stretched her to her limit. He rolled his hips, getting her used to his size. She arched her back, half afraid she would die from the sheer ecstasy of the sensation of him buried inside her. He eased out of her agonisingly slowly, and she dragged her nails down his back, begging him to reclaim his place.

"You're so tight, I want to feel you come," he panted, circled her clit, bringing her dangerously close to the edge. "I bet you sound so beautiful when you come."

She moaned as his hips drove into hers, driving her higher towards ecstasy.

"Come for me," he demanded, and unable to control herself, she splintered around him, her vision hazy as she lost herself to his caress.

She moaned as he eased himself from her, then realised something. "You didn't?" she asked with a frown, wondering if she had done something wrong.

He looked up at her with a devilish grin, trailing his tongue down her body before nipping her inner thigh. "Let's clean you up."

His tongue against her caused her to clutch his hair as he nipped and sucked. This time the wave burst over her before she had a chance to even know what was happening. He didn't give her time a chance to recover before sliding back inside her. He thrust relentlessly, and she knew nothing but him. She didn't know if she was moaning or crying as he erupted inside her and she was sent over the edge for the final time.

Her body was utterly boneless as he collapsed onto his elbows. They were both a mess of heavy breathing and sweat dripping onto the sheets. Will eased out of her, and Juliet only realised he'd left the bed when she saw the bathroom light turn on. She waited for her heartbeat to steady, wondering if she should leave, but she couldn't feel her legs.

Thoroughly fucked, she couldn't string a sentence together. Watching him return from the bathroom, the sweat glistening on his skin make her want to lick him clean, but she was too exhausted. He kissed her shoulder as he lay down beside her.

"If you keep kissing me like this, I might die," she mumbled, though it was a death she would happily accept.

"I think you've had enough for now." He chuckled softly and made his way up the bed.

Suddenly his words disappointed her. She didn't think she'd ever get enough of him, but she was reminded of their agreement: one night.

She didn't have the energy to think further on it as he pulled the soft white sheets over them, tucking her under his arm. Lost in the scent of his cologne, Juliet drifted off into the best night's sleep she'd had in months.

W ill loved waking up to find a beautiful woman in his bed, wearing his shirt. Distracted by her thighs on either side of his waist, it took him a moment to register that his Jingle Bells alarm was sounding, and she was reaching for his phone on the nightstand.

"Need some help?" Will beamed, staring up at the woman who'd ensnared him with her laugh. After weeks of studying Juliet's file, he'd never expected to feel for her as he did.

"I was trying to turn off your alarm." She climbed off him and leaned against the headboard, hugging a pillow to her chest. "I didn't mean to wake you, but Jingle Bells at five am is not the wakeup call I expected." She flushed, tucking her messy hair behind her ear. The gesture revealed the love bite he'd left on her neck, and he suddenly wanted another taste.

"Waking up with you on top of me is my new favourite form of apology." He sat up, so they were face to face.

She dipped her head shyly, her long hair fanning over her face. Its honey highlights looked like she'd been kissed by the sun. He found himself not wanting anyone to kiss her but him, not even a distant star.

"You don't like the classics?" he asked, pulling her close to try and make her more comfortable.

"Not at five am on a Sunday," she groaned, though not in the same way she had last night.

He liked to keep his schedule as close to Yule's time zone as possible so he wouldn't be in a constant state of jetlag, but he couldn't tell her he kept North Pole time. "What would you prefer? All I Want For Christmas? Maybe Rudolph The Red-Nosed Reindeer?" he asked, kissing the top of her head and hoping to distract her from the topic.

"Does it have to be a Christmas song?" The sadness in her voice surprised him as she stared up at him. God, those big brown eyes would be the death of him.

"I didn't think you'd be such a Grinch." He wanted to know more about her, more than what he had read in her file, but he didn't want to push too far.

"Don't get me wrong, I love Christmas," she told him. "My grandma always did her best to make it special, but in my experience, you can end up surrounded by people you don't want to and never see for the rest of the year. I'd rather spend it with those I love most." Her answer didn't specify if those she loved most included the Frost family, but he wasn't supposed to know she was a Frost, so he couldn't exactly ask without her thinking he was some insane stalker.

"Close with your family?" Will glanced to his wardrobe, where her file sat in his suitcase. Since she'd brought them up, it couldn't hurt to pry a little.

"To my younger sister, Beth. My Nana Rose passed over a year ago." The grief in her voice instinctively made him hold her tighter.

"I'm sorry to hear that," he said as she settled into his embrace, and he tried not to let his guilt spoil the moment.

"Thank you." Her forced smile told him he'd touched a nerve. "Since you've a selection of Christmas alarms, I take it you're the anti-Grinch?"

He couldn't count the number of Guardian rules he'd broken in the past twelve hours. What was a few more? Revealing some harmless details about himself couldn't hurt.

"I live for it. The smells, the snow, the people, the food. My family go all out every year, and the house is always crowded and chaotic. People will be fighting in one corner and laughing in the other – not perfect, but it's home."

It was true, even if the family he was referring to was the village Yule as a whole. Having been assigned to the Outside, he hadn't returned home for Christmas for the past two years; the festive season was the hardest time for those who'd left Yule. As a guardian, he needed to be on the Outside to help them adjust to living away from their concealed winter wonderland in the heart of the North Pole. Even with dozens of employees to support him, Will liked to be a hands-on boss.

"I'm jealous. I've always wanted a Christmas like that. Not perfect, but filled with love and not dictated by duty and guilt." Juliet sank against him, and once again his instinct to distance himself – as a guardian should – faltered. She didn't know about Yule, who he was or his true reason for approaching her, but he couldn't stay away. The moment they'd collided outside the party last night, all his training and logic had gone out the window.

"What if we could make your wish a reality?" he asked before he could stop himself.

Juliet leaned back from him, and he winced. He'd forgotten that to her they'd only met last night, whereas he'd been studying her for weeks.

"We've just met, and you want to spend the holidays with me?" She laughed, eying him suspiciously. "How many hot whiskeys did you drink before sending me one?"

"I'm not saying I'm going to keep you hostage in this

room, but what if you could just do what you wanted?" he asked, trying not to freak her out. *Maybe hostage was the wrong word to use.* Juliet hesitated, and he wished she'd say yes. *If she goes home to the Frost estate, I'll have to figure out a way to get myself invited without raising too much suspicion.* After weeks of planning, he hadn't expected to run into her in the way he had last night. He certainly hadn't expected to wake up beside her in bed.

"Tempting offer, but I can't leave my sister alone with our dad for the holidays. It wouldn't be Christmas without guilt. It's why we can eat so much – to bury the emotions." He thought it was meant to be a joke, but she mostly sounded resigned to her fate, and he wished this season was going to be so simple. She had no idea what was coming, and that he was part of it.

"I'd hate to spare you from a guilt-riddled Christmas, but what if I wanted to see you?" he asked, brushing his lips against hers.

"Aren't you going home for the holidays? I'd hate to mess up your plans."

Will sighed. She had no idea that *she* was his Christmas plans.

"Trying to get rid of me?" he teased. "I should've known you were just using me for my body." He kissed her shoulder.

She rolled her eyes. "You can hardly blame me." The way she looked at him nearly caused him to lose all self-control.

He cupped her face, his lips lingering inches from hers, but the sound of their rumbling stomachs interrupted the heated moment.

"I should go," Juliet said quickly, kissing him far too briefly. It was the last thing he wanted to hear.

"I'm not letting you leave without breakfast in bed." Will sat behind her as she tried to get up and wrapped his arms around her waist. She settled against him. Clearly, she was as reluctant to leave as he was to let her go.

"I thought you weren't going to hold me hostage?" she asked over her shoulder.

"I've changed my mind – at least until you eat. I'll call room service, if you want to hop in the shower."

"You've got to let me go first, unless you plan on showering together." She struggled against his arms, and he reluctantly released her.

Juliet scurried off to the bathroom, his shirt swaying with her hips as she went. Picking up the phone, Will realised she hadn't said what she wanted to eat, so he got everything – although he made sure to specify no fish of any kind, since her file mentioned how much she loathed it.

GETTING OUT OF THE SHOWER, Will wrapped a towel around his waist, all his thoughts on the woman waiting on the other side of the door for him. His steamy reflection judged him for overstepping. All he was supposed to do was make sure she got the chest and that she didn't reveal Yule's secret to the world once she learned the truth. But she'd invaded his mind the moment her file had crossed his desk, and his better judgement had disappeared the moment she bumped into him in the hallway.

Putting on a new pair of boxers, he heard a door slam. *Breakfast must've arrived.*

"Juliet?" He opened the door, roughly drying his hair with a towel. He was about to tell her there was tip money on the nightstand when he found his bed empty.

Confused, he scanned the floor. Her dress and heels

weren't on the bench at the end of the bed. *She must be on the couch; I can't blame her for not waiting for me.* They'd worked up quite the appetite last night.

He headed out of the bedroom, but his smile disappeared when instead of being met by Juliet's dark eyes, he saw a waiter placing breakfast on the table by the couch. "Oh. Sorry, I thought you were someone else."

"Sir?" The waiter frowned, clearly waiting for a response to a question Will had been too distracted to hear. "Is everything to your liking?" he repeated, putting the empty trays back on the silver trolly.

"Yes, fine. Thank you." Even if everything smelt delicious, his appetite had left with Juliet. *Why did she leave without saying anything?*

Again, the waiter stood waiting until Will remembered to tip him. In exchange, he pulled something from his pocket.

"Your friend gave me this in the hall. She nearly knocked me over on her way out." It looked to be a note scribbled on the back of their order receipt.

"Thank you." Will closed the door and sat on the couch. Ignoring the breakfast, he opened the folded receipt.

Thank you for last night. I won't forget it.
P.S. I'm keeping your shirt. ;)

That's it? Putting down the note, he scrubbed his jaw and wished he'd never let her out of his sight. *Why'd she run off?* The waiter had said she was in a hurry, and he wondered if he'd done or said something. She had been fine when she'd come out of the shower; what could've changed in ten minutes?

His heart threatened to stop when he realised he'd left her alone in the room. *Did she find the files?* Hurrying to the wardrobe, he found his suitcase exactly as he'd left it. The file with her information remained safely tucked inside a manila envelope marked *Property of the Guardians of Yule*. Yule's stamp, an embossed Christmas tree, would've exposed his identity if she'd recognised it from the chest. It was his job to protect Yule's secrets and its descendants, not add to the risk of exposure. Juliet wasn't technically his charge; her legacy case was a favour for his mentor.

Maybe she got a call, he thought, pulling on a pair of black slacks and a cream knitted jumper. Something must have prompted such a rush to leave. *I could call her, but there's no way to explain how I have her number.*

Tying his boots, he found the solution. Sitting on the table by the blueberry waffles was the manuscript with the Harley & Rowe address stamped neatly in the corner, giving him the perfect excuse to see her again. Now to figure out how to use this mistake to his advantage.

His phone vibrated in his pocket as he buckled his belt.

"Have you made any contact with Juliet?" The chief of the Guardians of Yule and his mentor, Eloise Heart, was clearly too eager for answers to waste time on pleasantries. Then again, he'd failed to check in last night as promised. Harvey had gone to great lengths to get him invited to Hugo's Christmas bash, but he'd arrived as Juliet was leaving and ended up staying for less than five minutes. Without her, there'd been no reason to attend.

"I didn't get to talk to Juliet at the party as planned, but she's fine. Nothing out of the ordinary to report – she's keeping to her usual routine. However, I've confirmed with the courier service that the chest has been delivered," Will informed Eloise.

He'd planned to talk to Juliet at the bar instead, but then Harvey had called him to scold him for leaving early. The poor guy had been deeply frustrated after all the strings he'd pulled, so Will had promised to bring him some of his favourite peppermint cookies from Yule, since he rarely went home.

Between Juliet's intoxicating laugh and rosy lips, he hadn't been able to resist the temptation when she'd kissed him in the elevator. He couldn't tell Eloise that Juliet hadn't had time to discover the contents of the chest because she'd spent the night with him. He wondered if she'd remember their night as fondly once she discovered he would be responsible for turning her life upside down. However, he was determined to be there for her every step of the way, as a guardian should be. If only his head and his heart would remember he was a professional, and not a teenager controlled by his urges!

His mentor distracted him from his thoughts. "If anything changes, I need to know. I'm worried Juliet will confront her father without having all the answers. The truth never came naturally to him."

Her anxiety could be heard from thousands of miles away. Will hadn't worked a legacy case in years, but he owed Eloise. That, and when Juliet's picture had slid across his desk, he'd found himself not wanting to let anyone else guide her home to Yule.

"I'm sure it's frustrating that you can't come and talk to her yourself, but when the time is right, she'll be prepared," he assured Eloise.

She sighed. "You're right. Learning the truth slowly will give her more time to adjust. I've waited twenty-six years, but now I can't seem to wait another day."

Will winced. He had definitely screwed this up. Hopefully his boss would never find out that he'd slept with her estranged daughter. He wasn't sure what she'd do to him.

"Juliet has the chest. Once she opens it, the next move will be up to her," he said.

"Be careful not to reveal yourself. Giving her the Frost chest could lead to our banishment, if we're discovered."

The words cut him like a knife, though not out of fear for himself. When Juliet learned who he was, he hoped that she'd see past his white lies.

"As discussed, I'll only reveal myself when and if needed. Adding her grandmother's letter to the chest should help cushion the news."

Eloise Heart had got the Frost chest out of Yule, and Will had made sure it was delivered along with the letter Rose Frost had sent him before her passing for safekeeping. He hoped he hadn't jeopardised their plans by mixing business with pleasure. When he'd offered to spend Christmas with Juliet, it had been to keep her and the chest away from her family when she learned the truth about her mum, Yule, and the Frost family's banishment. Since she was determined to return to the Frost Estate, he had to find a way into the Frost House to make sure that her father didn't find out about the chest.

"I never wanted to call in this favour, but if I can't be there to protect her, then I had to send someone I trust. You're the only one I could turn to."

Her words only added to his guilt. Will wouldn't have been able to become a guardian or started his own company to help dozens of people from Yule on the Outside if she hadn't trained him in the first place. Having spent the last twenty-six years devoting her life to Yule, and to becoming Chief Guardian, he'd never expected his mentor would ask for his help with Juliet. By reaching out to her banished daughter, Eloise was risking everything – and he'd put all their hard work in jeopardy because he couldn't control his emotions. All he'd wanted was to reunite his mentor with her daughter after all the years of guidance she'd given him. He promised himself he wasn't going to let his feelings for Juliet ruin that chance.

"There's no need to explain. I'm happy to help, and I won't let anything happen to her." He was used to helping people adjust to the Outside, but this would be his first time helping someone accept that they were a descendant of a Christmas village in the North Pole that was concealed from the outside world by magic.

"Once Juliet learns the truth about the Frost banishment, she can decide where she belongs. So long as she's safe and happy, I'll accept her decision, but she deserves to know where she comes from." Eloise's words seemed to be more for her own reassurance than his.

"You can rest easy. Juliet is happy. She lives with her friend Margot and enjoys her job at the publishing house. Like you, she isn't afraid to go after a promotion…" He picked up the manuscript from the table. "I'll call you with any further developments. Trust me to do the job you trained me for, all right?"

After saying goodbye to Eloise, Will grabbed his jacket and headed out. He didn't have much time if he was to get to the Harley & Rowe office before the meeting Juliet had mentioned. Sparing her from her boss's wrath might earn him some points, and he needed her trust if he was going to remain close to her – though he wasn't quite sure if he wanted that for his sake or that of his mentor.

In the hotel lobby, Jingle Bell Rock started playing through the speakers, reminding him of the early wake-up call. Fate was officially taunting him.

Stepping out into the cold, he was able to grab a taxi now that the roads were clearer. Giving the Harley & Rowe address, he tucked the manuscript inside his jacket to keep it dry and safe. As he stared out the window at the waking city, he was haunted by the knowledge that if Juliet reacted poorly to everything she was about to discover, he'd have to wipe her memory. He couldn't stomach the thought of erasing what little time they'd spent together.

He clenched his jaw. Regardless of his feelings, above all else, it was his job to protect Yule's sacred secret.

Instant gratitude washed over Juliet as a wave of heat hit her. Margot had remembered to turn on the heating. Unfortunately, she stumbled over her roommate's discarded shoes and cursed aloud. *There goes my plan to sneak in.*

Margot, still in her dress from the night, was awake on the couch. The smudged mascara under her eyes and the pint of water on the coffee table beside her gave away just how much fun she'd had on the dance floor.

"Morning, sleeping beauty. You look truly ravishing in the morning – I don't know how you're single," Juliet teased, hoping to deflect attention from her walk of shame.

"Don't even start. I think I'm still drunk." Margot winced, snuggling a fluffy blue blanket to her chest.

"What time did you get in?" The distraction seemed to be working. Juliet stripped off her jacket, and her feet cried out in relief as she took off her heels. She watched her friend place a gel hangover mask over her eyes and tenderly sip her water.

"Late, but I got you coffee from our favourite place. You'll probably need to microwave it – I already chugged mine. Speaking of late, you look like you had a good night." Margot eyed her neck, and Juliet's hand flew up to cover the hickey. *Damn.*

"Coffee first," she bargained, putting the mocha in the microwave.

"There's also a raspberry muffin for you on the table. Now, tell me what or who you've been doing!" Margot sat up, tucking her purple elephant under her arm – her favourite hangover snuggle buddy. It was technically Juliet's, but they shared pretty much everything.

"Spent most of the night reading Hugo's manuscript that we went to so much trouble to get. Then I got snowed in and had to stay at the hotel. I had to bribe someone for their taxi just so I could get home!" Juliet opened the brown bag of goodies from their favourite twenty-four-hour bakery beside their apartment building.

Taking a generous bite out of the muffin, she couldn't help thinking of the gorgeous man who'd been sweet enough to order her room service while she'd fled like a criminal from a crime scene. She'd tried to get his attention before leaving, but he obviously hadn't heard her over the running water, and she'd felt too awkward to ambush him in the shower. Ms Baum had texted her again, reminding her to be in the office at eight sharp, and she'd panicked, knowing that she had to make herself presentable. She hadn't wanted to ruin the memory of the night with an awkward goodbye anyway. Maybe it was better to let him continue to be the epitome of romance than allow him to spoil it by letting her down.

"I should've known you'd spent the night with a book! Still, I'm glad you didn't venture out in the snow. I only got back because one of the clients I was with had a town car," Margot said, sipping her water like it might hurt her if she wasn't careful.

"I didn't spend the whole night reading—" Juliet was

about to tell her everything when her stomach dropped. "Shit! I left the manuscript in his room!"

Leaving Margot to gape, she ran into her room and hastily stripped off Will's shirt and the dress. The clock by her bed taunted her. "How could I have been so stupid?! I don't have time to get back across town to get the manuscript."

"*His* room? I thought you said you were at the bar!" Margot appeared at her doorway, her interest piqued.

"I met a guy. I don't have time to explain, but I left the manuscript in his suite!"

"Oh God, please don't yell. My brain might fall out of my ears." Margot held her ears. "Take a deep breath and get ready. I'll ring Reception and see if anything was handed in. What room were you in?"

"Thank you!" Juliet exhaled, delighted that her friend had the ability to stay calm in a crisis. "I was in Suite 3. Just ask to be connected to the room." She didn't want to mention that she only remembered Will's first name, but she could tell Margot that he had a nice collection of freckles on his ribs.

Determined to focus on her monumental error, she shook away the memory and slicked her hair back into a high ponytail, even if tension headaches were no joke. Thank goodness Will had offered her the shower first, because she didn't have time now. When she'd finished hiding her dark circles and the hickey with concealer and thrown on some mascara and blush, Margot came to lean against the bathroom doorframe, phone in one hand.

"I tried Reception, but they said there was nothing left in the suite and that the guest has already checked out," she said apologetically, while Juliet grappled with a pair of wide-legged black slacks and a white cropped shirt.

Last night might have been heaven, but the morning was

quickly going to hell. "Did they mention if any papers were left behind?" Surely he'd have left the manuscript for her when he realised she'd left it. "There's no reason for him to keep it, and he probably assumed I'd come back and get it." *What if he trashed it when he realised I'd run out on him?!* But he didn't seem like the vengeful type.

Margot sighed. "Already asked. Housekeeping didn't see anything, and there was nothing left in Reception for collection."

"Great. Once Baum finds out I lost the manuscript, I'll never work in the publishing industry again. It's not like Hugo is going to hand me another copy after what happened at the party." Juliet's bag slipped from her shoulder as she lost hope. "Did they give you any contact details for him?"

"I tried, but they wouldn't give out guest information. I could access their computer, but it would take me at least an hour to get into their system," Margot offered, always willing to break a few laws for a friend.

"No hacking, but thanks for trying. Just pray for me – I'll need a Christmas miracle to stop me from getting fired." Juliet pulled on her long cream coat and grabbed her muffin on the way out. All those hours of humiliating work and fulfilling Ms Baum's endless demands were about to end in disappointment because of a stupid, exhilarating moment of weakness.

Margot tried to console her. "Baum might give you another chance?"

"There is a greater chance of Santa Claus being real than Baum forgiving me for losing one of the most expensive manuscripts we have." Juliet wrapped her red scarf around her neck, preparing for the cold – though nothing was going to be frostier than her boss's wrath.

"Good luck!" Margot called, cut off by the closing door.

Juliet pulled her bag onto her shoulder and hailed a taxi. Surprisingly, it didn't take long, and she couldn't help wondering if fate was eager to see her fired. With the thought of losing her dream job turning her stomach, she rolled down the window, not caring about the snow drifting in. Her cheeks would be as red as her lipstick by the time she reached the office.

The morning streets were busy as the Christmas season grew closer, but she couldn't get into the festive spirit. All she could hear was her father berating her for losing her job – a job he'd told her again and again was a waste of time, because she should have just come to work for Frost Industries.

After paying her fare, Juliet lingered on the shovelled path. It was layered with salt to keep her from slipping; a pity, because a twisted ankle might keep her from having to go into the towering office building. Staring up at the Harley & Rowe logo above the revolving door, she readied herself to head in for the last time.

"Clearly Harley & Rowe didn't want to spend extra on the heating bill over the weekend," Will muttered to himself, freezing his ass off in the frightfully white lobby. He had worried he wouldn't be allowed in, but thanks to a small bribe, the guard had let him wait out of the snow. Thankfully, it only took twenty minutes of pacing in the marble lobby for Juliet's clacking cream boots against the floors to announce her arrival. He watched her showing her employee ID to the security guard at the desk, who barely glanced up from his phone to check her in. Will couldn't blame the guard for his lack of attentiveness, given it was the weekend. Most weren't in the office anyway, and those who were, including himself, certainly didn't want to be there.

Will hesitated, hoping Juliet would notice him, but she kept her head down and headed past the waiting area to the elevators.

"Juliet!" he called, not wanting to miss his chance, as the elevator doors opened. His voice echoed through the large open space, making her jump; he cringed at his mistake, hurrying over. She'd dropped her ID, and he knelt to collect it for her. "I didn't mean to frighten you," he started, handing her the pass. Their eyes met as their fingertips brushed. Such a slight touch, yet his heart constricted, demanding more. "I waved when you came in, but you didn't notice me."

She might not have noticed him, but there was no way he'd have missed her, with those bright red lips and big brown eyes. He was beginning to think red was her favourite colour – and staring at her full lips, it was quickly becoming his.

"I'm sorry, I'm late for a meeting. I wasn't expecting to see you again. I mean, so soon!" She fumbled through her words, and he wasn't sure if she was blushing or if her cheeks were flushed from the cold. He'd hoped, after the night they shared, that she wouldn't look so disheartened to see him.

"I think you forgot something last night." His eyes searched her empty hands and troubled expression. Clearly, she hadn't noticed him on the way in because she was too busy thinking about the manuscript she'd abandoned in the suite.

"My grasp on reality?" she muttered to herself, studying her hands.

The only way to turn her frown upside down was to reveal the manuscript he'd hidden inside his jacket, and he definitely wanted to be the reason she smiled. "I'll happily take credit for that, but I think this is more important."

He didn't even get to hand it to her before her eyes lit up and she wrapped her arms around his neck, nearly tackling him. Will would've settled for a smile, but this was much better. Even if she was more than a foot shorter, he tucked his head into her shoulder, breathing in the smell of her sweet shampoo. *She's ruined me.*

"I can't thank you enough!" Juliet detached herself from him, and he told himself to get a grip when he immediately missed her touch. She hugged the manuscript to her chest. "How did you know to bring it here?"

"There was an address on the front, and you mentioned you had to get the manuscript to your boss this morning. I figured you ran out to make it to your meeting, since we lost track of time. I wasn't expecting to arrive before you, and security wouldn't let me leave it at the desk without you having signed in." He didn't usually ramble, but seeing her again made him nervous.

"I'm sorry…" She started fidgeting with the edges of the pages.

"For forgetting the manuscript, or leaving me this morning?" he asked, rather enjoying that he wasn't the only nervous one.

"All of it – and I didn't exactly run out. I tried to call out to you, but you couldn't hear, so I left you a note." She picked at the paper, clearly uncomfortable about her actions. He knew what it was like to have a demanding job, so he wasn't going to give her a hard time.

"You could've always come in and joined me," he suggested, closing the gap between them.

She smirked. "Then I definitely wouldn't have made the meeting."

"A meeting on a Sunday? Your employer needs a good talking to." Will shook his head.

Juliet only shrugged. "The senior editor doesn't believe in weekends, and if I want to be promoted then neither can I." He admired her for not badmouthing her superior, even if they were clearly unreasonable to call in staff in this weather on the weekend.

She looked to the elevator doors, and he knew they were running out of time.

"Thank you again for this, and I'm sorry for making you go out of your way in the cold," she said, and he reached for her before she could run off again. Her eyes settled on his hand on her forearm, and for a moment it looked like she was going to tell him not to let go. Did she feel it too?

"What if I wanted to see you again?" Will wished he'd been smoother in his delivery. His phone vibrated in his pocket, but he ignored it.

Juliet's lips parted, but she said nothing. Her hesitation killed him. He tried to remember that this was about work and fulfilling his promise to her estranged mum, but seeing her stare at him with those big, questioning eyes as if assessing whether he could be trusted, he wished he hadn't come at all.

He was about to speak when the elevator doors pinged opened at the end of the empty lobby.

"There's a woman staring at us," Will whispered, looking over Juliet's shoulder at a woman tapping her brown loafers impatiently by the elevator in the lobby.

Juliet followed his gaze, and her smile faltered. "That'd be my boss. If I don't want to get fired, I'd better go." She reached up on her tiptoes and kissed his clean-shaven cheek. "Thank you—for everything."

He clenched his jaw, worried that she was saying goodbye. Even though they'd escaped the snow outside, with her out of his reach he'd never felt colder.

"Maybe we'll meet again in the new year." She smiled, backing away.

He couldn't find words fast enough before she hurried off and followed the glowering woman into the elevator. Will ran his hands through his hair, cursing himself for getting tongue-tied. After scolding himself for acting like a lovesick teenager, and not a man with an important job to do, he thanked security on his way out.

CLIMBING into the back of his car, Will smiled to himself as he heard Jingle Bells playing again.

"Mr Bryce has called twice," Johnson, his driver informed him from the front seat.

He didn't get a chance to respond before his phone started vibrating in his jacket pocket. *Harvey must be desperate to ring my driver.* Will should've known not to ignore his friend's call. They'd attended Yule's academy of guardians together until Harvey was expelled after an arrest in the Outside had nearly exposed the village. A pity he hadn't become a guardian; he was talented at tracking people down.

"Hugo is demanding I cover his extensive hotel bill because you were invited on my behalf and you tossed him against a wall." Harvey Bryce, hotel and real-estate mogul – and Will's oldest friend – wasn't a big fan of 'hello'.

"That guy put hands on Juliet. One of the security guards was talking about seeing him on the cameras when I arrived. Thankfully, she had a friend to help her get out of there." When he'd entered the party, it had been a scene of slight chaos, with Hugo ranting and raving about how Juliet had disrespected him.

Harvey sighed, taking in the information Hugo had left out. "I'll have him escorted off the premises. He'll be black-listed from the Bryce chain." Harvey had very simple but strict rules: no discrimination, assault, or harassment of any kind at his hotels and clubs. Being thrown out was one of his lesser punishments, and Hugo was probably only getting off so easily because Harvey didn't want any blood on his hands during the festive season.

"I'll settle his bill for causing you the trouble." Will didn't want his friend to be out of pocket. He had ruined a painting when he'd tossed Hugo against the wall, causing quite the scene at the party. Juliet wasn't the only one who'd crippled the rockstar's ego last night, but it had been worth it.

"Don't bother, I'll make sure security ensures he pays up." Harvey's security consisted of retired guardians – no one valued protection or loyalty more. "At least you got to meet Juliet, so your evening wasn't a complete waste. It's already the 3rd of December, and you only have until the 26th to get her in front of the council. You'd better get a move on."

"I've made contact. Now, I need to find a way to get myself more involved in her life – gain her trust." Will didn't want to admit how many ethical lines he'd already crossed.

"I don't like this. Getting involved with a banishment case is risky. Even if you feel like you owe Eloise, communicating with someone banished could get you in serious trouble, and the way you talk about Juliet makes me nervous. Ever since you got that file, you've been far too invested."

Will hesitated, not wanting to lie to his best friend. Unfortunately, it wasn't hard to read the silence. Harvey knew him better than he knew himself.

"Fuck, I knew it – you like her. I knew this was going to get messy. Juliet's the job, a favour. Unless you want to end up like me, then I suggest you stay professional."

"Have we swapped places?" Will demanded. "Aren't I usually the one telling you to remember the rules? I think you still owe me for bailing you out last time."

"Evasion. Great. When you fuck up your life, I'll have head of security waiting for you." Harvey had been offering him the job for years.

"I'll be fine," Will lied to his best friend for the first time in his life. It did feel like they'd swapped places.

"If I remember correctly, I said the same thing before the Council of Yule expelled me from the academy. Be smart about this."

Harvey's warning didn't fall on deaf ears, but Will couldn't stop, not now. He had to get Juliet to Yule so she could meet her mum.

"Your concern is heart-warming. I didn't know you cared so much," he teased as the car pulled up outside an apartment building. One of the perks of being a senior guardian who spent more time in the Outside was having access to apartments in every city in the world. The downside was that he never felt like he had a real home on the Outside.

"Fuck you." Harvey sighed, never comfortable with displays of emotion.

"Love you too." Will knew it was the easiest way of getting off the phone before he confessed just how deep a mess he'd got himself into.

Juliet resisted the urge to fidget as she waited for Ms Baum to finish skimming through Hugo's manuscript. Her thoughts kept going back to Will. While they'd been talking, she'd spotted the town car outside the building and guessed it was waiting for him. She should've known from the hotel suite and the expensive tailored clothes, nothing marked with labels, that he came from real money. She feared that he belonged to the very world she'd spent years trying to escape. She hated that all it had taken was the smell of his cologne to tempt her.

"Congratulations, Ms Frost. You've proved you're not entirely useless," Ms Baum said, without lifting her eyes from the pages. Then again, she might turn to stone if she praised anyone while making eye contact. "I was beginning to think you weren't going to show up, or you'd call in sick, until I came down and found you flirting in the lobby."

"I'm sorry I was late." Juliet tried to think of some lame excuse, but Ms Baum had seen her standing with Will.

"I can't blame you; I'd forget about my boss waiting for me if a man like that paid me any attention." The woman's expression was as rigid as her jet-black bob.

Juliet didn't answer, worried her tardiness would be held against her. She hadn't meant to get so caught up talking with Will. She felt uncomfortable that she'd worried him by running out, and she wished she could've confessed how much she'd wanted to stay, but if he really was from the social circles she'd tried so hard to stay away from, maybe it was a good thing she hadn't.

"Don't look so terrified. I was only teasing. You really are too sensitive." Ms Baum extended her hand, offering Juliet a seat.

It wasn't the first time she'd been called too sensitive, but it *was* the first time Ms Baum had offered Juliet a seat in her office since she'd interviewed for the position at the publishing house.

"I got a call from Hugo himself while you were occupied downstairs. He informed me of how well you handled yourself, and he promised that in the future his pages will be in on time." Ms Baum eyed her suspiciously through her thick square glasses.

Juliet forced herself to smile under the scrutinising gaze. "It took some convincing, but with the work you've already put in, he just needed an extra nudge. First-time authors are always nervous to get started." She was surprised that he'd called Ms Baum to praise her instead of getting her fired. Maybe he hadn't wanted to lose out on the contract for assaulting a staff member now that he'd sobered up. Juliet was just relieved she'd never have to stand in the same room as Hugo again.

Ms Baum's suspicious gaze slipped away. At the end of the day, all that mattered to her was the manuscript.

"About the other manuscripts you wanted me to finish before the holidays… I didn't get to finish the report because I had to go to the Bryce." Juliet waited for her boss to use the missing report as an excuse not to promote her to Junior Editor despite getting Hugo's heinous pages.

"Reports? You can forget about the other manuscripts." Ms Baum waved it off, leaning back in her chair. "A deal is a deal, and though I may be many things, I keep my word. The Junior Editor position is yours." Her smile didn't reach her eyes, but it was the effort that counted.

Speechless, Juliet wondered if this was a dream or some practical joke.

"Thank you! I promise I won't let you down." She shook Ms Baum's hand before the woman changed her mind.

"Don't thank me." Ms Baum scoffed, like gratitude was an insult. "You've earned it. Hugo has been dragging out the process. I don't know what you did, but this is a major win for us. And before I let you go, HR has been nagging me. You've got some vacation days remaining for the year. I don't know how you could leave it so late to take them – it's against policy." She acted as though she wasn't the one who'd denied Juliet's every request for time off. Hell, she'd even worked when she was sick.

"Must've slipped my mind, so caught up in work," Juliet lied, not wanting to rock the boat. Now was not the time to argue, not when she was so close to getting her dream job.

"Make sure you don't let it happen again. HR is insisting you take them this month before your promotion can be processed. Even though it'll leave us awfully short, there's no arguing with policy. When you return in the new year, the Senior Editor of the Young Adult division will go over the new contract with you." Ms Baum shoved Hugo's pages in her drawer, probably not to be looked at again until January. The gesture confirmed that the last twenty-four hours had been a test, to either promote or fire Juliet. At least if she was fired, she wouldn't have to spend another miserable year as Ms Baum's servant.

"So... I'm off until we return on the fourth of January? If

you can't spare me, I'm happy to work." *A month off? Maybe I wasn't the only one who got laid last night.* The last time she'd had that much time off was before college.

"We're well able to manage without you, and I don't like to repeat myself. Are you accepting the position or not?" Ms Baum tapped her foot impatiently.

Juliet wanted to jump for joy and throw her arms around her hateful boss, but neither would be appropriate for the office. "Yes, I accept!" she practically shouted, before correcting her tone. "I'd love nothing more." Being an editor was her dream, and the Young Adult department was a highly sought-after position. And in a separate building to Ms Baum.

"Excellent. I don't know where I'll find another assistant such as yourself, and I'm loath to let you leave, but I'm sad to say that our time together has come to an end." Ms Baum sighed. "I hope you won't embarrass me. I expect great things from those who leave my desk. Make me proud."

Juliet glowed at the first praise she'd received in years. "You won't regret this!"

"I hope not." Ms Baum picked up her coffee cup and turned her attention to her computer screen. "Now, I suggest you go and enjoy your holidays before I decide to rescind the offer."

Juliet didn't need to be told twice; she practically danced out of the office.

For the rest of the work week, she slept in, caught up on her reading, finished the Korean drama she'd been forsaking, and celebrated Margot's birthday without having to worry once about Ms Baum calling her into the office. The Christmas season was turning out to be too good to be true.

But even if she'd forgotten about the chest under her bed, she hadn't forgotten about Will, as much as she tried to.

Dropping her Christmas shopping on the couch, Juliet sighed in relief. She'd never got her Christmas shopping done as early as the 8th before. The best part of being off during the week was being able to get her shopping done without crowds and never-ending queues. Even on a Friday afternoon, she'd barely had to queue after finding the perfect gifts for Margot and Beth. Now she just had to hide them from her sleuth friend.

"What scandals need tidying up this week?" she asked Margot, who was in front of her blindingly bright computer screens with her knees tucked under her chin.

"Just finished up with my last client, and then the weekend can begin. His mistress was stealing from his company. I almost feel bad for hacking into her account; I think she deserves a Christmas bonus for sleeping with a man three times her age." Margot winced, tossing back the last of her long-melted iced coffee. "Also, my Aunt Gabby texted me to say she hasn't received your RSVP for the Christmas Gala tonight." Margot set her fluffy-sock-covered feet onto the corner of her desk. One of the things they had in common was that they'd never mastered being able to sit at a desk 'properly'.

"I didn't get the invitation. They usually go to my dad,

and if he hasn't requested my appearance then I'm not going to remind him." Juliet shrugged, relieved he hadn't called to force her to attend this year. The last four years had been painful enough.

"Strange that you haven't heard from him by now."

"Please don't jinx it."

"Not attending again this year?" Juliet asked, wondering if she'd escaped this year or if her dad was just waiting to pounce last minute. Invitations were only extended to the esteemed parents and their eldest child of the wealthiest and most powerful families in the country. Throughout the dinner, everyone boasted about their achievements and that of their precious darlings. The event made the Met look like a public affair.

"No, Dad still isn't talking to me for not joining his security firm so he'll probably take one of my brothers." Margot plaited her hair over her shoulder, as she did when she was anxious. "He doesn't want me stealing any of his precious clients, and even if I'm technically invited, I'd probably be turned away. No one wants to fall out with him."

"What about your aunt? I'm sure she'd bend the rules for you, since she helped you get your business started." Juliet took her shopping to her room.

"She would if I asked, but I'm sure the others on the invitation committee wouldn't accept it." Margot's voice travelled down the hall.

"I wish you could go in my place in disguise. Although you'd have to deal with my stepmother trying to match you up with someone *suitable*. I think she believes marrying me off will get me out of the family once and for all. Then again, what wife wants the illegitimate child hanging around?" Juliet ranted. "And if being made to feel like prized cattle isn't bad enough, the *worst* part of the evening is the whispers from those who think I shouldn't even be there because I was born 'out of wedlock' and to a woman nobody knows anything about. As if I even want to go!"

"I'd be surprised if Gillian tried to set you up again this year – not after last year's scandal." Margot smirked as Juliet flopped back down on the couch.

"Don't start. The jerk deserved it. A prince should know to keep his hands to himself." Juliet winced, remembering how she'd slapped the Prince of Maldonia when he had groped her during a dance. She left the room again, in search of a sweater and to avoid the conversation.

"The video got over one million hits in twenty-four hours. The media should've cut you a cheque – and it did raise awareness for the charity." Margot chuckled, having been the one to remove it from the internet after Juliet had pleaded for her help. The money raised on the night always went to war orphans, who probably suffered from a war some people at the gala profited from.

"I would've preferred if the precious prince hadn't grabbed my ass at all," Juliet called, grabbing her warm cream cardigan from the storage box beneath her bed. *Oh shit, the box!* She had forgotten about her nana's chest in the chaos of the week. She was about to reach for it when the landline phone rang.

Juliet stuck her head into the living area, where Margot was reaching to pick it up. *Who is it?* Juliet mouthed, as her friend sat up and pushed away from her desk.

"Mr Frost! I'm afraid Juliet's still at work." Margot was well used to lying on her behalf.

Juliet mouthed a pitiful *thank you*. She reached for her phone to check her messages.

"That's odd. Her office told you she's left for the holidays?" Margot grimaced. "Oh, right – I forgot she went

Christmas shopping. I'll get her to call you when she's back. Yes, sir. I will."

Twenty missed calls pinged as Juliet turned on her phone. Even her stepmother had tried to call her.

"Why did you turn off your phone? I hate when he shows up when you don't respond." Margot shut off her screens from prying eyes, as though Juliet's dad was about to burst through the door.

"I've got four weeks to do whatever I please, and I didn't want to get caught in my father's festive plans," Juliet muttered, picking up a pastel pink blanket from where it lay in a heap on the floor and tossing it over the cream couch.

Frantic, they tidied up the apartment as best they could, covering the dishes in the sink with a wooden cutting board and closing their bedroom doors to conceal the mess within. They both knew there was no way Mr Frost wouldn't come himself, and he'd report whatever he saw to Margot's father, his lifelong frenemy.

After twenty minutes, both surveyed the sitting area. *Legally Blonde* was still frozen on the TV screen from breakfast, and the bookshelves that sat across from Margot's desk needed a dust, but they'd done their best.

"If we get out of here before my dad arrives, he won't know you lied and it'll spare us both an argument," Juliet said, much preferring for them to flee.

"Don't have to tell me twice." Margot pulled on her trainers and wrapped a giant scarf over her NYC jumper. She didn't like coats – they made her claustrophobic. Juliet shoved her laptop in her bag, hoping to get some writing done during her break, and threw open the door.

"You've got to be kidding me!"

Her father, Jeremy Frost, stood in the hall with an intimidating grin. As usual, not a strand of his black hair, peppered with grey, was out of place. Even his navy suit was probably too afraid to wrinkle. It was at moments like this that Juliet knew God had a warped sense of humour.

"Is that any way to greet your dear ol' dad?" Mr Frost brushed past her smugly, not waiting for an invitation. He watched Margot backing up towards the couch. Even though Margot was taller, he had an aura that made people shrink.

"Wonderful timing, sir," Margot lied, forcing a wide smile. "She just got in."

To take the heat off her friend, Juliet tried to apologise. "I'm sorry I didn't answer your calls. I was out and left my phone behind."

"Am I truly so frightening?" Mr Frost raised his greying eyebrows, and she noticed the suit bag occupying his other arm. *Maybe he just came from the dry cleaners?* Juliet hoped it wasn't anything for her. Gifts always came at a steep price.

"Yes," Margot muttered. Both Frosts turned to look at her. She quickly moved to the kitchen. "I'll put the kettle on."

"How is your father, Margot? I haven't seen him at the Club recently," Frost commented, though he knew they weren't talking.

Margot's shoulders stiffened as she filled the kettle. "You know him – he prefers to work rather than spend his time idling away."

Mr Frost clenched his jaw at the insinuation, and Juliet felt herself sweating. Only Margot could get away with talking to him like that, thanks to her family name and connections. It would only take a snap of her fingers for Mr Frost to end up in some unmarked grave. She'd even offered once. Juliet wanted her dad out of her life, not dead. However, it was nice to have the option.

"Aren't you going to give your father a hug?" Mr Frost wrapped his free arm around her. She froze; his calm and happy demeanour confused her. "Don't frown, you don't want to get wrinkles."

Juliet's expression softened.

"Better. I already pay enough for your stepmother's Botox." He surveyed the apartment, no doubt wondering again how the girls could possibly live in this shoebox. But they loved it – and it came with no strings attached, even if it wasn't up to his square footage standard.

He's only this cheery when he wants something. "To what do we owe the pleasure? I'm sure your calendar is overwhelming; a visit wasn't necessary." Juliet cut to the chase, even though he had hundreds of employees to keep the Frost industrial empire going without him.

"Don't play dumb, it doesn't suit you. Your attendance at tonight's Christmas Gala is requested, and Gillian has kindly selected two dresses for you to choose from." Her father lifted his suit trousers and sat down on the lilac stool by the kitchen counter.

"I thought requests could be accepted or declined?" Juliet hid the irritation in her voice to stay on his good side. Mr Frost wasn't like Margot's dad, who'd iced her out when he was mad at her for leaving the family business for a less murderous career. Juliet's dad only inserted himself more into her life if she didn't give in to his requests.

"I would love to give you the option," he started.

Liar. She kept that to herself.

"However, after last year's incident, you've no choice but to attend and make amends. As a Frost, you have responsibilities, and you *will* act accordingly," he told her, his thick brows pulled together. As if she could ever forget who she was. "Be at the Museum of Natural History by eight tonight."

Margot set a cup of coffee in front of him, but there was no way he'd drink it. Not unless it was an Irish coffee.

"Don't be late. Gillian doesn't like guests coming in once the speeches start. She won't be embarrassed again, and I don't want to spend another Christmas in sullen silence," he added. His wife co-chaired with Margot's aunt, making the exclusive event all the harder to skip.

"I wouldn't want to embarrass the family. Again." Juliet resisted the urge to smile at the thought of his displeasure. As punishment for last year's embarrassment, her stepmother had refused to talk to them for the entire week Juliet had spent at the Frost estate. It was one of the best Christmases she'd had to date, despite it being the first without her nana.

"That's the spirit! It's the Christmas season, after all. We shouldn't be at odds with each other."

Juliet didn't even dignify that with a response. Wanting to see the damage, she unzipped the suit bag, wondering if Gillian had chosen something more tasteful than last year's pink, ruffled monstrosity. She pulled out a strapless emerald dress with a slit up the leg. *Huh, maybe she's starting to hate me a little less.*

"My assistant booked your hair appointment for four at the salon Madame, so be prompt." Gillian would probably have the spies in her favourite salon confirm that Juliet turned up for her appointment.

Juliet darted her eyes to Margot. It seemed like so far all she had to do was dress up and attend…

"There is something else," Mr Frost said, heading toward the door and leaving his coffee untouched.

And there it is.

"There's someone we want you to meet. A Mr Duncan. His real-estate portfolio is impressive, and I want him on our books."

"Dad, does it ever disgust you to pimp out your daughter to the highest bidder?" Juliet asked, opening the door for him. The name sounded familiar, but she couldn't place it. Not that it mattered; he was sure to be some leech trying to please her father.

Her dad let out a bark of a laughter. "That wit! One of the many traits we share."

Juliet's skin crawled at the thought of sharing anything with him.

He put his thick-knuckled hand on the door before she could close it. Still strong for a man in his early fifties. "Is it a sin to want my daughter to have a good life? If we both benefit from tonight, then I see no harm done." He headed towards the stairs, not waiting for her answer. "See you tonight, chickpea."

He only called her "chickpea" when he wanted to pretend they had a normal father-daughter relationship. Juliet slammed the door, then opened it and did it again. It helped relieve some of the anger, but not all. She'd have done it once more, but the door was rather old, and she didn't want to break the frame.

"I should've just gone to some abandoned island for the holidays and left my phone behind."

"He still would have tracked you down. Probably would've hired one of my brothers to do it too," Margot pointed out, handing her the coffee her father had abandoned. *I need something much stronger.* "At least the dresses are pretty, though. I think Gillian actually wants you to look nice this year." She held the second dress from the suit bag against herself: a silver midi with crystal-beaded straps. With her icy hair, it made her look like a snow queen.

Juliet smiled into her coffee, knowing exactly what would make the night more bearable.

Margot grimaced. "I don't like it when you get that look in your eye."

"Well, I've got two dresses, and it'd be a shame for one to go to waste… and having back-up might disrupt whatever sordid plans my father has in store."

"You're supposed to be making up for last year's scandal, not scheming for another," Margot accused her, but Juliet could see the twinkle in her eye as she held the silver silk against her body.

"Like you said earlier – technically, you're already invited. I don't want to go alone, and you can keep me in check." Juliet grinned. "C'mon, it's not like your aunt wouldn't love to see you, or she wouldn't have checked in earlier."

Margot hesitated, chewing her lip. Juliet resorted to begging.

"Please! Frost is trying to marry me off again to this Duncan guy for the sake of a deal, but if I've got a stunning friend with me, he'll be too distracted. You said you wanted to find some new clients, and this is the perfect opportunity!" She gave her the biggest puppy-dog eyes she could.

Margot wavered. "It is kind of a pity to let this dress go to waste…"

"It was made for you," Juliet agreed. The slinky outfit complemented Margot's golden skin perfectly.

"Okay, I'm in."

Juliet threw her arms around her. "I'll call the salon! Leave it all to me." Buzzing with excitement over her plan, she grabbed her phone to find the number for the exclusive hair salon, Madame.

"Madame." The receptionist spoke with a thick British accent.

"Hello! It's Juliet Frost," Juliet said brightly.

"Ms Frost, how are you? Mr Frost called ahead already; you're scheduled for four o'clock."

"That's wonderful – only, I've got a small problem," she

admitted, copying her stepmother's half-apologetic, half-whiny tone whenever she wanted something.

"There's never a problem at Madame, especially for a Frost! What can I help you with?" the receptionist begged, eager to please. Juliet's stepmother had helped Madame Brigit gain legal ownership of the hair salon when her ex-husband had tried to divorce her and take it from her. Mrs Frost's methods, though successful, hadn't been altogether ethical.

"My father, Mr. Frost…" Juliet knew she was milking it, but she needed all the luck she could get. Everywhere else would be fully booked. "He was meant to make the appointment for two, myself and a Ms Roth, but silly Dad only made the appointment for one." She cringed at herself.

"I'm sorry, Ms Frost, but with tonight's event we're already fully booked." The receptionist sounded gutted not to be able to help, and Juliet used that to her advantage.

She let out a long, audible sigh. "I understand completely, and I'd hate to put you under any pressure. I'll have to go to Claudia's instead—"

"That won't be necessary! We can accommodate you!" the receptionist said quickly. "Just a moment, please."

Juliet heard her fingers flying over the keyboard. She felt awful for causing the woman such panic when she'd never intended to cancel, but this was an emergency.

"We've got a free seat at ten past four. Will your guest's treatments be charged to Mrs Frost's account also?" the woman asked, making Juliet's day even better.

"Yes, all on the Frost account. Thank you for all your help." She had some cash left in her purse after shopping for a nice tip; she made a mental note not to forget.

"For the daughter of Mrs Frost, it's a pleasure. Please tell Mrs Frost we look forward to seeing her very soon," the receptionist said. Juliet knew Gillian would be there at noon for her standing appointment; she helped plan the Christmas Gala, and she'd be sure to arrive before all the guests. Juliet was relieved to hear they wouldn't run into each other.

After exchanging polite goodbyes, she put her phone on the kitchen counter. "Done!" She winked at Margot.

"I can't believe you got me in! They book out months in advance." Margot beamed. "I'll have to put it on one of my credit cards until my next client pays up. They charge hundreds for a freaking manicure." Margot might have come from money, but she'd put everything into her business, and her family had cut her off once she announced she had no intention of following their plans for her future. Juliet could never thank her enough for always supporting her. Hopefully, this would be a good opportunity for her.

"No need – it'll be charged to Gillian's account. I'd pay to see her reaction when she gets the bill," she said mischievously.

Her stepmother had always begrudgingly given her what she thought was appropriate to keep up appearances befitting a daughter of the Frost family, but Juliet had been the first Frost to work her way through school and college because her stepmother had kept the money her dad had originally planned to give to Juliet for expenses. She'd claimed Juliet wasn't mature enough to handle her own finances, but Gillian obviously just didn't want her to have any financial freedom. She'd only been able to attend college because Nana Rose had paid for what her scholarship didn't, and she'd covered the rest herself. An education meant freedom, and they'd wanted to keep her on a tight leash.

Yet when they'd learned about her plans to go whether they liked it or not, and the power was out of their hands, her dad had suddenly loved to brag about her excellent grades and her academic scholarship, as though it hadn't been out of necessity.

"Thank you, but it's too much!" Margot argued.

"It's not nearly enough, and you can thank Gillian." Juliet smiled. For the first time in years, if ever, she was looking forward to attending the Christmas gala.

"Are we going to talk about the man's shirt I saw in the laundry basket the other day?" Margot whispered as their stylists worked on them side by side.

Despite it being one of the busiest days of the year, the salon still maintained a quiet, peaceful atmosphere. Every inch, decorated with white marble and gold-trimmed mirrors, screamed expense.

"It's Will's. The guy from the night when I collected the manuscript from Hugo." Juliet tried to sound like she wasn't still thinking about him. The flashbacks of his lips on hers, and the weight of his hands on her hips, were never far from her mind.

"You kept his shirt? How romantic." The manicurist glared at Margot as she snatched her hands out from the heat lamp to clap. "Are you going to see him again?"

"I don't think so. I was going to return the shirt to him, but I've no way to contact him. It's expensive, so I wasn't going to throw it out." Juliet wished she had his number, so she could have at least thanked him for helping her get her dream promotion. But she figured that if he'd wanted her to have it, he could have given it to her in the lobby.

"You could donate it?" Margot suggested as her stylist

sprayed her icy locks, slicked into a low bun and decorated with white pearls, with an alarming amount of hairspray.

Maybe Margot was right and she should get rid of the reminder. After all, they'd agreed on one night, and she needed to stop thinking about him. But it felt wrong donating what wasn't hers, and what if their paths crossed again?

"I will, when I get the chance," Juliet lied, focusing on the bald stylist clipping back her soft waves with emerald-winged clips. A few wispy bits were left out to frame her heart-shaped face.

Thankfully, they couldn't really speak once the make-up artists started. Juliet nearly fell asleep in the chair. When she opened her eyes, she admired the blushed cheeks and dark brown eyeshadow that highlighted her features without masking them.

"Your eyes look incredible," she told Margot, whose dark, smoky eye gave her a vampiric yet sultry look with her sleek hair.

"Still, I'd kill for your lips. The red is perfect on you," Margot returned as they pulled themselves from the comfy leather chairs. They said their goodbyes, and Juliet made sure to add a generous tip to the bill.

"I need another coffee if I'm going to last the night." Margot shivered outside the salon. Luckily it hadn't started snowing again, but she was grateful for the litre of hairspray, because the wind had picked up.

"You read my mind." Juliet took her arm, and they huddled together to keep warm.

BOTH APPRECIATED the large coffees once they got to their chilly apartment.

"Victor should be here to pick us up at seven," Juliet said, carefully slipping her green dress over her hair and make-up.

"I'll be ready. I haven't seen him since he brought you back from the estate last year—" Margot cut herself off. "Sorry, I didn't mean to talk about it." She fidgeted with the crystal straps that did little to support her chest.

"It's fine, you don't have to tiptoe around it." Juliet shrugged off the memory and put on the gold necklace with the small bell she'd found in the chest. She didn't like talking about the Frost estate, even though Margot knew about her cottage – how her grandfather and stepmother had kept Juliet out of sight and out of the main house when she turned fourteen. Her dad had agreed, needing to keep his wife and father happy, when it was suggested Juliet had better not live in the main house – that it was too upsetting to have her in *Gillian's* home, except for at parties and during the holidays, when appearances had to be maintained and Gillian could show her friends how generous she was to accept her husband's pre-marital child.

Even if she had never felt wanted at home, Victor, the groundskeeper and driver, had always been like the dad she'd never had. He'd taught her to drive, and taken her to the emergency room when she'd broken her arm when she'd failed at her first and last attempt at skateboarding.

Pushing aside the memories, Juliet searched for her silvery heels. They weren't in the wardrobe; lifting up the blanket at the end of her bed, she found them resting against the chest she'd been procrastinating about opening again. She grabbed her heels, but couldn't resist her curiosity. Margot was still getting ready in her room, so she had a moment to spare.

The letter she'd shoved inside still sat on top, and this time Nana Rose's handwriting hit her like an emotional freight train. She forced herself to swallow her grief so her tears wouldn't ruin her makeup.

Dear Juliet

My darling granddaughter, I'm sorry I couldn't give this to you in person and explain its contents. This chest was entrusted to me by your mother, to be passed on to you only after the passing of your grandfather. I'm afraid that in keeping my promise to your mother, I've had to keep you in the dark. There are many elements of our family's past and your own story that have been kept from you, for both your own safety and that of others. However, the time has come for you to learn the truth.

Having watched you grow into such a thoughtful, kind and honest woman that I'm proud to call my grand-daughter, I feel you should be allowed to make your own decision and find where you truly belong. I hope you can forgive me – us – for what we've kept from you over the years. Please keep your mind and your heart open, and I promise you'll find the home you've always deserved. One I'm afraid that we failed to give you.

I wish now that I could go back in time and protect you, but you have to understand that your father's relationship with your mother put us in an impossible position. Your grandfather and I did what we thought would protect our family. Our family history is rife with secrets that will seem impossible for you to understand at first. I wanted to spare you any undue longing for a home we could not give you. I've been in contact with your mother, Eloise, and I promised her that I would get this chest to you when the time was right. It is of the utmost importance that you keep this chest and its contents to yourself. I know I'm asking too much and you'll want to confront your father for answers, but please have patience. Your mom will reach out when the time is right. The last thing I ask of you is to give her a chance to explain.

All my love,
Nana Rose

Taking a deep breath, Juliet resisted the urge to crumple up the letter, to forget all she'd just read and move on from her past. What she didn't know couldn't hurt her.

She settled on the edge of the bed, reminding herself to breathe as she absorbed her nana's words. She loved her grandmother, but what had she – what had her family – been hiding from her that could be so terrible as to wait until death to expose it? Her grandfather was dead, so she couldn't confront him for answers, and she doubted her dad would tell her what the hell this letter meant.

She read over the last part again. *Your mom will reach out when the time is right. The last thing I ask of you is to give her a chance to explain.*

Reach out? It'd been days since she'd received the chest. There'd been no calls or emails, letters – nothing. *She's been talking to my mom since when?* She'd always been led to believe that her mom wanted no contact with her, that she was a mistake to be forgotten. *Did Mom know how I was being treated over the years? How I was never welcome and raised by the driver and chef? Did she know all this and never come for me?* Her grief quickly morphed into rage.

"I buzzed Victor up. You almost ready?" Margot popped her head around her door. Luckily, her friend was too busy stuffing hard candy into her tiny satin clutch to notice Juliet's solemn expression. Watching her friend trying to squeeze her phone into the already stuffed clutch made Juliet chuckle, softening the ache in her heart. She would've suggested less candy, but Margot never went anywhere without it, always saying she couldn't offend anyone if her mouth was full.

She thought of the gala, and in spite of Margot's presence a cold sweat took over her body. Strapping on her heels with shaky hands as Margot headed down the hallway, she reminded herself that in a few hours she'd be home and safe. It was too late to cancel now, and despite what her nana had requested, she *had* to ask her dad if he'd known his mother was talking to Juliet's mom. If he and his deceased mother had concocted this cruel plan to dangle the woman Juliet had never met before her to bring her back into the family fold…

She heard Margot greeting Victor as she shoved the chest back under her bed. Forcing her best smile, she prepared herself for the night ahead.

"Victor! Prompt as always." She beamed, kissing her father's driver's cheek.

"Ms Juliet, beautiful as always." He spun her round, ever the gentle giant. His grey beard was longer than when she'd last seen him. However, he still wore the grey suit and white shirt he'd worn for as long as she could remember. "Ms Margot, you look wonderful also," he said politely. "Though I wasn't aware I was bringing both of you tonight?"

"I've a little surprise and a favour to ask," Juliet wheedled, playing with the waves that framed her face.

"I'm listening." His dark eyes narrowed, and his weathered wrinkles deepened.

Juliet glanced at Margot, who looked incredibly nervous. "Margot is invited, so I thought we'd ride together."

"I don't know." Victor always knew when she was up to something. "I didn't receive any notice, and I don't want a repeat of last year…" He had escorted Juliet to the Frost estate last year after the scandal with the prince, and it was Victor who'd brought hot cocoa and an icepack for her cheek to her cottage after Gillian had slapped her – with her rings on – for embarrassing the family. Juliet guessed he was erring on the side of caution to protect her.

"We can always take a cab," she suggested, knowing he wouldn't let that happen. "Please, Vic! Don't make me go alone. Margot will keep me in check."

Her voice got a little pitchy at the last part. It was more likely that Margot would have to keep her in check when she confronted her father about her nana's letter.

"You left this to the last minute, so I can't argue." Victor checked his watch. "Ms Roth, I'd be delighted to offer you my services." It wasn't the first time he'd met Margot; he'd helped them move out of their college dorm and into their current apartment almost five years ago.

"Thank you. I promise our girl will be on her best behaviour," Margot said with a smile.

"I can only hope the other guests will do the same," Victor said, eying Juliet sympathetically. He knew how the other guests thought she was an easy target because of how she'd come to be a Frost.

Then again, if I confront my dad about private matters at the biggest event of the year, I might not be a Frost for much longer.

By nine o'clock, the steps in front of the museum were empty since they'd missed everyone arriving. Thanks to the icy roads, what should have been a twenty-minute drive had taken nearly an hour. The moment Juliet saw the press weren't waiting on the steps, her nerves settled, and she thanked whatever god was responsible for the weather for delaying them. Her father would be furious with her for being late, but she got some amusement from knowing he'd have to swallow it for the night so he wouldn't make a scene in public.

"Thanks for the ride!" Juliet hugged Victor from behind the driver's seat before hurrying out of the black sedan.

"Have a good night! Call if there are any issues," he called after them. His nervous gaze unsettled Juliet.

"As always." She saluted him through the window.

Victor saluted back, always in her corner. It had been Nana Rose's gesture, a way of saying 'stiff upper lip'; Victor had adopted it after her death. The thought reminded her of the letter. She wished she'd read it sooner. She needed to get to the bottom of all these secrets, but for now she'd have to be patient.

"Ms Frost, Ms Roth, welcome. If you'd both please follow me." Clearly, the suited greeter had done his homework on the guests. They were swiftly led down a long corridor adorned with artefacts from various centuries. The pillars that separated each exhibit were ornately decorated Christmas trees. The pine smell was a touch overwhelming.

Even with the festive decorations, the museum, empty save for the music drifting from the event's room at the end of the corridor, gave Juliet the creeps. Margot seemed right at home, admiring each dimly lit exhibition. Then again, when else would you get a private tour of one of the busiest museums in the world?

"The main course will be served momentarily; I suggest you take your seats. The speeches have already begun." The greeter checked his watch, his nostrils flaring. They'd clearly ruined his timing.

"This is so embarrassing." Margot blushed as he directed them to the centre table, where Juliet's father sat with some men Juliet had never seen before. It was by an overwhelmingly white Christmas tree so tall that she wondered how they'd even got it inside.

"It's fine, don't worry," she whispered, steering them to the two empty seats to her father's left. As usual, Gillian would be sitting at the head table with the other event-planners.

In fact, she was midway through her speech about the importance of this charity gala. Juliet winced as she caught her stepmother's eye. If looks could kill, Gillian's could slaughter.

"They weren't kidding when they said the theme was Winter Wonderland," Margot whispered, distracting her. It was true – the Roman-style statues were made of ice, and the large, ornate snowflakes hanging from the snow-speckled glass ceiling looked like they were straight from the film *Frozen,* if Elsa had been given a bigger budget. With the glow of fairy lights amongst them, it almost appeared to be snowing within the function room.

"So glad you both could make it." Mr Frost winked at Juliet and rose to kiss her cheek. He clearly wasn't surprised to see Margot in the slightest, so he'd either anticipated her plan, or Victor had messaged ahead to spare Juliet from getting into trouble.

What is going on with him? He should be quietly seething, but he seems downright cheery. Maybe he's dying, she thought, unkind as it was.

He sat Juliet next to him, and Margot sat beside her as waiters in white uniforms and perfect silver bow-ties cleared the starters. Juliet noticed the table was missing a guest. She wondered who else was late.

"Sorry we were late," she said quietly to the table, "the icy roads really slowed down traffic." A few of the guests acknowledged her with waves that said 'no need to apologise' and 'at least you made it safely', and Margot introduced herself.

There was a round of applause for Gillian, and Juliet joined in.

"Thank God that's over with," her father said, giving them his full attention. "You both look beautiful. It's lovely to see you again, Margot. I'm delighted we've a member of the Roth family joining us; Gillian was so disappointed to hear that your father had to pull out last-minute."

"I'm delighted to be here, and I'm sure my family would want me to send their regards." Margot made bullshitting look easy, not even looking slightly fazed at the news of her family's absence.

Mr Frost tucked into his steak without responding, but his eyes lingered on Margot. *Gross.* Juliet downed the flute of champagne and squeezed Margot's leg under the table, trying to reassure her that he was only looking for a reaction. This was not how she'd wanted the evening to go.

"I took the liberty of ordering you vegan mousse, Juliet; Gillian mentioned you were on a diet," Mr Frost said, while the white-gloved waiter laid a bowl of cold green goo before her.

Margot stifled a chuckle with her napkin as Juliet poked it with a fork. "I wouldn't feed that to the stray cat outside our building," she whispered.

"Looks great – thanks, Dad," Juliet said, not wanting to fall into a trap. Gillian was the master of subtle digs. Juliet had been curvy ever since puberty had hit her like a freight train. Once she'd despised the tiger stripes on her hips or that her thighs dared to touch, but once she'd left the Frost estate, she'd learned to love her body, to eat what she wanted, and to exercise because she wanted to and not because she had to.

Margot ate her steak with great enthusiasm while Juliet filled up on the bread and champagne. *The only thing that should come in mousse form is chocolate.* At least her dad had stopped staring at her friend.

"That steak! There are no words—" Margot put down her knife and fork as the waiter began to clear their plates.

"The slurping noises were a bit of a giveaway." Juliet smirked.

"How was your delicious vegan mousse?" Margot asked, once the table was clear.

"I think I've pulled stuff out of the garbage disposable that looked more edible."

"Probably would taste better, too."

They cracked up laughing. Thank God for dessert – Juliet's favourite, two scoops of peppermint ice-cream in a beautiful crystal bowl. Having a good time was easy with Margot to chat to.

"Tonight isn't so bad, is it?" Margot reasoned, looking to all the people engaged in polite conversation at their table. Thankfully, Mr Frost had been too engrossed in a private conversation with the man on his other side to pay them any more mind. Juliet wondered what had happened to the mysterious guy he'd wanted to set her up with. Hopefully it was his seat that remained empty. *He probably backed out when he learned about the set-up and wanted to spare us both an evening of awkward small-talk.*

Once dinner finished, the dance floor, made to look like a frozen lake, filled up with guests, and the bandstand commenced with classic Christmas songs sans lyrics. Margot got up to mingle with the other guests with an ease that Juliet had never been able to achieve. She was satisfied to enjoy the music and observe the party, ignoring the occasional disapproving looks she received, possibly due to last year's scandal.

"Holy crap, do you know who's here?" Margot squealed, meeting Juliet at the bar – the perfect hiding spot, as it was in the corner. If only her tiny clutch bag could've fitted a book.

"Considering you were dancing with a future king when I last looked, it must be someone good."

That was when Juliet saw him. Will. His black suit matched his dark gaze as he found her across the room. He winked at her and raised his glass. One look, and she felt utterly exposed.

"Will Duncan, the CEO of Duncan Recruiting! He finds people to do *any job* anywhere in the world. My dad's been trying to get him as a client for two years. I tried to get an interview a while back to handle his company's tech security, but they're strictly in-house only." Margot sighed, staring across the room at the business opportunity that could change her life.

"*Will* Duncan? Are you sure?" Juliet stammered, hoping Margot was talking about one of the men standing with Will and *not* the man she'd spent the night with. Worse, her father was also heading towards him. This didn't look good. Could Will be the Mr Duncan her father had mentioned? She remembered suddenly that the receptionist had called him Mr Duncan, but she'd never connected the dots – it was a common surname.

"Are you okay? You look a little pale," Margot said, as Juliet watched her father shake Will's hand. Her stomach dropped. She'd already slept with the man she was being set up with. *I should've known one night of fun would come back to bite me on the ass.*

"Too much champagne," she said, downing her glass. "I need some air."

Margot's brow creased with worry. "I'll go with you."

They'd just passed the table nearest the terrace doors when Will and her father blocked their path. Given Will's devilish smile, one Juliet remembered from a much more intimate setting, the humour of this moment wasn't a surprise to him.

"Juliet, let me introduce you," Mr Frost said, shoving Will towards her.

"Will," Will corrected him, eyes on Juliet.

"Juliet." She didn't know what else to do but to play along.

"Have we met before?" he quipped. Her father frowned, looking between them.

"No," Juliet said, a little too quickly. His stubble was gone, and his dark hair had been combed. But his eyes hadn't changed, nor the way they looked at her.

"My mistake." Will took her hand and brought it to his

lips. The sensation was enough to make her hate herself. *Had this been a set-up all along? Did he approach me on purpose the other night?*

He was still holding her hand. Disengaging rather abruptly, she decided to make up some excuse to leave, only to stop herself when she remembered she had to talk with her father about the letter. Now wasn't the time to get distracted by a devastatingly handsome man in an expensive suit.

"Dad, could I talk to you?" Juliet tried to draw him away, but he refused to budge.

"About what chickpea? Now isn't the time – unless you'd like to praise me for having picked a good one? I was bound to get it right one of these days." He looked at Will like he was a champion racehorse. Margot was doing her part as buffer and client hunter, introducing herself to Will with ease.

Juliet clenched her fist, wishing he'd focus. "No, it's about Nana Rose. Did you know she was talking with—"

The breaking of glass interrupted them. A waiter passing Will had stumbled and dropped his tray, spilling red wine and glass shards all over the white tablecloth and floor.

"How clumsy of me! Sorry, man, I didn't see you behind me," Will said, helping up the frazzled waiter, who hurried off without a word. Will grabbed a napkin and placed it over the stain on the white tablecloth before it spread further.

"Sorry, what were you asking?" Mr Frost said, handing Will a new glass of wine. Juliet watched him put it down immediately.

"Did Nana Rose ever—"

"Might I ask your daughter to dance?" Will interjected. Juliet could've sworn he was doing this on purpose. Before she could protest, he added, "Perhaps it might bring back a memory of having met before."

Juliet glared at him. If he revealed just how well they 'knew' each other, her dad would be planning their wedding before the end of the night.

"I'm sure she'd be honoured." Mr Frost nudged her towards him.

Will offered her his arm. Juliet looked for Margot, hoping for an escape, but her friend had been distracted by a man who'd apparently decided against a jacket and tie, in spite of the stringent dress code. Trust Margot to find a rebel amongst the guests.

Will followed her gaze. "Don't worry, your friend is in safe hands," he whispered with a wink.

Her buffer had clearly been intercepted by his friend. Juliet forced a smile, wishing she'd confronted her father earlier so she could have left before Will arrived.

"There aren't many dancing quite yet, and I don't want another spectacle like last year," Juliet said, not wanting to be gawked at.

"Don't be silly, when has a dance ever hurt anyone?" Frost said, eager to forgo the rules to get them together. "If you'll excuse me, I believe Gillian is talking to the CEO of City Bank. I should go and save her."

"I'm sure the Prince of Maldonia would speak to the contrary," Will murmured over her shoulder as she watched her dad go. He wore the same aftershave as when they'd met, causing her body to remember some of the other, finer details of that night.

Juliet wanted the ground to swallow her up. Clearly he knew far more about her than he'd let on. "You do know this is a set-up, right? I suggest you run for the hills before the wedding venue and theme is decided."

"I do – and thankfully my friend can keep your buffer company." He looked to his friend, who'd whisked Margot away to the bar.

Traitor, Juliet thought, but she couldn't blame her.

"As for a wedding venue, what about the Bryce hotel? I think it would be romantic to end it where we started. I know the owner, so I could probably get us a good rate." Will snaked his arm around her waist, leading her to the dance floor.

Of course he knows the owner. Who the hell is this guy? Juliet hushed him. "I'd keep what happened between us quiet, unless you want to be dragged to City Hall. Dad would make you a Frost by dawn."

"I can't blame him for being protective of his daughter," Will said, taking her in his arms.

"More like protect his property." The words flew out before she could stop them.

His hand brushed her lower back, making her heartbeat quicken and distracting her from her worries. "I have to say, I thought I'd receive a warmer welcome," he said quietly, as she tried to follow his steps without treading on his toes. He had a way of throwing her off balance.

"I've got a lot on my mind." She'd spent so many hours wanting and wishing to see him again, but knowing he knew her dad made her question his motives. She tried to keep her distance, but he pulled her close – close enough for others to notice and whisper.

"I don't remember you being so quiet." Will stared down at her as though trying to read her mind. Memories of the other night flooded back: his skin against hers, his lips tasting every inch of her. "You've gone red. Are you alright?"

"Just the champagne," Juliet lied, unable to meet his heavy gaze. She glanced down, and his cufflinks caught her eye.

The Christmas tree… the symbol looked familiar, but she couldn't place it. So where?

The chest under my bed. Juliet froze in his arms, realising he'd turned up the very night she'd received the chest. She had so many questions, but no idea where to start, and she couldn't leave the dance floor without causing a scene, since they'd been joined by other couples. She tried to picture the chest in her head, to figure out if it was truly the same symbol.

"Did you know who I was when you approached me at the hotel?" she blurted out, needing to know if what had happened between them had been some game.

"Yes." Will didn't even hesitate. "And I knew you'd be here tonight because Harvey, who is currently charming your friend in the silver dress, is part of the charity that helped arrange all this."

"So, seducing me was all part of some twisted set-up?" Juliet felt the muscles in his shoulder tense at the question. She stared up at him, needing to know he was telling the truth.

"There was no set-up. I didn't know you'd be in the bar that night. Is there a rule about not being allowed to approach a beautiful woman just because I know her last name?" Will asked, spinning her round so her back was flush against him.

She gritted her teeth, trying to ignore his charm. "How did you know what I looked like?" At least he was being upfront about it, and given that she hadn't known she'd be at the Bryce that night, he couldn't have planned it in advance.

"Society pages." He sighed out the answer like it was obvious and turned her back to face him. "Can you stop looking at me like I'm some evil spy? I'm not planning on kidnapping you or becoming a Frost. I only met your father recently because when I saw my friend for drinks the other night, he was having a business dinner with Frost and his wife. I'm not scheming with your father, if that's what you're worried about." He pulled her close again, forcing her to meet his eye, and she didn't know if it was naivety or lust, but she trusted him.

"I'm choosing to believe you."

"I'm glad I passed the interrogation," Will teased, spinning her around again so they were chest to chest. He dipped his head, and she couldn't take her eyes off his lips. "Have I told you how gorgeous you look tonight? I might change my mind about stealing you away."

His deep voice resonated through her, and she realised how much she missed his touch. *How can a stranger make me feel so safe when my actual family sends me into fight or flight mode?* She didn't realise she'd settled so deeply into his embrace until the round of applause at the end of the song snapped her back to reality.

Juliet clapped for the band, but spotting Gillian and her father whispering to each other ruined the moment. The paranoia of being watched like a bug under a microscope got the better of her.

"Gotta go to the ladies' room, if you'll excuse me." She hurried off before Will had a chance to stop her.

WITH SOME SPACE, Juliet could finally breathe again. The salmon-pink ladies' room startled her more than the guests who went silent when she entered. The white doors separating each cubicle broke up the bold pink shade, but not the tension her presence created.

Forcing a smile, Juliet passed the women touching up their already perfect make-up at the marble sinks. Once she'd run some cold water on her wrists, her heart rate started to return to normal, as did the surrounding conversation.

"Juliet?" Fiona Caldwell – the darling of society and editor of GlaMORE magazine – stood behind her in the mirror. It was the type of magazine filled with societal and celebrity gossip, along with ads for products very few could afford.

"Fiona! It's good to see you," Juliet lied, forcing a fake hug. Last year Fiona had written a two-page exclusive about how appalled she was by Juliet's incident with the prince.

"We have to catch up soon! Maybe coffee?" Fiona beamed as they released each other.

"I'll text you. If we survive the night," Juliet said, referencing the article. It had ended by predicting that the charity event wouldn't survive another year if Juliet Frost were to pull another such stunt.

Fiona patted her arm playfully. "I hope you weren't offended by that little article. We live for the gossip you stir up; the event would be nothing without you."

"I'm afraid there'll be nothing to write about this year. I brought a friend to keep me in check." Juliet wished she'd stayed with Will, even if she was suspicious of his intentions.

"A friend?" Fiona powdered her surgically perfected nose. "Would that be Will Duncan? We saw you dancing. He's quite the catch – surprised you got to him first." She giggled.

Juliet got out her lipstick. "No, I've only just met him. I came with Margot Roth. Last time I checked, she was at the bar with Harvey…" She trailed off, realising she didn't know his last name.

"Harvey Bryce," Fiona filled in. "I wondered if they were

dating, considering the rest of her family aren't in attendance. Not that I'm surprised; everyone knows about their little family tiff." Fiona liked to be involved in everyone's business. Juliet wondered how she had the capacity to remember so much gossip. "Bryce is quite the catch, and you with Will Duncan – seems you're both doing quite well for yourselves." Fiona nudged her, and Juliet nearly streaked her lipstick across her cheek.

"I'll introduce you," she said through a forced smile, merely wanting the conversation to end.

"Oh, no need. There's no one here who doesn't know Mr Duncan, and Harvey Bryce is not a man whose radar I want to be on. I hate to mention it again, but I thought I really should mention how the ladies were put out that you seemed to get the catch of the evening." Fiona rested her hand over Juliet's, feigning concern. "But I don't blame you for wanting to get there first."

"Will asked me to dance, and it would've been rude to decline. If he wants to ask anyone else to dance, then that's up to him." Juliet didn't like the insinuation that she'd ensnared him. She couldn't imagine Fiona's reaction if she knew they'd already been... acquainted.

"No need to explain; I'm sure the ladies will understand when I explain you were merely doing as instructed. At least Will fared better than the prince!"

Fiona's laugh grated on Juliet's last nerve and made her want to pull out the woman's expensive hair extensions. "Will knows where to keep his hands," she said pointedly.

"I'm sure you'll put his hands to great use by the end of the evening." Fiona winked. Juliet gritted her teeth. "We should meet up soon. I'm serious – maybe a night out with Margot? She must need a good cheering up. I heard Mr Roth cut her off," Fiona went on, clearly rooting for the truth of the situation. "I suppose her aunt took pity on her and allowed her to come."

"Ms Roth was invited. Some of us can make it just fine on our own," Juliet snapped, and Fiona's lips formed a tight line. This woman could insult her all she wanted, but no one went after her friend. "Speaking of, I was so sad to hear about your marriage, and after such a beautiful wedding! I hope it didn't set you back too much, but at least you won't have to return the wedding gifts." She didn't like to stoop so low – and she didn't want to get Margot into trouble either, given that she only knew about Fiona's husband buying his mistress an apartment because Mr Caldwell had hired Margot to make the purchases untraceable – but she couldn't resist reminding Fiona that her shit did in fact stink. "To be divorced after only two years of marriage must be humiliating."

Fiona straightened her narrow shoulders, gathering herself. "You'd know all about humiliation." She stepped so close, Juliet could smell the alcohol on her breath. "Given that your mother was a gold-digging social climber who left you on a doorstep after failing to snare your father. It's amazing how you find the strength to face the world."

Juliet glanced at the other women in the bathroom. Either they hadn't heard or didn't want to get involved. She refused to crack, to let Fiona see how her words had cut her. She simply picked up Fiona's glass from the sink and handed her the flute.

"Drown in it," she whispered, before pressing her red lips against the woman's cheek. Fiona gaped; Juliet left her standing there like the trout she was.

Her bright smile dropped as soon as she spotted Mark Hume at her table. He was Ms Baum's boss, and had clearly dropped the news before she could.

"Juliet, we were talking about your work. Apparently you've been promoted! How could you not tell me?" her father said, as she reached their table. Hurt and anger at Fiona swirled in her gut, making it hard to focus.

"It was only just made official," she said, trying not to let her emotions into her voice. "If you'll excuse me, I'm not feeling too well. I'm afraid the champagne has gone to my head." It was code to her father that she'd been insulted and unless he wanted a scene, he should let her leave.

"I wouldn't want to keep you if you're unwell." Mr Frost rose from his chair and glanced around the room as if to see who had upset her, but she knew he only wanted to know who'd spoken against a Frost, not out of a desire to defend her.

The first tear fell. Juliet swiped it away as she kissed her father's cheek and wished the table goodnight. Concern creased Will's brow, but she couldn't explain here, even if she didn't want him to think he was the reason for her leaving. Glancing around the room, she spotted Margot dancing happily with the man she now knew as Harvey Bryce and couldn't bring herself to interrupt them.

"Could you make sure Margot gets home?" she asked her dad. He might have his failings, but he wouldn't let anything happen to his friend's daughter on his watch.

"I'll have Victor pick her up when she is ready," Mr Frost agreed curtly.

"It was lovely to meet you," she said to the table in general, before grabbing her clutch from the table and leaving without looking back. She didn't know where she was going, but she just had to get out of there.

Will

Watching as Juliet left the room, Will lost track of the conversation. He didn't want to run out immediately, but the tears he'd glimpsed in her eyes tested his willpower, and he desperately wanted to know what had caused her to become so upset.

"Sorry you didn't get to spend more time together. Perhaps we can arrange another get-together over the holidays?" Mr Frost said, clearly eager to bring them together again. Not that Will would complain. He needed an in, and her father was throwing the door wide open.

"That would be great," he agreed, "but if you'll excuse me —" Unable to think of an excuse, he simply left the table.

Once he was in the clear, he hurried down the corridors, hoping he wasn't too late to catch up. He was about to give up his search when he spotted Juliet sitting on a bench in front of the elephant exhibit with her back to him. He heard sniffling as he approached her and felt an overwhelming urge to comfort her, and strangle whoever had upset her.

"Are you okay?" he panted.

"You frightened the life out of me!" Juliet's hand flew to her chest, and he noticed her necklace. He tried not to react. *She has the Yule bell necklace! So she's been in the chest.* The bell wouldn't work for its intended purpose unless she truly believed in the spirit of Christmas.

"I'm sorry – I got worried when you disappeared. I wanted to make sure you weren't upset with me about the other night," he explained, wishing his arrival into her life hadn't been so rocky. It wasn't exactly winning her over.

"I didn't leave because of you. I just needed to get away from that room, so I found some other mammals to hang out with." She wiped the smudged mascara from under her eyes, as though trying to conceal her tears from him, and moved over on the bench so he could sit down.

He eagerly accepted the silent invitation, relieved she wasn't pushing him away, given how she'd run off the dance floor like a woman possessed.

"Elephants?" He wanted to distract her from whatever had upset her. "I'm more of a lions and tigers kind of guy." Her teary eyes increased his desire to wrap her in his arms. Not the most professional urge to have, but screw it. He'd already gone too far to turn back now.

"Claws and sharp teeth. How about wolves?" She looked to the grey wolves in the corner of the exhibit.

Will shivered, having had first-hand experience with the wolves of Yule. "No, definitely not wolves. I do have a soft spot for pandas," he admitted, taking his phone from his pocket to reveal his wallpaper was a panda eating bamboo.

Her soft smile was a warm welcome after the tears. "Elephants have always been my favourite. I watched a documentary in school where a mother elephant who had lost her baby returned to the same spot every year in hopes of finding them. That type of pure love makes it hard not to love them." The sadness in her words tugged at his heart. "I just find it unfathomable how an animal with less intelligence than us can't stand to abandon their child, but a human can."

He wondered if the sudden mention of motherly love and her earlier questions to her dad, though successfully interrupted, were because she'd read her grandmother's letter and learned about her contact with Eloise.

"Ignore me," Juliet whispered. "It's the champagne making me emotional."

Will gripped the edge of the bench, resisting the urge to confess.

"I just want to forget tonight and go home," she sighed, fidgeting with the small bell on the end of the necklace.

Will didn't say anything; there was nothing he could say. He simply put his arm around her, and she leaned into his embrace.

And then his blood ran cold as he heard the chime of the bell.

"What the hell is happening?" Juliet held onto him tightly as the museum slipped away.

Will cursed himself for not removing the Frost bell from the chest before he'd given it to his courier. Then again, he'd never expected it to work. She must not hate Christmas as much as she'd claimed, because not ten seconds passed before they found themselves transported to the heart of Yule's Village.

Of all the places the bell could've taken us – her flat, Frost Manor – it took us to her true home. She must have been thinking about her mum and home, and the bell did its damn job. My job, on the other hand, just got a hell of a lot more complicated...

"Are you alright? Take a few deep breaths. Travelling by bell can be disorientating the first couple of times," Will said firmly as Juliet swayed slightly, steadying her. He was afraid she was going to pass out or, worse, scream.

She stared, wide eyes taking in her surroundings and the giant Christmas tree glowing beside them. Will let her adjust, not wanting to overwhelm her with explanations.

"This isn't… I don't… I feel a little sick," she stuttered, her eyes darting from the snow-covered cobbles beneath their feet to the surrounding stores and workshops.

"That's normal – you get used to it," Will assured her.

"Travelling by bell?" Her hand flew to the bell around her neck. "This brought us here!" Thankfully, it was a little past eight in the evening, so the streets were mostly empty and there was no one close enough to hear her panicked squeal.

"Juliet, it's okay," he said, gently turning her so she was facing him – and because he was worried she'd run off. Her eyes frantically jumped from the candy-striped lamp post to a passing reindeer sleigh; he couldn't make out the occupants, so hopefully they wouldn't notice anything unusual. He took off his jacket and wrapped it around her shoulders as her teeth started to chatter, either from the sudden drop in temperature or the shock. Keeping her warm was key.

"Breathe, Juliet. You're safe here; no one and nothing is going to hurt you," he said, unsure if she'd even heard him. He let her process for a minute, her breath steaming between them.

"I'm fine. I need some space." Juliet backed out of his grasp slowly as another reindeer-pulled sleigh passed by, taking a couple home after a romantic night out. Her brow furrowed. "I think that last glass of champagne really did a number on me. This can't be real." She squeezed her eyes shut.

Will wished he could tell her this was a dream. It wasn't every day you learned about a magical Christmas village hidden within the North Pole. It would take her some time to adjust, and this certainly wasn't what he'd wanted her first impression of Yule to be. He'd planned to introduce her to this place slowly, once he had her complete trust.

"Why aren't you freaking out?" Juliet rounded on him, her eyes wide with confusion. Her lips were faintly tinged with blue as the climate took its toll on her in the strapless gown, though she seemed unaware of her shivers. "What is this place?"

"This is Yule, my home. In the simplest terms, it's a protected village in the North Pole." Will settled his hands on her waist, trying to stop her from moving in case she slipped on cobbles slippery with ice. A head injury was the last thing she needed. Also, he needed to protect her from being seen by anyone still out this late. He didn't want people asking questions about a newcomer. No one could find Juliet here. A Frost hadn't stepped foot in Yule for three generations, and she was nowhere near ready to learn the whole truth.

"You live here? In Christmas land?" She frowned at the giant Christmas tree, thankfully not pushing him away.

"I come and go, but yes, Yule is my home. That small bell charm on the necklace you're wearing took us here. You weren't supposed to find out this way." He was surprised by how well she was taking this. Some people screamed; others went silent.

"A bell took us to the North Pole? There isn't anything in the North Pole. This is insane. You're insane, or this is a dream." Juliet let out a long breath, grasping the bell.

He wished they'd landed somewhere more private. "I'm sorry this is happening this way, but Yule is very much real, and the bell is the only way in or out. I wish this was a dream, but it's not. I'll explain as much as I can to you, but for now, we need to go." He tried to get her walking, but she refused to budge.

"You make it sound like the bell is magical." Her laugh was staggered with panic.

"Exactly like magic."

That did it. Juliet paled and swallowed. He wasn't sure if she was going to be sick or pass out.

"C'mon, let's get out of the cold and find somewhere to sit down." He held out his hand; she ran hers through her hair, her unfocused gaze telling him she was deciding whether to trust him or bolt. She glanced at the dimly lit alley next to them, but there was nowhere to go.

"Juliet?" he asked, trying to get her to focus.

"I don't understand," she mumbled, and he knew he had to get her somewhere warm. He caught her before she hit the hard cobblestones and pulled her into his arms.

"I've got you, don't worry," he said softly.

He'd have to wait a few hours before he could bring her back to her apartment; travelling by bell soon after a shock wasn't recommended. He turned down Cane Lane and walked until he reached the red brick townhouse marked 59. This certainly wasn't how he'd imagined bringing her to his place for the first time.

Then again, nothing in the past few weeks had gone to plan.

Juliet snuggled her knees close to her chest as a cold breeze nipped at her toes. *Thank God, it was just a crazy dream* was her first thought. With a lazy stretch, she reached for her bedside lamp. Instead, she knocked over an old red alarm clock that didn't belong to her.

Juliet leapt out of a strange bed, stumbling over a blanket on the floor as she went to the frosted window. *This is not the view from my bedroom.* There were no skyscrapers or beaming lights; instead she found fairy lights decorating the rooftops. Rubbing her eyes, she hoped the foreign view would change, but groaned when it didn't. No, this was definitely not the view from her apartment, this was not her room, and she wasn't home.

Her gaze darted up and down the street until she spotted that same giant Christmas tree standing above the village from her dream. Her stomach dropped; the dream was quickly becoming a nightmare. Her hand flew to her bare neck. *The necklace! The bell is gone.* Her dress had been replaced with a T-shirt and a pair of sweatpants that weren't hers.

"You're awake! I was beginning to worry." Will tapped lightly on the door as he entered.

Juliet backed up to the window. "Where am I?" She hated how shaky she sounded.

"We arrived last night, and the alcohol you consumed before bell travel caused you to pass out. This is my house. I know you're scared. The constant darkness can take a while to get used to, and you probably have a thousand questions, but I couldn't bring you back to your apartment because it would worsen the effects, and Margot can't find out about the bell or Yule," Will explained, staying by the door to give her the space she desperately needed. He looked far more relaxed in his grey sweats and white t-shirt than when she'd last seen him in his penguin suit.

Margot is probably wondering where the hell I am. How am I ever going to explain this? Still, her best friend was the least of her concerns.

"Travel by bell? Right, okay. Well, I'm sober now, so I want to go home," she said firmly, thinking he had to be insane. There was no way she was in the North Pole, or whatever the hell Yule was. "I want my clothes, my phone and my necklace, and I want to go home."

"I'm sorry for taking the bell from you. I was afraid you'd use it once you woke up and hurt yourself. It's not my intention to keep you here. You absolutely can go home, but I need to explain some things first." Will laid some breakfast on the bed. Blueberry pancakes – her favourite. Her stomach rumbled, but her nerves had ruined her appetite.

"Whose clothes are these?" she asked, pulling at the T-shirt. "Did you change me?"

Scratching the back of his head, he suddenly found the pale green carpet fascinating. "My older sister's. She stays here occasionally when I'm out of town, so she won't mind. Please don't misunderstand, I took no pleasure from changing you, but your clothes were damp from the cold… and when you came to from passing out you threw up."

Juliet dug the palms of her hands into her eyes, mortified. At least she didn't have any memory of it.

"There are some new clothes on the chair. I doubt you want to put on a ruined evening gown," he said, frustratingly calm. But the kindness in his eyes tempted her to forget how angry and confused she was by all that had happened.

She glanced at the woolly navy sweater and sweatpants with leg warmers draped over the pink armchair in the corner. Judging by the bold floral print on the walls and the dressing table well stocked with makeup, this *had* been his sister's room. And he'd left her a pair of winter boots by the door, making her think he was being honest about not keeping her here. *He wouldn't give me shoes if he didn't intend for me to go outside.*

"I don't know if they'll fit, but it'll take some time before you acclimatise to the weather," he said, following her gaze.

Juliet ran her hands through her hair, wishing he'd stop acting so normal. "They don't need to fit, because I don't plan on going back out there unless it's to go home," she snapped, turning back to the window. It was rather beautiful. Frighteningly festive – magical, even. *What if this is real? What if I'm really in the North Pole?* Her head was beginning to throb.

"This isn't how I wanted you to find out about Yule, but you can trust me and trust that you're safe here. I didn't know the bell in the chest would work—" He cut himself off with a grimace as he stepped deeper into the room.

Juliet forgot how to breathe. *He knows about the chest.*

"How the hell could you know about that? I didn't even know about it!" She crossed the room to stand before him, demanding answers.

"Because I sent it to you," he snapped, clearly *not* as calm about the situation as he'd wanted her to think. He took a deep breath, pulling at his neck. "Well, I helped get it to you anyway. You should have read the letters first. I didn't expect you to wear the bell as soon as you found it!"

"Why would I ever think that a magical bell necklace would transport me to a supposedly uninhabitable part of the world?! Where is the next letter going to take me to – Oz? How can you expect me to believe this is all real? You could've drugged me at the gala. I barely know you, and there are plenty of places in the world that could be festively decorated and covered in snow this time of year!"

"Oz is from a fairytale. You don't have to worry about evil witches and munchkins here. But you're right, you don't have to believe anything I say. You'll learn the truth in time." Will shrugged, apparently sticking to his magical village story. "No, I didn't drug you. If you remember, you were the one who left the gala alone, *you* wished to go home, and here you are. I was only responsible for having the chest delivered to you and making sure you didn't do anything stupid with its contents." He clenched his jaw, seemingly not impressed by her accusations. "And since you're here, clearly I failed at that last part."

"Home? This isn't my home." Juliet pointed to the window. "I look like I landed inside a snow globe. Love the mountains – are you going to tell me the Grinch lives there?"

"No Grinch, but there's a lumberjack called Ted who doesn't come to town much during the season." Will half-smiled, and she wished it didn't melt her insides. *If he weren't so damn attractive, I'd consider this kidnapping…* even if she did believe him, for some reason, when he said she'd been the one to take them here. She couldn't believe she was contemplating the idea that magic was real.

"Can you please not make jokes right now? I'm trying to

figure out whether you're a psycho or Santa Claus." Juliet sat on the edge of the bed, hanging her head between her knees.

"Sorry. I wish I was a psycho, if it made this easier to digest. Not a Klaus either, but I can introduce you."

She scowled at him, sitting on the edge of the bed. "Santa Claus? Is real?"

"Yes, in a way. Sorry – no more jokes, I promise." He crossed his heart and knelt beside her. "I swear that no harm will come to you here. You weren't supposed to come here for a few more weeks – not until you already knew about Yule."

"Who are you? Really?" she begged. She'd felt bad enough finding out that Will had known all along about her dad wanting to set them up, but this felt like a new level of betrayal. How could she trust anything he'd said to her?

"I'm still me. The only part I left out was that I'm a Guardian of Yule. I help those who live in Yule assimilate with the Outside world when they leave. My recruitment company helps them with new identities, colleges, work – whatever my charges need to go to and from Yule with no risk of exposing its existence."

"So… you're my guardian?"

"No, but being a guardian gave me access to you. Getting you the Frost chest was a favour for a friend."

"A favour? For who?" Juliet asked, remembering the letter had mentioned her mom. Her heart began to race. "Was it my mom? Is she from here?"

"I can't tell you that for now." Will clenched his jaw. "I was supposed to keep an eye on you while you discovered the truth about Yule and the Frost family, and to make sure you didn't do anything to put Yule at risk. That night at the hotel bar, I crossed the line."

He was watching me; that's how he knew who I was. Oh God,

how could I have been so foolish as to trust a stranger? Still, she couldn't help feeling a little peeved that he sounded like he regretted what had happened between them.

"Too late for regrets, considering we've already slept together. Can't really get more involved than that – or was that just a favour as well?" she demanded, glaring up at him. She felt like a fool. *Of course he said all the right things that night. He already knew so much about me.*

"I don't regret that night or meeting you. I regret making this situation more complicated for you," he said earnestly. "You might not trust me now, but I need to get you out of here. As I mentioned, you aren't supposed to be here – not yet, anyway. Please get dressed and get some food into you. Eating will help with bell travel. We can get you home before Margot realises you're gone, and I'm trusting you not to tell her anything about this place."

She let that sink in. "You aren't going to keep me here? Not afraid I'll betray your secret village once I get home?"

Will shook his head, and she wished she could see into his mind. "As I said, I'm trusting you. I believe you're more interested in finding out the truth. Until you do, you won't say anything. You never told Margot about the chest, right?"

She was annoyed that he'd guessed right. "No, she doesn't know anything."

He smiled, and she realised she'd confirmed he was right about her wanting answers.

"Dressed, breakfast, and then I'll get you home," Will ordered, closing the topic. "When you get home, I suggest you go through the chest, and you'll discover that I'm not lying to you."

We'll see about that. I need to see Yule for myself. Seeing was believing, and she definitely needed to see more of the winter wonderland outside the window if she was going to believe him one hundred percent.

"I'm going to take a shower. Try not to run off while I'm gone. Coffee is in the kitchen; I wasn't sure how you liked it. Eat before it gets cold." Juliet stared at him, bewildered. *He's just going to leave me alone?* "I'll give you some privacy – everything you need is in the bathroom. My sister keeps the ensuite well stocked in case she comes to stay." He pointed to a door by the bed.

Juliet nodded, then glanced at the dresser and picked up a wedding picture of one big, happy family. A groom stood next to his bride, who was in a wheelchair. The beaming smiles of the family members around them made Juliet feel safe. Will and a woman who had the same features stood behind the groom, who she guessed was also related to Will.

"My sister was the maid of honour," he told her as she tried to place everyone. "It was my cousin's wedding."

Juliet wondered if she'd get the chance to meet his sister and confirm his story, but he read her mind. "She isn't here often, so you don't have to worry about unexpected visitors. She lives with her wife in a cabin up the hill."

"Good – I wouldn't want to surprise her if she came home and found me in her room," Juliet said, putting the frame back.

"Don't worry, it's just us," Will said, putting her at ease. He reached for the door handle, and hesitated. "I know it's a little late to say this, but I wish we could've met under different circumstances. I never wanted to cause you any hurt or confusion."

With Will in the shower across the hall, Juliet felt better once she'd eaten and washed up in the ensuite. Finding the courage to investigate, she changed before creeping down the narrow staircase. Pausing by some family photos, she stared at a picture of a smiling Will in his teens with a group wearing ski jackets that read 'Yule U18 Ski Team'. *Yule might exist as a town, but there's no way we're really in the North Pole, right?*

At the front door, she spotted her clutch on the coat stand. Good, she'd have money for a car to take her home. Grabbing a pair of gloves from the stand, she unlocked the door. The lock clicked loudly and she winced, but hopefully Will wouldn't hear over the shower. Icy air hit her lungs, nearly changing her mind about venturing out, but her desire to call Will's bluff and get home won out.

"Where am I even going?" she muttered as she stepped into the street, breathing into the over-sized gloves. Wondering down a series of streets and alleyways, she tried to avoid the hustle and bustle of the early risers in varied coloured overalls and excessive layers. She'd never seen any place so elaborately decorated to look like some kind of Santa's village. Every door was marked with a wreath, and the shop windows each had a countdown clock to Christmas Eve.

"Sorry, could you tell me where I can catch a taxi?" Juliet asked a man carrying a stack of presents in one arm and a small child in the other.

"There's a sleigh rank at the end of this street, though it'll be a bit of a wait because of the morning rush," he said, tipping his head down the road she'd already come from.

"Right. Um, sleigh rank?" *He must not have understood.* Before she could correct herself, he'd gone on his way, the child waving at her over his shoulder.

Across the street, a sign read 'Yule Postal Office', and Juliet recognised the symbol in the window as the same one from the chest back home and Will's cufflinks. Inside, the brightly lit post office was crowded with people waiting to send their parcels. She squeezed past the queue to get a look at the map on the wall. Everyone else seemed too busy to notice her.

Scanning the old map, she frowned when she saw a pin over the North Pole with the inscription 'Village of Yule'. Along the side of the map was a list of all the delivery times for those wishing to send a parcel from Yule to the list of Outside countries.

Everything Will had told her rushed through her mind, and it felt as though all the oxygen had been sucked out of the post office. Desperate to catch her breath, Juliet hurried out of the post office and hunkered down in the closest alleyway.

I never should have left the house! Why didn't I listen to Will? How can I be in the North Pole? Her mind struggled to believe what her eyes had told her. A sleigh passed her alley, mocking her ignorance. *I must get back to the house.* How hard could it be to find her way back? However, looking up and down the narrow alley, she had no clue which direction to start in. Burying her face in her knees, she tried to steady her heartbeat so she could figure out her next step. *Hell, how am I supposed to think rationally when I'm thousands of miles from home in a magical winter wonderland that isn't even supposed to exist?*

A gentle voice from above interrupted her racing thoughts. "Are you okay?"

"I'm lost, and I just want to go home." Juliet hated that she sounded like a pathetic child as she talked into her knees.

"Don't worry, you wouldn't be the first! With all the alleyways and lanes, even I get turned around. Maybe I can help? I saw you rush out of the post office. I figured either you saw the price of shipping to the Outside, or you're new to Yule. I'm Lyla, by the way." Lyla came down to her level, greeting her with warm eyes and a mess of snow-frosted dark curls. "Can you tell me your name?"

"Juliet, but can I just ask, before I lose my mind completely… are we really in the North Pole? Did a bell really bring me here?" She needed to stabilise her sanity before she lost it completely.

"Afraid so," Lyla nodded, "but you're safe and this reaction is totally normal. The first time Klaus brought me here, I thought it was some dream."

"I think I'm going to be sick," Juliet warned, wondering if it was the hangover or fear of being in a strange place straight from some Christmas movie on steroids.

"How about we get you somewhere warm? I promise nothing is going to happen to you, and we can try and get you home," Lyla reassured her, offering her a hand up.

Juliet took it, needing the support, and stood on shaky legs. Lyla's kindness thawed her distrust, and it was nice to get some confirmation that Will had been telling the truth, even if she felt like she couldn't trust him entirely after everything he'd hidden from her.

"You're not from here?" she asked, following Lyla out of the alley. She guessed they were around the same age.

"No, it's how I was able to spot another newbie. I'm from Dublin but my fiancé, Mason, is from here. I've only been coming here for about a year now," Lyla explained. "I know finding out about a secret village and magical bells can be very overwhelming at first, but even though you don't know me, I promise you can trust me."

Lyla was so open, and there was something so welcoming about her energy, that Juliet couldn't help but feel safe.

"I was staying in one of the townhouses near the giant Christmas tree, and I went out for some air. I think the end of the road said Cane Lane? Then I got lost in the alleys," she admitted, worrying about how much Will would want her to reveal about herself. Thankfully, Lyla didn't push for more information.

"We'll figure it out, but the snowfall is due to get heavier soon, and we should get something hot in you. I know where we can get the best hot chocolate in the world."

Eager to be indoors, Juliet followed Lyla down a busy street, noticing how others smiled and waved at her new friend, wishing her a good morning as they passed.

BY A FROSTED FRONT WINDOW, Juliet sat in the armchair nearest a small fire and read the name on the dark green napkin: Peppermint & Pumpkin Coffee Shop. Lyla ordered their drinks at the counter. Juliet had offered to pay, but when Lyla removed some gold coins from her pocket, Juliet realised she had a lot more to learn about Yule. Yet it all seemed so normal, like she was back in the city during the morning rush and everyone was grabbing their morning coffee and pastry.

"Here we go, drink this. Hot chocolate – I don't think you need caffeine right now, but the sugar will help with the shock," Lyla said, placing two giant spotted mugs on the antique table. She removed her bright orange scarf and sat opposite her.

"Thank you, and I'll pay you back when I figure out how."

Juliet grasped the mug, letting the warmth sink into her bones.

"Don't worry about it. It's my treat."

There was something calming about Lyla, with her wild curls and bright colours. Juliet felt herself starting to trust her; she was going out of her way to help a stranger when not many would. The strong smell of chocolate assaulted her already overwhelmed senses, but once she took a sip she was won over by the bittersweet chocolate and the giant pumpkin-shaped mugs.

"When did you arrive?" Lyla asked, removing her fluffy purple gloves as they got down to the nitty-gritty.

"Last night. I was at a Christmas party in New York. I said I wanted to go home. Before I knew it, we were here, by the big Christmas tree." Juliet reached for the phantom necklace.

"Sounds familiar. Was there a gold bell involved?" Lyla asked with a sigh. Juliet nodded frantically. Clearly, she wasn't the only one who'd had a bell mishap.

"I didn't know what it could do. I thought it was just a family heirloom, but in future I'll be a lot more careful with what jewellery I wear. It was only a charm on the end of a necklace, I didn't expect…" She still struggled to believe such a dainty bell could transport her to the North freaking Pole.

"Travel by bell can be rather volatile the first time. I take it you didn't know about Yule until you got here?" Lyla asked, taking a sip of her own drink.

"Not a clue, or I sure as heck wouldn't have worn the damn thing. Will should've warned me—" She cut herself off, not sure whether she should mention him or not. She didn't want to get him into trouble.

"Will? Not Will Duncan?" Lyla nearly choked on her coffee.

"You know him?"

Her new friend's eyes widened. "A *guardian* brought you here?"

Juliet nodded, unsure of what that meant for her situation.

"It all makes sense now. You must be a legacy! Though Will should've explained the situation to you before giving you the bell. Legacies can return to Yule should they wish to, once they turn twenty-six," Lyla told her, as though Juliet would understand exactly what a legacy was.

"What's a legacy? And Will isn't technically my guardian – he didn't really get a chance to explain before we ended up here," Juliet said, unsure of how to explain. Lyla was right about one thing; he should have warned her about the bell when she got the chest. Even a note would have spared her the past however many hours.

"Some families or individuals decide to leave Yule, and their descendants can return to Yule should they wish. Some descendants, or as we call them, legacies, aren't informed about their origins, so it can be a bit of a shock. Happy Christmas, your family comes from a mystical winter wonderland that's kept secret from the rest of the world!"

Nana Rose's letter mentioned that the Frost family had secrets, but this is far from what I could ever have imagined. The chest was delivered a month after my 26th birthday. That explained why Nana Rose had waited, at least.

"I don't know why the age is twenty-six – I'm still learning these things," Lyla went on, then paused, seeing that Juliet was struggling to take it all in. "Sorry, I ramble when I'm nervous. It's nice to meet someone who's also new to Yule. Anyway, you're in luck, because I know where Will lives. He's a friend of Mason's, so I can vouch for him. His townhouse is only one alley over on Cane Lane. If he isn't your guardian, are you together? He is such a stinker for keeping his life private. Guardians can know everything about everyone, but Rudolph forbid they let anyone in on their secrets."

"Tell me about it," Juliet muttered into her creamy hot chocolate, before taking another sip. "You were right when you said this is the best in the world. I love the hint of spice."

"That would be the chilli. My personal favourite flavour – thought you could do with a kick. Will hasn't been home in a few months, so we figured he'd met someone while working on the Outside." Lyla frowned, picking at the rim of her mug as though the idea troubled her.

"The Outside?" Juliet asked, diverting the topic away from dating to facts about her supposed ancestral home. *Dad has a serious amount of explaining to do once I get home.*

"The world outside Yule. Anything beyond the mountains that our little festive world sits in."

"I don't mean to sound rude, but you do know this is crazy? No one lives in the North Pole. It's uninhabitable."

"It's—"

"If you say magic, I might scream." Juliet buried her head in her hands.

"Scream all you like," Lyla chuckled, "won't make it any less true. I had a hard time believing when I first arrived, but it's about faith. Yule is the heart of faith and hope in this world. I think I should leave the rest to Will to explain, though. I'm sure he's going crazy wondering where you've gone."

"He was in—"

Juliet didn't have time to finish her thought before Will himself frantically opened the door. The bell chiming over the door made her jump, afraid she'd end up in some other magical universe.

Will glared at her. His cheeks were pink from the cold,

and suddenly she thought that being transported anywhere else but here sounded good.

"Juliet! You scared me! How could you run off like that? Do you know what could've happened to you?" His outburst caused more than a few people to stare. Ignoring Lyla, he towered over Juliet as though protecting her from the onlookers.

"Will, can I talk to you for a moment?" Lyla asked, an edge to her voice that said it was a request, not a suggestion.

Will didn't budge, his eyes on Juliet. He clenched his jaw as Lyla rested a hand on his forearm.

"Outside, before you cause a scene," Lyla said quietly. "Juliet, do you mind if we catch up for a moment?"

"I'm not going anywhere," Juliet promised, mostly to reassure Will. Where was she supposed to run to? He had her necklace.

Will's nostrils flared; he stared at the ceiling for a moment before finally looking back down at her. "Don't move." He leaned over her chair. "And don't mention your last name to anyone."

"I won't." She gritted her teeth, trying not to let her irritation show.

He hesitated, holding the arm of the chair. She rolled her eyes. He could doubt her all he wanted, but he'd have to take her word for it if he didn't want to cause a bigger scene than he already had.

"Cross my heart," she mocked, making the X on her chest.

He huffed out his frustration before following Lyla outside.

A few eyes fell on Juliet once they left, and she shifted uncomfortably. She was used to people staring at her because of who she was; now they were staring because of who she might be. She didn't know which was worse, but neither were pleasant.

Outside the window, Lyla appeared rather animated while Will crossed his arms over his chest, only nodding at intervals. Judging from Lyla's flushed cheeks and the way she pointed at Juliet through the window, she was giving Will a piece of her mind about bringing her here with no warning. Juliet almost felt bad for him as he ducked his head. Lyla didn't know that it was her mistake that they'd ended up in Yule. Then again, this was the last place she'd imagined when she said she wanted to return home.

Even if the shock was still wearing off, she took some comfort in knowing that Yule was real, and that somewhere in this snow-coated land was her mom. She was sure of it, especially after Lyla's explanations. She was one step closer to figuring out the puzzle of her past. She sipped her hot chocolate while Will and Lyla went back and forth, finding that the sugar and warmth did wonders for her anxiety.

A tense silence fell over the table when they returned. Juliet wasn't going to be the first to speak in case she revealed something she shouldn't.

At last Lyla took a deep breath. "Well, you've both got yourselves into quite the pickle."

"You're not one to judge," Will muttered, and Lyla rolled her eyes at him.

"Don't start, Will. Mason was grieving when he brought me here from the Outside. Whereas *you've* broken several rules while under orders from the Chief of Guardians!"

Juliet had no idea what they were talking about, but she got the impression she wasn't supposed to.

"Like I said outside, it was an accident," Will snapped. "She didn't know the bell would bring her here, and we were going to leave before Juliet decided to run away from me."

Juliet was about to defend herself, but Lyla got there first.

"Can you blame her? A strange man enters her life, and all of a sudden she's transported across the world and—"

"Are you talking about me or Mason?" Will cut in lightly, but Juliet wasn't sure what the joke meant. Had Mason brought Lyla here under false pretences?

"Leave him out of this!"

"I'm not strange," Will muttered.

Juliet had grasped enough to realise that Will must have told Lyla who she was. "You told me I shouldn't tell anyone who I am!"

"I had to tell her, or she'd have blabbed to her fiancé about her new outsider friend. Mason would've enquired further, and we'd have *both* been outed," Will said crossly.

"I don't blab!" Lyla protested. Juliet believed her; she seemed genuinely concerned. "Don't worry, you don't have to marry him."

"What?!" Juliet was feeling rather lost.

"Mason rewrote that rule when he took over as Klaus. Now, partners can be brought to Yule so long as there's an intention to be together for the foreseeable future," Lyla explained.

"You don't have to make it sound like marrying me is a death sentence," Will said.

"I didn't even know there used to be a rule about being engaged," said Juliet slowly.

Will shook his head. "You're a legacy. You have a right to be here."

"She's a banished legacy – it's different. Frosts are legends here, and not the good kind. You should remember that, Will, before you bring her back. There's a procedure to all this, and Juliet will suffer the consequences if she doesn't abide by it. Talk about throwing her to the wolves!" Lyla eyed her sympathetically. "Both of you should leave, and only return when you've got everything in order. I'll help you handle things with Mason when the time is right." She gave Juliet a reassuring smile. "Don't worry, Mason has a big heart; it's the council you have to worry about," she added, which was less reassuring.

"I agree, and we should go before we're spotted," Will said.

Juliet didn't fancy running into any of these council members, but she was relieved to know she had one person on her side within Yule. It made the magical place seem more real, instead of some fever dream induced by the horrid mousse she'd eaten at the gala. She'd better start reading those letters in the chest before she made any other life-altering mistakes.

"Thank you for being so kind and for helping us keep our secret," she said to her new friend.

"Happy to help. I know how hard it is to get used to the idea of this place. If you ever need any help, just ask," Lyla said, giving her a small hug as they said goodbye. "And keep her safe!" she added sternly to Will.

Neither of them spoke on the way back to Will's house. Juliet had barely had time to think of what to say when the door slammed behind her.

"Why are you always running away from me? I don't think it's safe to shower around you." Will glared at her, backing her up against the door.

"I didn't mean to run off! I just went to get some air and I got lost." She fumbled through the excuse, while he stared at her like he was trying to decide what to do with her.

"How am I supposed to trust you?!" he hissed. "Next time I'll have to bring you in with me – I clearly can't take my eyes off you."

"You can't be angry and flirt with me at the same time." Juliet narrowed her eyes. "I left you at the Bryce because I had to work, not because I didn't want to stay. Also, you can't lecture me about trust when you've been stalking me for weeks!"

"I wasn't stalking you. It's complicated." Will paced in front of her. "If you'd just stayed with me for breakfast, I could've explained everything. You're lucky that it was Lyla who found you."

"Why would I believe anything you say now?" Juliet asked firmly, trying to keep her composure.

"I wish you could understand what might have happened to you by running off like that. If Lyla hadn't found you—" He buried his face in his hands. The deafening silence nearly killed her.

"I'm fine. I'm sorry I worried you. I panicked; this is all so overwhelming." She reached for his arm, needing him to see that she was okay.

"The cold alone could've killed you, since you haven't acclimatised. I need you to trust me, and if you can't, then please listen to me while you're here," he pleaded, taking her hands in his. "There are rules in Yule about outsiders—"

"How am I supposed to know what the rules are or aren't? You haven't told me anything! I've just found out that my family is meant to be from some isolated magical village in Yule that I never knew existed until a few hours ago."

"Lyla told you about legacies," Will said slowly, letting every word sink in. "The Frost family was banished from Yule three generations ago for reasons I'm not going to get into. The banishment applies to you, and if someone discovered who you were and that you had brought me as well, then we'd *all* risk banishment. The council could remove your memories of this place and everything related to Yule, including me."

"Banished? Why? What did my family do?" Juliet gasped, before the last thing he'd said sank in. "How can memories be altered? Would they really go so far?" Losing her memories was unthinkable, if it was even possible. But then she also would have said that being transported by a tiny bell to a village in the North Pole was impossible.

"I can't be the one to tell you why. I'm sorry, but I promised your mum that I would only reveal what was necessary to keep you safe."

As frustrating as the response was, she could see how

much he was risking by helping her. *Was that the point of the chest? So I could discover all this myself? Or was I supposed to wait until my mom just magically appeared and revealed the dozens of magical secrets that have been kept from me for over twenty-six years?*

"This is all so crazy! I don't even know how to take it all in," she confessed, trying to make sense of the snippets she knew so far.

"Being overwhelmed is completely normal. If the situation was different I would tell you everything in a heartbeat, but some things shouldn't be revealed by a stranger."

"I hardly think we're strangers; we've seen each other naked," she mumbled.

He grinned. "Flirting with me won't distract me. Promise me you won't do this again? Because if Lyla hadn't found you today, I don't even know what I'd have done…" His troubled expression squeezed her heart.

"I get it, but I'm here and I'm safe. Can we start the day over?" Juliet closed the gap between them, and his hands travelled up her arms to her shoulders as if making sure she was real. She realised how much she'd missed his touch.

"You're so lucky that I can't resist those damn eyes," he sighed, and she rolled her eyes. "Did you just roll your eyes at me?"

She stilled as he tipped her chin up to make him look at her. "Maybe, but only because your mood is giving me whiplash."

"Trust me, I'm giving myself whiplash. I'm trying to remain professional – and then I see you, and all my self-control goes out the window."

Juliet tried and failed not to smile, slightly smug that it wasn't just her.

"When you smile at me like that it makes me forget that I'm mad at you," he murmured.

She chewed her lip to stop herself, but he tugged it free with his thumb, then tucked a strand of free hair behind her ear with his other hand.

"And your flushed cheeks tell me you want me just as much as I want you. I think that's the only truth that matters right now."

Juliet swallowed as his breath brushed her neck. Being this close to him was dangerous. Her body responded to him in ways she had never really felt before, but she knew she wanted to feel them again.

"And if I do?" She looked up at him through her eyelashes, praying for him to make a move before she lost her mind.

Will pulled back slightly, eyes carefully searching her face.

"Juliet." He rested his forehead against hers. Juliet felt a shiver pass down her spine at her name on his lips. "What do you want from me? If you want to go home, tell me now."

"Kiss me." She had wanted to say those words for longer than she cared to admit.

Will's lips were on hers before she was aware he'd moved, his hands in her hair so he could control her as he wished. Juliet's stomach churned with excitement. His body had her trapped against the door, and she brought her hands up to rest on his biceps, holding on to him as though she'd collapse under his touch.

He dropped his lips to her neck, and she instinctively rolled her head back to give him better access. His mouth was warm and surprisingly soft against her skin, and she felt her eyes begin to close as he trailed urgent kisses from her jaw towards her ear. A flood of warmth passed through her, and she opened her eyes. She wasn't fighting this or over-thinking it, only letting the desires that she had been denying since the first night they'd spent together come to the surface.

"You won't run from me again, will you?" His teeth captured her bottom lip, and she shuddered as he growled low in his chest. She couldn't get enough of the feel of his lips against hers. "Answer me."

The pressure on her lip increased; his hand slid up over her stomach, and Juliet inhaled sharply as it reached her breast. Even through her clothes, her skin burned for him. A small moan escaped her.

"I'll take that as a yes." Will's rough tone spoke of his own desire, and the hard length of him pressing into her hip confirmed it.

He grabbed her ass, lifting her up so that her thighs wrapped around his waist, and carried her to the stairs. There he positioned himself between her legs, peppering kisses down her neck as his fingers trailed along the waistband of her sweatpants. He made quick work of the knotted drawstring. Juliet swallowed hard as his fingers grazed her lower belly, and felt her cheeks grow warm with embarrassment. She was so ready for him, and neither had even lost a stitch of clothing.

"You're blushing. Are you wet for me?" Will whispered.

Juliet found herself nodding, unable to speak, as his fingers slid inside her underwear. Her hips bucked against him as he brushed against her core.

"So fucking eager, I love it," he groaned, claiming her lips once again and pulling her sweats and underwear down her legs, teasing her with his touch. "Did you want something?"

Juliet's laboured breathing gave away her desire to be touched, claimed by his hands, his lips. She was aching to feel him against her, inside her, again.

"Fuck me," she breathed. "Please."

Will's eyes darkened. Slowly, he dipped his fingers into her.

Juliet leaned her head back against the stairs. Gentle moans escaped her as she felt him leisurely slide his fingers in and out. There was no denying how much she wanted, *needed* him. He had lied to her, followed her, but she couldn't deny how much she yearned for him. She wanted to turn her brain off and let her body take all it desired from him.

"I want you, Will," she breathed. "I want this."

His hand dropped from her breast to her knee, pulling her leg up around him roughly enough to make her gasp sharply. He pulled himself free from his underwear, moving his hips against her, and suddenly she remembered just how impressive his size had been in her hand last time.

"I missed this," she panted as his hand gripped her thigh, holding her in place.

"I missed this too." He grinned wickedly, then leaned down and kissed her again. She let out a small, shaky breath, but nodded when he pulled away and looked down at her for confirmation. He grabbed a condom from his wallet, and she smiled.

Feeling the pressure of him at her entrance and biting her lip to silence her moans, Juliet lifted her other leg and wrapped it around him as well, unable to wait any longer. Will smiled against her lips. Taking the hint, he pushed into her. Juliet dug her nails into his hips as he stretched and filled her, crying out into his mouth as he groaned into hers. Her body tensed and tightened as he pulled back a little before pressing forward again, getting a little farther this time.

"Oh fuck," Will muttered as he lifted her up, burying his face in her hair.

"Oh my God, Will!" Juliet gasped as the pressure inside

her built. It felt good, but it also hurt, and she felt her body clench.

"You're so tight; relax for me." Will's voice was deep and commanding. Juliet tried her best to loosen her muscles. "I'm sorry, I should've taken this slower."

"Don't you dare stop or apologise. I need this. I need you," Juliet told him, pulling him back to her. Slowly, she accepted more and more of him inside her. Will's eyes clouded over with lust; he dropped his hand between them, heightening her pleasure with his touch. Juliet's heart began to race as his fingers teased her.

"Yes," she gasped, tightening her legs around him and angling her hips for better access. Will thrust into her, and Juliet arched against him, taking all of him.

"You feel so good," he grunted. "You were made for me."

Juliet could barely catch her breath as he thrust in and out of her at a steady pace. His lips found hers again, swallowing her moans as he sped up gradually. The ecstasy sent shivers through her body.

"Oh fuck, Juliet, tell me you're close," Will rasped. Juliet leaned back, sensation rising within her, and moaned loudly enough for it to echo around them.

"I'm close..." She clenched around him, and pleasure exploded in her. "Will!"

He groaned as he reached his own end, and they both took a moment to catch their breath, his face pressed into her neck.

After regaining their senses, they pulled apart, situating themselves and adjusting their clothing. Juliet had her shirt halfway buttoned back up as Will bent down and scooped up her underwear from the wooden floor. Blushing, she reached for it, but he quickly pulled it back out of her reach.

"I'm keeping these." He smirked, tucking them into his pocket. "So that you'll remember this lesson."

Juliet rolled her eyes, but her heart threatened to melt as he eased her sweatpants back up her legs.

"Lift your hips for me," he asked, and she did as she was told. He made a little knot in the drawstring, the furrow in his brow as he concentrated an adorable contrast to his firm orders.

Juliet tucked her hair behind her ears before glancing back up at him. His smile had been replaced with something she couldn't quite name… fear, concern. Guilt cut through the moment; she hadn't realised how much her leaving him had hurt him.

"I'm sorry I worried you."

"It's my job to worry about you." Will secured his belt and knelt to press his lips to hers. Juliet shook her head, but he ran his fingers over her jaw and down her throat, and her breath caught. "I should get you home before Margot starts to wonder where you are, but we should wash up first." He sounded disappointed that she'd have to leave.

"She's probably going out of her mind with worry," Juliet agreed.

"Don't worry, I told Harvey you were with me. Though I left out where." He smiled, and she wished it didn't make her insides melt. Another hour or two wasn't going to make a difference.

They left Will's home after finally getting around to breakfast. She was full and satisfied in more ways than one, but it still felt like she'd got back too soon. They arrived in the alley a few streets over from the apartment block, since randomly appearing inside probably wouldn't be good for Margot's heart. Even with some fresh air and the short walk to her building, Juliet's stomach churned a little thanks to travelling by Air Bell.

"The next few weeks aren't going to be easy, but you need to keep the past twenty-four hours to yourself," Will warned, opening the door to her apartment building. He followed her inside, and she wasn't surprised when he stopped at the bottom of the stairs. She was better off facing Margot alone.

"I don't like lying to Margot," she said, hesitating to make a promise. If only she could tell Margot *something*, just to have someone to share all this craziness with.

"I know, and I wish you didn't have to, but this is for her own good."

She nodded reluctantly, wishing they'd spent less time on his stairs and more time getting back to how he'd got caught up with the chest and her family. There were so many answers she needed, but she didn't even know how or where to start asking.

"I put my number in your phone," Will said, kissing her cheek. He handed her back her dress from the gala and her clutch bag. Good thing he'd taken it, or she probably would've tried to ping her location to Margot in a panic, and how would she have explained that she was at the North Pole? Then again, she doubted her service provider even covered secret winter villages. "I suggest you go through the letters in the chest, and call me if you need anything. Even if it's just someone to talk to."

"When will I see you again?" She didn't want to be too far from the only person who knew what she was going through.

"Soon – and be careful with the bell. I don't want to have to chase you down again." He winked.

Since he had a habit of just appearing, Juliet didn't doubt him. She watched him head out, and took a deep breath before taking the stairs. Getting out her keys to her apart-ment, she saw her phone was truly dead. At least she wouldn't have to lie about that.

"Where have you been?" Margot snapped before she even had a chance to take her shoes off.

"I'm sorry—" Juliet barely got out the apology before Margot suffocated her in a hug.

"Don't leave me like that ever again! When I got home, you were gone. Victor didn't have a clue where you went. I called the hospitals, but the cops wouldn't do a thing until forty-eight hours passed. You scared me to death!" Margot dragged her to the couch. "Tell me everything, and leave nothing out!"

Juliet winced, realising she had forgotten about the time difference. The kitchen clock told her it was already well past two in the afternoon. She tried to conceal her guilt as she lied, staying as close to the truth as possible. She went over how Fiona Caldwell had humiliated her in the toilets, and despite standing up for herself, Juliet had got upset and ended up leaving the party before crying in public. Will had followed her to check if she was all right, and one thing had led to another, so she'd ended up staying the night with him, and he'd given her some clothes to come home in. She pointed out that her phone had died – thankfully Margot was too engrossed in the gossip to ask why she hadn't just charged it. She left out the travelling bell, now concealed in her pocket, Lyla, and most importantly, Yule.

"On the stairs? Interesting choice, but bravo," Margot smirked, snuggling with her hot water bottle.

"How was your evening with Harvey?" Juliet hadn't mentioned that Will had brought his friend as a distraction.

Margot sighed, resting her head on the back of the couch. "He wants me to come and work for him, but I refused. Then he wanted to sleep with me, but I refused that too. Now he won't stop calling. If the rumours are true, then he's used to getting what he wants. I plan on making him work for it." She smirked, enjoying the game.

Juliet grinned. Margot had a way of making men fall at her feet – but Harvey might be her match, given that he'd managed to convince her to have dinner with him tonight.

Once she'd showered and climbed into her comfiest pjs, she decided to spend the day lounging in front of the TV to give herself time to absorb all she had learned.

With the apartment to herself that evening, Juliet pulled out the chest from under her bed. A small part of her needed to verify what Lyla and Will had told her, even if she'd seen

Yule with her own eyes. To believe that such a magical place could exist for thousands of years without discovery seemed impossible, implausible – not in the modern world, where information was power and technology made nothing secret.

Unfolding one of the oldest letters, dated twenty-five years ago, Juliet took a deep breath and settled into the pillows on her bed.

Dear Ms Eloise Heart…

Juliet ran her fingers over the name. Eloise Heart. *Mom.* Tears stained the paper before she could stop them. She hurried through the next few sentences, desperate to learn something, anything, about the woman who'd left her with the Frost family.

I was under the impression that we had come to an agreement last winter that you would leave my family alone, which is why I was surprised to receive a letter from Mr Klaus stating that the banishment of the Frost family and its descendants will not be voided by order of the Council of Yule.

I appreciate your effort to confer with the Council of Yule on our behalf, but I'm afraid there is no undoing the past. The Frost family has lived in banishment for three generations, and we are at peace in the Outside. Unfortunately, your relationship with my son, forbidden by Yule law, has opened a wound that will not easily heal.

As per our agreement, your daughter Juliet will be provided for as a Frost, but she will never know of Yule, or our history. As a guardian, you swore an oath to protect Yule's secret and obey its laws – an oath you and my foolish son broke. Going forward, I hope you will honour it and leave my son and granddaughter in peace. As hard as it must be to leave your child, I hope you will put her needs before your own. I wish you and my son had considered the weight of your actions before engaging in a relationship that could only result in heartbreak and a daughter losing her mother.

I hope you will heed my advice, and accept the situation as it is. If not, and you try to reach out to my son or your child, I will be required to report your infraction to Mr Klaus and the Council of Yule. Let us all find some peace.

Reginald Frost

P.S. I have enclosed a photo, taken on Juliet's first birthday. I hope it will bring you some closure to see that she is healthy and well looked after.

Juliet's heart threatened to fall out of her chest as she read the letter again and again until the words bled together. *Why did my grandfather threaten my mom into staying away from me when he never treated me as anything other than a burden?*

There was clearly more to her mom's relationship with her father than she knew. And her mom was or had been a guardian of Yule, like Will! *Am I making the same mistake my parents made?* Pacing back and forth, she wondered why Will had approached her in that bar if he'd known he was risking his own banishment by helping her. Wasn't he making the same mistake as her mom, breaking his oath to Yule because he was getting emotionally involved with a Frost? All the questions gave her a tension headache. Biting her lip, she turned to the other letters. There were a few shorter notes that she almost immediately realised must have been written by her parents. Heart hammering at seeing her mom's handwriting, she picked them up and read them next.

Dear Jeremy,

I'm sorry, but we must end our relationship. Regardless of our feelings for each other, it's against the law and I never should have revealed myself to you that day. I know you feel that we can overcome Yule's laws, but if it were discovered that we are in a relationship, it would be my job to erase your memory. The thought of losing that day and every day since would be a painful fate. The 22nd of December 1995 will always be imprinted on my heart, along with the time we've spent together; I don't wish for you to forget me, to forget us. The time we spent together has been the happiest time of my life. As hard as it is, we have to focus on how lucky we've been to have it. If we're discovered, the harm done will only be to ourselves.

Forgive me.

E x

JULIET TRACED the letters as if she could feel an echo of her mom's anguish. Had this been before she knew about being pregnant, or after? She moved on to the next letter.

Dear Eloise,

You haven't responded to my last two letters. It breaks my heart to think that you've returned to Yule and that I might never see you again. I'll keep writing to this address until I get a response – please don't leave like this. Just come to me, and we can figure this out. We can petition the Council of Yule. I can go with you and we can plead our case. I'll move to Yule, I'll give up the Frost name, anything you want.

Yours eternally,
J x

Juliet read it again, stunned. *Could that really be my father pleading, willing to give everything up for my mom?* He sounded like an entirely different person to the man she knew. Why hadn't Eloise agreed? She ripped open the last letter from her mom.

Dear Jeremy,

It breaks my heart to read your words. Before I'm reassigned, I'll go to our place at ten pm on the 7th January and we can say our goodbyes. That's all I can give you; please understand. I'm trying to do what's best for everyone, but please don't think my heart doesn't ache as much as yours.

E x

JULIET SAT BACK on her heels, her heart aching. The date of the 'one last goodbye' was roughly ten months before she'd been born. If her dad had let her mom go when she'd first written, without that final meeting, Juliet never would've existed. She couldn't help but feel like her conception had been the final nail in their coffin.

Underneath the letters was what looked like documents relating to the Frost family's banishment. They didn't tell her much, but it was enough to confirm what Will and Lyla had told her. After skimming through a bunch of legal jargon, the page marked 'Final Verdict' was the only page she could make heads or tails of.

The Frost Family are charged with crimes against Yule and will be banished from the village henceforth. Their descendants will also carry the penalty of their crime. No legacy will be granted clemency, and their ancestorial Bell granting them access to Yule and citizenship will be stripped from them. However, to help the family assimilate to the OUTSIDE, and as a show of respect for the good deeds of the past Frost ancestors, all funds and assets will be transferred to OUTSIDE establishments. In accordance with our laws, a guardian will be assigned to watch over the family to make sure they follow the laws of secrecy. All contact will be prohibited. Any contact will result in memory erasure, monetary penalties, or imprisonment.

JULIET GASPED at the last line. *Could Will go to prison? Does Yule have a prison?* She'd hoped the memory erasure was just a figure of speech, but it certainly didn't sound like it. She dreaded to think of what was being risked to reunite her with her mom. She ran her fingers over the faded signatures of the Frost ancestors she'd never known, and the names of those binding the sentence. She understood punishing those responsible for committing a crime, but condemning the following generations of her family for something they'd had no part in felt extreme. She needed to know more, but she'd read everything in the chest. *What could their crime have been, to receive such a terrible punishment? Theft? Murder?* She shuddered. It would have been helpful if Nana Rose or her mom had given her a little more information on what exactly had happened all those years ago so she didn't jump to conclusions. She guessed her dad might have more letters at the estate, if he hadn't destroyed them to cover up the forbidden relationship.

"WHY ARE YOU STILL UP?" Margot arrived home at three am after her night out with Harvey to find her sitting at the kitchen counter, rubbing her tired eyes. Juliet couldn't believe the night had passed so quickly.

She shoved the papers under her thigh. "Couldn't sleep. How was your dinner with the persistent gentleman?" She couldn't believe how many hours she'd spent lost in the letters, dissecting every word.

Margot poured herself a cup of coffee from the pot Juliet had been nursing. "Persistent is an understatement – and no, we didn't sleep together. It was all business; we were in the dining room of a hotel he owns for hours, just talking. I didn't even realise it was just us! He has a way of hypnotising me with his mouth – something about his lips – but I refuse to be tempted. Signing him as a client would be a great fuck you to the family business. However, he wants me to work for his company exclusively, and the money he's offering is insane. I'm not surprised by either point, since he does have a rather ruthless reputation in business."

Juliet remembered what Fiona had said in the bathroom about Harvey Bryce being the type of man you didn't want to get on the wrong side of. On the other hand, the biggest mistake anyone could make was underestimating Margot.

"So why are you pouting? At least you wouldn't have to worry about money or having to take on clients you detest," she pointed out, surprised Margot wasn't more excited.

"You know I don't mix pleasure and business. If I work for him, I can't fall for that damn rugged smile. And those cheekbones – swoon. I could barely listen to his pitch!" Margot plonked down on the chair opposite her.

"Seems like we're both torn between our hearts and minds," Juliet muttered as Margot drained her mug.

"I didn't catch that?" Margot got up to put the mug in the sink and came back.

"Nothing. I'm sure you'll decide what's more important when it comes to Mr Bryce, business or pleasure. No matter what you decide, you win." Juliet wrapped her arm around her friend's shoulder and gave her a reassuring squeeze. "I'm going to bed before my eyes fall out of my head."

"You're right, and it's not like I have to decide right away," Margot said, almost to herself.

"Ever the victor." Juliet chuckled. "Before I forget, I've got to go to the Frost estate for a couple of days. Victor is picking me up tomorrow – well, technically in a few hours." She didn't want Margot to think she'd pulled another vanishing act.

Margot followed Juliet to her bedroom, where she quickly tucked the Yule papers under her pillow.

"The Frost estate? Are you sure you're okay? I don't think I've ever seen you go back to that place willingly." Margot used some of Juliet's face wipes to remove her makeup at the dresser while Juliet finished packing a bag. "You can tell me if something happened with Will. Is your dad mad at you for leaving the gala?"

"Nothing happened. It's just getting close to the holidays, and I want to spend some time with Beth while she's on winter break." Juliet shrugged. It was only half a lie; she *did* want to see her sister, who was home as much as Juliet was thanks to the expensive boarding school she attended.

"Doesn't she usually go skiing with her friends?" Margot

frowned. Juliet wished her friend didn't know every detail about her life.

"The last time we spoke, she said not this year. Maybe she's going later in the season. Either way, she's home now," she mumbled, tucking some final sweaters into her suitcase. They concealed the small chest that took up most of the space.

"Okay, give Beth my love and remind her she's always welcome to visit." Margot hesitated in the doorway. "Are you *sure* everything's okay? I'm worried you're not telling me something. I don't mean to bring it up again, but leaving the gala like that without a word isn't like you. You can tell me anything, you know." She'd always been able to see right through Juliet. Being raised with secrets and society tended to make one more attune to sniffing out secrecy.

"Thanks. I guess I just got caught off-guard seeing Will again and wanted to get away from my dad and Fiona. I promise I won't disappear again." Zipping her suitcase shut, Juliet placed her favourite Rudolph scarf on top and wheeled it through the apartment to the front door, ready for the morning.

"I'll stop nagging, but I'm here if you need me."

Every fibre of Juliet's being longed for her best friend's opinion on the real situation. Maybe in time she would be able to reveal everything, but for now it was best to do what Will had asked.

Margot's phone buzzed in her pocket, breaking the tense moment. She smiled down at the screen. Harvey must be good with his words; Juliet had never seen her roommate grin like that so late at night.

"Now, go to bed and take your smiles with you," Juliet teased, and Margot scrunched her nose at her.

"Okay, last question. How good was last night?" Margot winked.

Juliet didn't answer. If she knew the whole situation, she wouldn't be encouraging her to think about Will, let alone reminding her of how he'd made her toes curl.

"That good, huh? I don't think a guy has ever made you silent before," Margot giggled. "Aaaand I'm going to bed."

"I won't wake you when I leave, so please let me know if there are any further developments with Harvey. I want updates!" Juliet headed back to her room, ready to snuggle under her duvet and catch a few hours of sleep before having to face going home.

Margot rolled her eyes. "Text me if you need some back-up, okay? I can be down there in an hour."

She closed the door behind her, and Juliet let her smile slip. She thought about reaching out to Will, staring at his number in her phone, to tell him about going home. To tell him about the letter, and to ask him about the guardian connection between him and her mom.

Deciding she needed sleep over answers, she set her phone down on the nightstand and turned off her light, hoping she hadn't made a mistake trusting him.

"Juliet?" Victor said softly. "We're here."

Lifting her head from the black leather backseat, Juliet squinted in the sunlight flooding through the tinted windows. When he'd picked her up outside her apartment building, it had still been dark. The pothole-free streets had made for a smooth ride and her nerves had settled after some sleep, but her body ached from curling up in an uncomfortable position.

It was too quiet this far from the city; the small, exclusive town of Hartdale might only be an hour away from the bustle of New York, but it felt like another world of perfectly manicured trees and litter-free sidewalks. Not even animals dared to make a mess on these streets. The Frost estate was vast, but just one of many in the area. The bigger the estate, the more privacy – not that there was such a thing in a small town of busy-bodies with too much money and time on their hands.

"Stop the car!" she blurted out.

Puzzled, Victor braked, and Juliet scrambled out before he'd come to a full stop outside the large gates of the Frost estate. She nearly slipped on the path up to the gate – trainers and ice were never a good combination. However, all she could focus on was the sigil, half concealed by snowy vines, that she'd never taken the time to notice before in the metal. Like a woman possessed, she ripped away the greenery to reveal delicate iron snowflakes around the central *F*. Wide-eyed, she clenched her fists to prevent an outburst. The sigil on the chest, the sigil on the gate – they were the same. Her gut twisted at yet another confirmation.

"What are you doing?" Victor snapped, climbing out the car. He grabbed her wrists to make sure she wasn't injured. "You're lucky you didn't cut yourself; that gate is old and rusty!" He sighed, releasing her once he saw that she was unharmed.

"Sorry, I didn't mean to frighten you," Juliet said meekly.

He watched her with troubled eyes. "Is there something going on I need to know about? You aren't yourself, and it's not like you to come home early for Christmas. Your dad's not coming home until Monday," he told her, his brows pulled tight together. She was almost disappointed her dad wouldn't be home to confront, but him not being home gave her two days to discover what secrets he was hiding in the expensively decorated rooms.

She hated to worry Victor, but as he looked to the sigil and back at her, she suddenly wondered if he knew. He had served the Frost family for as long as she could remember. She took a step back, unsure of who to trust. He'd practically raised her, and somehow the thought of him lying to her hurt far more than her dad's betrayal.

"I need some air; feeling a little car-sick. I'll walk up to the house," she said.

"It's freezing," he protested, pointing to the snow-lined driveway. "Please let me drive you the rest of the way."

Juliet barely heard him as she stared down the long gravel drive. Frost House looked exactly the same: four stories, long draughty windows.

"Some air after the long drive will do me good." She forced a smile.

Victor didn't push the issue. He drove ahead with her bags while she admired the old home, crowded with more rooms than anyone could possibly have use for. Then again, they'd been pretty useful when it came to hiding from her grandfather. He had never liked having her in the house, preferring that she kept to the groundskeeper's cottage, except for dinner or social events, when her attendance had been mandatory. Still, she'd often snuck into his library to hide in the window seat, concealed by the burgundy curtains – she'd learned from a young age to make herself invisible. With his back to the window, Frost Sr. had never even noticed her hiding while he worked at his desk.

Walking up the icy driveway, she struggled not to slip once or twice, but the fresh air helped settle her stomach, and she started to feel like she could face being home. She startled when the perfectly varnished black front door opened before she even knocked.

"Mr Frost said you were coming on Monday! Victor called from the car; this is such a lovely surprise!" Diana beamed. "Beth is so excited to see you." She hugged Juliet, practically strangling the life out of her.

"Di, I love you, but you're crushing me," she grunted, though she didn't really mind. Diana, who had married Victor when Juliet was eight, was like the mom she'd never had. They'd all lived together until she turned fourteen, when her grandfather had decided they should have the gate lodge, while Juliet remained in the cottage by the gardens, as if he'd rather she live alone than with the 'help'. Victor oversaw security and the grounds, while Diana was the chef and housekeeper. They'd both been hired by her grandfather. She wondered again if they knew about the Frost secret.

"Come in, come in, what are you thinking standing out there in the cold? Victor already arrived with your bags." Diana ushered Juliet inside, as the tips of her fingers were as red as Rudolph's nose. The delicious warmth of the house was a sharp contrast to the crisp air outside. Her bags sat by the staircase, which was decorated with wreaths and fairy lights.

"Just wanted to stretch after the long drive."

"I'm not surprised – Victor said you slept most of the way. I was going to put a tree up in your cottage and everything!"

"We can get one together! It's been too long since we did anything together." Juliet remembered how Diana used to take her to the Christmas tree farm a few miles from the estate, and Victor would cut down the smallest one to fit in her cottage. Christmas was Diana's favourite season, and the house screamed it as they walked through the hall; even the rug had been changed from her stepmother's signature beige to a ruby red.

"Beth is in the kitchen making Christmas cookies," said Diana, explaining the flour-caked apron, her smile deepening the creases around her eyes. Neither of the Frost daughters were gifted in the kitchen, no matter how hard Diana had tried to teach them. Then again, Juliet was sure Gillian didn't even know how to turn on the oven.

"I didn't know Beth would be home. I thought Dad mentioned she was skiing with friends for the holidays?" She was glad her lie to Margot had turned out to be true; she hadn't seen her thirteen-year-old sister in a year.

"The trip was delayed – the resort closed due to severe weather." Diana glanced over her shoulder to make sure she wouldn't be overheard before adding, "The lady of the house wasn't all too pleased, but we're keeping her busy." Gillian didn't like to parent anyone, not even her own child, especially when that child had been a surprise.

"Where *is* the lady of the manor? Charity brunch or shopping?" Juliet shook away the thought that maybe her sister was better off this way and took the arm of the short, stout woman who had more heart than anyone she'd ever met.

"Neither – volunteering at the library. They have a Santa giving away books, and she's helping to put together the stockings," Diana said, smirking at Juliet's clear shock.

"My stepmother? Mrs Frost? Is stocking-stuffing at the library?" Juliet stopped in her tracks as they reached the open-plan kitchen. "What's she stuffing them with? She knows children can't have Xanax and red wine, right?"

"Don't be unkind; Mrs Frost has been getting into the holiday spirit." Diana nudged her. "She even let Beth help decorate the tree in the main room."

Juliet shook her head. "No way! She let someone touch *the* tree, the focal point of the season?! Have you been putting something in her smoothies?"

Diana tutted. "Mrs Frost is trying; don't be unkind. She's missed Beth. Her being away at school can be hard on her."

Diana had a terrible habit of seeing the best in people. Juliet would never speak ill of her stepmother to Beth, but she had trouble believing that the woman who'd cast a pre-teen out of her home had suddenly found a kind streak.

"What's the angle?" She narrowed her gaze, not wanting her sister to hear her talking poorly of their 'mom'.

"No angle. The library in town was struggling. Mrs Frost bought it from the city council and added a bookstore, so you can buy or rent a book, and a small coffeeshop."

It was a great idea, but books weren't exactly Gillian's thing. *She used to scold me for always having my nose in a book, and now she's managing a bookstore?* This was almost as strange as learning a magical village existed. Oh well, if her stepmother was out of the house, Juliet had more time and freedom to snoop.

"Look who's here!" Diana called.

Beth sat cross-legged on the counter, covered in icing sugar, decorating cookies with various shades of green and red icing. Her head snapped up, and Juliet smirked when she saw the gold sprinkles tangled in her dark plaits.

"Excuse me, but have you seen my sister?" she asked, making a show of looking around the kitchen.

"Very funny, J! " Beth jumped off the counter, and Juliet couldn't believe how tall she was. There was no way the little girl she'd seen last was now wearing eyeliner and almost the same height as her.

"No, no, you're far too tall and grown up to be my Beth." Juliet shook her head and winked at Diana, who was cleaning up some of the mess on the counter while the youngest Frost was distracted.

Beth groaned, wrapping her arms around Juliet. "It's me! Stop messing, or I won't give you any cookies."

"Let me get a good look at you." Juliet leaned out of her tight embrace, staring into her familiar brown eyes. "We do have the same eyes."

"I'm not playing this game with you." Beth released her. "We're making your favourite gingerbread cookies!"

Juliet wondered if they were edible. "You must be my sister – only she would know my favourite Christmas treat. However, I forbid you from growing anymore. You'll be taller than me soon," she teased, regretting how long it'd been.

"That wouldn't be too hard." Will Duncan stepped out from the pantry with a bag of icing sugar. "We thought you wouldn't arrive until Monday."

He acted like him being here was completely normal. *What the hell?*

Slack-jawed, Juliet tried to find her words. Even if they'd left each other on good terms, she wasn't sure how many more surprises her heart could take. Given the snowman apron he was wearing, he'd been here a while. From the flour on his cheek and food colouring stains on his hands, he'd been enlisted as Beth's assistant in the baking.

Juliet shook away the thought; cookies were the last thing she was concerned about. When had he arrived, and why the hell was he here? *How'd he know I'd come here?*

"I couldn't wait to see my sister. Why are you here?" She hadn't meant to snap, but if he was here, she wouldn't be able to snoop without his interfering. *Is it to stop me from confronting my dad?*

Diana frowned as the two stared at each other. "Mr Duncan is our guest for the holidays. Please remember your manners!"

"Sorry, tone delivery problem," Juliet said. "I just wasn't expecting him to be here."

"Mr Frost said you two were already acquainted; he's staying in the guest wing," Diana explained, clearly delighted to have a helpful, handsome guest. "He only arrived last night."

"Yeah, we've met… but surely you have your own plans for the holidays?" *Arrived last night? Was it his plan to come here all along?* She remembered his questions about her Christmas plans that first night in the hotel.

"I'd say we're more than acquaintances." His eyebrow arched playfully. Juliet gritted her teeth at the insinuation. "Mr Frost kindly invited me to stay when I informed him I'd be stuck in the city, working over the holidays."

Juliet narrowed her eyes. She knew what he was working

on over the holidays – her. She was his mission, and that damn chest he'd brought into her life. *I can't believe Dad would welcome a stranger into the house in the hopes of working with him! If he knew who Will truly was, he wouldn't have got past the gate.*

"I should get my bags to the cottage, settle in," she said, suddenly finding the kitchen suffocating despite it being nearly the size of her entire apartment.

"Let me give you a hand," Will offered, removing his apron. He clearly didn't plan on letting her escape.

"Fine." She wanted to talk to him alone anyway.

"Same!" Beth chimed in, eyeing the pair as though she was enjoying the show.

"You need to help Di clean up this mess. While you finish, I'll unpack and then we can watch a Christmas movie in the cinema room – your choice," Juliet suggested. She couldn't let Beth find out about Yule; she was too young to handle such truths.

"Muppets' Christmas Carol?" Beth didn't hesitate. They'd watched it every Christmas they'd spent together, while hiding from the Annual Frost Christmas Eve party.

"Absolutely!" Juliet agreed. Beth hurried back to the counter, picking up the bag of frosting to finish the cookies.

"We aired out the cottage and I've lit the fire, but it'll need time to warm up," Diana called after her. "Are you sure you don't need a hand? I can call Victor?"

"We'll be fine," Will interjected. Clearly, he wanted to talk too.

"I didn't think you'd be so upset to see me," Will said, following Juliet through the house.

"I didn't think you would stalk me all the way to Frost House." She picked up the suitcase in the hallway, not wanting him to know she had brought the chest with her. He grabbed her handbag; pink wasn't really his colour.

"I'm not stalking you, I was invited! After you ran out of the gala, your dad mentioned we should spend some time together over the holidays. And I figured you would come back here for answers. I thought you could use some moral support."

"The last time you tried to comfort me, I ended up in some magical village. I can figure this out by myself," Juliet said, trying not to sound rude. She'd still be in the dark about Yule without him, but right now she didn't want to be distracted by him or his cologne. "You've done enough; you don't need to watch me 24/7. I promised to call if I needed you."

She opened a sliding door in the dining room, and the chill hit her as she stepped into the frosted gardens. They walked through the perfectly trimmed short hedges that separated each species of flower and the various statues and fountains that made up the gardens.

"Being a guardian of Yule, I'm here to protect our secret and for your protection, even if you need to be protected from yourself." Will followed close behind as she navigated the covered pool.

"I don't need to be protected," she huffed, weaving her suitcase through the garden path, careful not to crush any plants.

"Says the woman who'd have frozen to death in an alley if Lyla hadn't found you," Will mused.

Juliet clenched her jaw, not wanting to think about that, or what had followed. She turned on him and grabbed her handbag, leaving him with the heavier suitcase that contained the chest. Since he wanted to help, he could be the one to struggle.

"You're cute when you're petty," he said, taking it.

"Don't flirt with me when I'm mad at you." Careful on the icy path, she passed the rose bushes that surrounded her small cottage.

"Where are we going?" Will asked, side-stepping a plant pot mostly camouflaged by thick snow.

"Home," she told him, fishing in her bag for her keys. "The cottage predates the estate." It was a quaint patchwork of old stones and cement.

"Don't you live in the main house?" he asked, looking back towards the main house.

She chuckled to herself. "So, you *don't* know everything about me."

"There was only so much in your file," he muttered, his leather shoes struggling to find grip on the icy path.

"You have a file on me?" Juliet stared at him, and his eyes widened as he realised his mistake.

The lanterns on either side of the door had been turned on, highlighting the front door that she'd painted baby pink years back. The shade had faded to cream after years of weathering.

She shook her head. He'd probably broken another rule by telling her about the file, and they were in enough trouble as it was. "Well, looks like that file left out some important details. I lived here for most of my teen years." She was putting the keys in the door when she heard a loud curse and a thud. Turning around, she found Will in a hedge.

"Are you alright? I thought you'd be used to some icy steps." She chewed her lips to stop herself from laughing as he pulled a twig from his woollen jumper.

"Fine. The weight of the suitcase threw me off. Did you smuggle Margot in here?"

"A woman can never have enough shoes." If he knew she had the chest, he'd probably want it as far away from the Frosts as possible, but she needed it in case she found anything in the house and could compare details.

"Didn't you want to stay with your family?" he asked, apparently trying to move past his rather inelegant stumble.

"It was my grandfather's idea, and my stepmother preferred me being out from under her feet," she sighed. She had to admit that she loved her little home away from the house, even if she'd never forgive her grandfather for denying her the family she'd always wanted growing up.

"Didn't Beth ever ask why you don't live in the main house?" Will asked, unwittingly picking at a mostly healed wound.

"When she was born, I'd already been living here for a few years. And I like having my own space. Grandfather Reginald even gave me a nice allowance every few years to do it up the way I wanted."

"How kind of him," he muttered, placing her suitcase by

the couch in the centre of the pastel pink sitting room, just off from the small lavender kitchen.

Diana had been right about the heating – Juliet quickly added a log to the fire. Thankfully, there was no visible damp. Diana or Victor must've been maintaining it in her absence.

"It *was* kind of him. It was probably one of the only times he did something for me because he wanted to. He could've let my stepmother decorate it the way she wanted, which would've included a lot of beige and cream." She didn't know why she was being so defensive of the old man. Maybe she didn't want to taint one of the few good memories she had of him that wasn't tainted with neglect and hurt. "He even left it to me in his will. My stepmother wanted to knock it down when I went to college and put in a tennis court." She couldn't help but wonder if Reginald had done it so she'd have her own place on the estate, not just to keep her out of the main house when she came back for visits.

Will surveyed the fluffy white cushions on the light grey couch and her stacks of DVDs by the small TV. "Miracle on 34th Street, The Grinch Who Stole Christmas, The Holiday," he murmured, looking over the collection. "I thought you weren't all that into Christmas?"

"Christmas as a holiday I love. The expectations that come with it, not so much," she explained, taking The Holiday out of his hand and putting it back on the rack. "And movies can be enjoyed at any time of the year." She loved Christmas movies, with their messages of hope and love. "Do you have these in Yule?" she asked, wondering if a town dedicated to Christmas would indulge in such things, or if they distanced themselves from what outsiders believed.

"We do, but I haven't watched any in a few years," he said.

Juliet guessed he enjoyed them, given the smile he tried to conceal.

Desperate for a cup of coffee with swirls of the chocolate sauce that Diana always remembered to stock her cupboards with, she boiled her ridiculously bright orange kettle by the small sink in the corner of the kitchen. Having Will in her home, the one place in the Frost estate she felt was her own, made her feel far too exposed, considering how much he already knew about her.

"Here. You got a bit wet when you fell into the hedge," she said, tossing him a pink towel from the bathroom cupboard, trying to distract him from looking over her Christmas snow globe collection. It didn't seem to faze him as he dabbed the droplets from his navy sweater.

"The snowman is smoking." He frowned, picking up the figurine.

"Nana Rose loved to find ridiculous Christmas trinkets. We used to collect them from thrift stores during the holidays," Juliet said, taking a reindeer driving a Santa sleigh from his hand.

For a moment, only the sound of the boiling kettle filled the space. Will turned to her, and she considered taking a step back, but his gaze held her still.

"I couldn't imagine being forced to live on the grounds when there are plenty of rooms in the house."

It wasn't what she had expected him to say, and the concern in those dark eyes melted her insides. Still, she changed the subject, not wanting to dwell on the past. "If you're here because you're worried, I'm not going to tell anyone about Yule, you don't have to be. Anyway, even if I told someone about a village in the North Pole, they wouldn't believe me," she said, leaving his side to go to her bedroom. She wanted to hide the chest in the secret compartment in her floorboards she'd made in her teens. She'd considered leaving it in the apartment, but then Margot might find it.

Lifting out the jumpers and putting them on the bed, she removed the chest from the suitcase and was about to lift the floorboards when she heard footsteps. She froze when she saw Will in the doorway.

"That can't be here! Are you insane? Do you have any idea what your father would do if he got access to that or the bell?!"

"If you're so worried about the contents, why would you help my mom get it to me?" Was he going to take it back? She wasn't going to let that happen until she had answers. "I'm not going to let you take it." She stepped back towards it, protectively.

The shock on his face told her she was wrong. "Why are you so determined to think I'm the enemy? After all the trouble I went to get it to you, I'm not going to take it from you. As a guardian, it's my job to make the learning process easier for you. Learning about Yule can be overwhelming. Given your family's history, I don't want you to be alone in this, regardless of my personal feelings for you."

His admission made her heart pound. Why did her body respond to his words, when her mind told her it could only end in heartbreak? He was from Yule, the very place her family had been banished from. She couldn't help but wonder what her life would've been like if her mom hadn't given her up, if she'd grown up in Yule. Sadness washed over her. She could have been raised by two parents who loved each other enough to break laws. Part of her resented Yule for ruining the family she might have had.

"What do you mean by trouble? How did you get it?" she asked.

"Your mum got the Frost chest from Yule's ancestral vault, a crime punishable by banishment. I got it out of Yule and passed it on to your grandmother, another crime punishable by banishment," he explained. "If your father found the chest, he could use it to get to Yule, and the council would know someone got the chest out."

Well, that explained why he was so determined to protect it. He'd risk losing his home to help her?

"Put that away and let's sit down. You don't look so good." Will reached for her as she swayed. She'd never been a fainter in the past, but now was as good a time as any to start. He helped her lift the floorboard and secure the chest inside before covering it again, then led her to the couch in the sitting room and sat down.

"There was a letter from my grandfather to my mom. He mentioned that she was a guardian who broke her vows," she said quietly. "That her relationship with my father was forbidden – it's why she had to give me up. I came home to find answers. There were other letters where she tried to end things, and Dad wouldn't let her. I want to see if I can find out more."

"That's why I got here first. In case you got the overwhelming desire to confront your dad," he said, sitting down beside her on the couch.

"I don't want to confront him. I need to find the letter my mom sent Reginald about petitioning the council."

"The council of Yule will do anything to keep our secret and return that chest to its rightful place if they discover it's missing. Your father can't find out you have the chest; he can't get his hands on the bell."

"Because he could use it to prove Yule exists?"

He nodded. "And that can't happen."

"One more question. If guardians aren't allowed to get

involved with their charges, like it said in Reginald's letter, why did you approach me in the hotel but let me believe you were just a stranger?"

"Selfishly, I wanted you. I'm sorry I couldn't keep my distance." He tipped her chin up to him, and she blushed. "The moment I saw your photo in the file, I couldn't imagine anyone else by your side through this, even if it's mostly my job to protect the chest, and Yule. I couldn't stop myself from approaching you, but I'm also not sorry for the time we've spent together," he admitted. Conflict raged inside her. *How can I repeat the same mistake as my parents?* She wanted to be angry at him for putting them in this complicated and potentially heartbreaking situation, but it didn't matter how much she rationalised, because her heart skipped a beat as he rested his hand on her thigh. His head dipped towards her, and all she could think was how safe she felt beside him.

A door slammed open, making them both jump, and Beth rushed into the room and leaned on the back of the couch. "Sorry to interrupt the flirting, but the cookies are ready, and I set up the movie."

"Did you clean the kitchen?" Juliet asked, thankful to her sister for breaking the tension before they got carried away. Her cheeks were hot with embarrassment.

Beth nodded furiously. "Did you have time to hide my presents?"

"Stop thinking about presents – do you want to watch the movie or not?" She got up to playfully shove her sister towards the door.

Beth looked so like their father with her dark hair and eyebrows, the narrow cheekbones. Juliet couldn't help but wonder if when her father looked at *her*, he saw only her mom, the woman he'd shared a forbidden love with. Perhaps that explained their tumultuous relationship, one she was glad her sister didn't have to experience.

"Are you going to join us?" Beth asked Will. "There are plenty of cookies, and I don't want you to feel left out. Dad wouldn't like for us to leave out a guest."

"I'm sure Will has far more important things to do. We shouldn't keep him to ourselves." Juliet smiled at him, hoping he'd reject the offer so she wouldn't have to sit in a dark room in such a proximity with him for hours. "Right, Will? Places to go, people to visit."

"But he just got here." Beth's frown melted her resolve.

"And I've nowhere else I'd rather be. It'd be rude of me to reject such a kind offer," Will said with a grin, rising from the couch.

Beth beamed. "Good, because I've made all of us some hot chocolate. I don't want it to get cold, so hurry up!"

BETH FELL asleep within the first twenty minutes of the movie, and Will, despite being from a place far more magical than any Christmas movie, couldn't have been more engrossed in the antics of muppets messing with Michael Caine. Juliet was surprised when he took her hand, threading his fingers through hers as though it was the most natural act in the world, but she couldn't bring herself to pull away. His touch put her more at ease than she'd felt in weeks.

The next day, Juliet watched the sunset from her small kitchen and decided to take the opportunity to search the house while Diana worked on dinner with Beth. Will had left after breakfast to run some errands, which she hadn't asked about; she wasn't sure she wanted to know more about his guardian duties for fear of breaking yet another rule. Since she'd spent the day helping Beth wrap presents for her friends, this was her only chance to snoop before Will came back for dinner.

Her dad's office on the second floor was locked. Luckily for her, he was a man of habit and kept the key above the family portrait on the wall opposite the stairs. Not that anyone would dare enter his office without his approval, and she'd never been so bold – until now.

In the grotesquely maroon office, her phone rang. Cursing herself for not silencing it, she answered before the sound made its way down the hall. The problem with big houses was that they loved to echo, and she'd barely managed to sneak past Beth and Diana on her way upstairs.

"Margot! Sorry, can I call you back? I'm in the middle of something," she whispered, closing the door with a soft click. She pressed the phone to her ear with her shoulder, searching the papers on her father's desk to no avail. Not that he would keep information about skeletons in the Frost family closet out in the open.

"No problem. I just wanted to check in. I just got in from seeing Harvey. We went ice skating and then to a Christmas market. Talked for hours – I think I might keep this one." Margot's smile could be heard in each word; Juliet didn't think her friend had ever sounded so giddy, though it was difficult to concentrate while she was crawling on her hands and knees on the Persian rug that concealed the family safe.

"Got it!" she exclaimed, staring at the safe after flipping up the carpet.

"Are you alright?"

"I was looking for something. What were you saying?" It wouldn't be long before she'd be called for dinner. She needed to hurry, but she didn't know the safe's password.

"Harvey mentioned Will is spending the holidays with your family. I didn't believe him, but he was certain. Should I be worried this guy is a little obsessed with you?" Margot chuckled in disbelief.

If only she knew just how obsessed. "Dad invited him – business connections and stuff. He arrived a couple of hours before me. He was making cookies with Beth and Di when I arrived," Juliet told her as she tried birthdays, anniversaries, and other important family dates. Nothing worked.

"I should've gone with you. Are you sure your dad isn't trying to set you up again?"

Juliet snorted at the irony. Given her father's history with guardians, if her father knew who Will really was, he'd make sure they never saw each other again. The thought caused a sudden ache in her chest.

"I can handle Will and my dad's schemes," she said. The last thing she needed was Margot turning up and complicating the matter further. "If you'd come, you wouldn't have had your date with Harvey."

Perhaps Dad used a date no one would know... It hit her like a bucket of cold water. *The date he met Mom!* She screwed up her face, trying to remember the date her mom's letter had mentioned, then typed *22-12-95.*

The door on the safe clicked. *Yes!*

"Once I get through the season, I'll come straight home, and you can tell me everything about Harvey." She let out a sigh of relief as she pulled out the contents of the safe.

"I can't wait to see you, but give Will a chance. He might just make the season more enjoyable. If he's willing to spend the holidays with your family, he might be a keeper," Margot pointed out.

Juliet barely heard her, too distracted by the file concealed within a manila envelope marked with the Christmas tree sigil that was becoming all too familiar.

"I really have to call you back," she said hastily, and promised she'd call later before hanging up.

Inside the envelope, she found the original letter her grandfather had sent her mom. The letter in the chest must've been a copy her Nana Rose had made. What *hadn't* been in the chest was her birth certificate. Juliet ran her fingers over her name and her mom's signature. It was the closest she'd ever been to the woman who'd given her up.

She wiped her tears with the back of her hand, not wanting to stain the official document. In the right-hand corner, a red stamp read **Citizen in Banishment by order of the Council of Yule**. This document and the banishment papers in the chest were the only evidence of what both worlds wanted to conceal. Seeing her father's signature right by her mom's was everything she needed to confront him, but today wasn't the day. She wasn't going to ruin the holidays for her sister.

She turned on the printer behind the desk, watching Yule's golden seal shine through the back of the document as it copied.

"What are you doing in here?" Will snapped.

Juliet spun around to find him standing in the doorway. *I should've locked the door behind me.* She hurried over and pulled it closed before they were overheard.

Will stumbled on the overturned rug as he came towards her. He glared at it, then the documents on the floor by the open safe. "I guess that answers my question."

"Did anyone see you come up here?" Juliet hissed, wanting to distract him, but the printer interrupted with a beep. She winced.

"No, I was on my way to my room when I heard someone walking around. I thought your dad had come home early." Will reached around her and removed the evidence from the paper tray. "I see you've been doing your own research."

"I had to find something concrete, and since you said I can't reveal the stolen chest, I figured I can tell him that Nana Rose left me a letter about Yule and Mom, and I can use this birth certificate to confront him without using the chest. This way Dad can't say Nana Rose or my mom are lying. My birth certificate with Yule's official stamp can't be refuted." She removed the original and turned off the printer, careful not to leave any trace of her presence.

"Okay, you have your evidence. Now let's get out of here before we're found snooping," Will said, pacing by the door. Juliet enjoyed seeing him unsettled – nervous, even. It made a change from her being the one driven up the wall.

"You can leave. I'll be downstairs in a minute." She carefully folded the photocopy into her back pocket before putting the documents back and sealing the safe, only to hesitate when she spotted a red envelope dated before her grandfather's response to her mom.

"You shouldn't take any originals in case your father checks when he gets home," Will warned.

"I'll return it before he comes back," Juliet reasoned, but the way his eyes darted to the letter made her think that he didn't want her reading it. *Did Mom warn him to conceal certain letters?* She didn't care either way; she *had* to know what her mom had written to her grandfather before deciding to give her up for good.

Before Will could argue, they both froze at voices in the hallway.

"Did you hear something?" Diana's voice was barely audible through the thick door. With Will distracted, Juliet slipped the red envelope into her back pocket.

"Maybe Dad came back early?" Beth suggested.

Their footsteps grew louder as Will and Juliet stared at each other in horror.

"Mr Frost?" Diana knocked on the door to the office. The doorknob turned.

Before Juliet could think, Will wrapped his arms around her.

"What are you—?" But she didn't get to finish her sentence before the room around them melted away.

Instead of being greeted with Diana's questioning gaze, Juliet found herself standing in a library surrounded by narrow shelves. *Not again!* she grumbled to herself.

The terrifying part wasn't where she was, but that she was alone. Her heart hammered as she searched row after row of books for Will with no luck. She leaned over the wooden balcony to see if he was on the floor below, but all she saw were readers perusing shelves, unaware about her freak-out.

She tried to call him, but her phone wouldn't connect; Yule clearly wasn't part of her phone plan. Shouting his name through the library might work, but wouldn't be the most subtle option.

Eventually she decided to make her way down a winding staircase decorated with garlands in hope of finding him. A large Christmas tree stood behind the reception desk, decorated with huge, sparkling ornaments which, on closer inspection, were books. Engraved in the wall behind several staff members organising carts of books was a sign that proclaimed **Library of Yule**.

Wandering off last time was a mistake, so if I stay put, he might find me? Juliet didn't have much of a choice. *If he doesn't turn up in the next few hours, then I'll find my way to his place.* She was only wearing a thin cardigan, so going outside was the last thing she wanted. Luckily, she was wearing her boots.

Taking a seat at one of the long tables lit by antique lamps, she removed the red envelope from her back pocket. It looked like it'd been crumpled up more than once. Her desire to know the truth, to know what Will wanted to keep from her when he'd already revealed so much, won over her need to protect herself.

Mr Frost,

I hope this letter finds you and your family well. I promised to stop all communication with your son, and I have. As a guardian of Yule, I'm ashamed to admit to the part I played in my relationship with your son. I won't pretend that I didn't know any better, but I loved your son as I love my daughter, who is now in your care. The council of Yule and Mr Klaus have agreed to allow me to keep my position and to spare the Heart name the shame of my actions. However, I hope you'll understand as a parent yourself why I've opened a petition with the council of Yule to grant me custody of Juliet. I need you to support my petition, otherwise I will not be allowed to have any contact with my daughter for the next twenty-six years in accordance with legacy laws. I know I'm in no position to ask for your help, but for the sake of Juliet's happiness, I'm asking for your assistance.

Thank you for taking care of her while I can't. I understand if you need time to consider, but I beg of you to help me reunite with my daughter. Again, I apologise for the hurt my actions have caused your family.

Eloise Heart

. . .

JULIET WIPED the tears from her cheeks and placed the letter back in the envelope. *Twenty-six years... This confirms why Mom sent Will now. This legacy law came into effect.* She wasn't surprised her grandfather hadn't helped Eloise with the petition, but to know her mom had tried to fight for her told Juliet she had never been just a mistake to be forgotten. Still, for a moment she was relieved never to have known this. Over twenty years of waiting would've been an unbearable pain.

"Excuse me." A guy in his late teens tapped her on the shoulder. "I didn't mean to interrupt, but I wanted to ask if you were alright. I was studying at the table across from you and noticed you crying."

Embarrassed to have made a scene, Juliet tucked the envelope in her pocket and out of sight. "Sorry if I disturbed you – I'm fine. Just got a little choked up. Family stuff." She wiped her eyes, making sure there was no trace of smudged mascara.

"The holidays can be emotional; can I help at all? I noticed you searching different rows. I wasn't watching you or anything, I was just procrastinating studying and wondered if you were looking for something?" He ran his hand through his sandy blonde hair as it flopped over his eyes.

"I was, but I couldn't find it," Juliet admitted, knowing she wasn't supposed to be talking to anyone. She didn't want to reveal that Will was the 'it'.

"Okay. Sorry again for disturbing you."

As he started to walk away, she noticed the Klaus name embroidered in gold thread on his black backpack. He might not be able to help her find Will, but what if he could help her find answers about her family's past? It was someone in his family who'd written to her grandfather about upholding the Frost family's banishment.

"Sorry." She got up and followed him down the row. He paused, turning back to face her. "Actually, I'm doing some research on old families in Yule. Specifically, those who've been banished, and legacies," she explained, taking a gamble in trusting a considerate stranger.

"Banishment records?" His brows pulled together as he thought it through, clutching his laptop to his chest. "They would be in the archives beneath the town hall, and you'd need permission from the council or the current Klaus to see them."

"Right. I just thought since you're a Klaus – sorry for bothering you," she said quickly, not wanting to overstep more than she already had.

He merely chuckled. "I could ask my brother; Mason would be easier to convince than the council. Being the Klaus, he wouldn't need their permission. However, as it's December, he's rather swamped getting everything ready for Christmas Eve. He's in Santa mode right now, so it's not the best time to ask for a favour."

Given that this was a magical village in the North Pole and she'd used bells that could bring you from one place to the next, Santa Claus, or Santa Klaus, being a real person didn't seem all that far-fetched. Still, the fact that Juliet was apparently talking to Santa's brother threw her for a loop.

"As for information on legacies, I'm doing some research myself on Yule's history for a game I'm designing. Depending on how far you want to go back, I might be able to help," he said, motioning for her to follow him up the stairs.

"Anything would help. I'm Juliet, by the way. Thank you for helping me." From what she'd gathered, the Klaus was the leader of Yule, with the council being some sort of government. Getting this close to a Klaus was probably dangerous, but she'd be careful not to reveal her last name.

"Kevin," he said over his shoulder, "and I'm happy to help."

They climbed the stairs to the third floor, where they were the only visitors. Judging by the dust on the shelves, this section of the library didn't get much love.

"Was there a time-period you were looking into? Any family you want to focus on? Are you looking for someone?" Kevin asked, searching the rows of dusty shelves.

Juliet only knew about one event in particular. She tried to be as nonchalant as possible. "Um, the Frost family? I heard about their banishment in passing. I'm new to Yule, and my boyfriend is from here. I want to learn as much as I can about the history, rules, and laws. I wanted to know if it was true that people *can* be banished." She comforted herself that it was mostly the truth, hating to reward his trust and kindness with deception.

Kevin hesitated, pointing to a row of F names. "A Klaus is the only one who has the final say on who is or isn't banished, but the council make the recommendation. The Klaus family is the most powerful in Yule," he explained with a self-deprecating grin. "A few generations ago, the Frosts were second to them; they looked after the protections of Yule. Unfortunately, they broke our most important rule." He said it as though she should be able to fill in the blanks herself.

"About revealing Yule's existence?" she guessed.

He nodded. "There hasn't been a Frost in Yule for three or four generations, I think. I believe their legacies were included in the banishment, so I doubt they even know about Yule. I'm surprised you've even heard about them. The closest we've ever come to exposure was because of them –

until my great-grandfather stopped them." He scanned the last of the Fs. "Sorry, there's nothing here. Everything must be in the archives."

"You said your great-grandfather stopped them?" Juliet dared to ask.

"The story is pretty much legend now! The Frost family believed the world should know of Yule and its magic, so that those on the Outside could understand the hope and magic Yule brings to the world. They tried to use their influence to destroy the protections that safeguard the village from the Outside, but my great grandfather Klaus discovered their plot and stopped them in time," Kevin told her. "The Frost name has become synonymous with the very threat of exposure in Yule."

Juliet swallowed, wondering what he would do if he knew who he was talking to. "How were they going to destroy the protections?" she asked, wondering how much was known about them.

"I don't know; that part of the story is always left out. It was the only time since Yule was founded in 270AD that our existence was almost outed. They don't reveal details, probably to stop anyone else from figuring it out." He shrugged.

"Do you think they would ever be allowed to return? I mean, can anyone banished return?" Juliet tried to hide the desperation in her voice, but the hint of suspicion in Kevin's gaze told her she wasn't being so subtle.

"They could petition the council, or the sitting Klaus, but they'd have to plead a pretty good case. Banishment is rare, and you have to do something pretty terrible to be cast out. I might be wrong, but I think my grandfather received a petition about a child in the Frost family." Kevin's eyes narrowed, deep in thought, as he scanned the books. It must be for his own work, because the titles he removed were beyond her comprehension.

"A child?" Juliet followed him to the next row, a cold sweat creeping up the back of her neck.

"I could be wrong, but I think the latest scandal had something to do with a guardian falling in love with the eldest Frost son. It's not confirmed, but apparently, they had a kid. Every banished family is assigned a guardian to make sure they don't step out of line. No one ever expected the guardian to be the one to overstep."

"What happened to the guardian?" Juliet was practically tripping over herself to get to the answers.

"I wouldn't dare ask; the Heart family always dismisses the tale as mere rumour. No one knows for sure which guardian it was. Gossip would say that the guardian was given a choice, give up the kid or keep her position in Yule. Only the sitting Klaus or the council can confirm or deny the details. I think the story would make for an interesting game. Forbidden love is always a winner." He beamed over his stack of books.

Juliet clenched her fist at the idea of her family tragedy being made into a game for other people's amusement, but she needed his help. He was a Klaus. Even if she wasn't sure what the deal was with this whole Santa Klaus thing, the Klaus family clearly had power in town, and she needed help.

"All sounds like some romantic tragedy. What about now? Are the Frosts still so feared?" Was there any hope for her future with her mom… or Will?

Kevin sighed. "Mason would probably be lenient. He's broken a few laws himself. However, considering that the Frost family wanted to expose us, and the latest scandal being a perfect example of them defying the rules for their own desires, I don't know. In Yule, everyone works together

– so betrayal cuts deep," he said, leading her out of the stacks and back to the main floor of the busy library.

"But those who wanted to expose Yule are long gone. Couldn't your grandad have lifted the banishment and let the couple be together?" Juliet asked, trying not to think of how she was talking to a member of the family who'd kept her from her mom.

"It's complicated. When someone, anyone, leaves Yule, they're assigned a guardian. However, those banished are forbidden from interacting with their guardians and vice versa. Guardians are supposed to be invisible – the banished shouldn't even know the identity of their guardian. They're only tasked with making sure the banished doesn't reveal Yule's secret. To forgive such an infraction might encourage others to commit it. That, and I think the council were dead against it – and since a Klaus needs the support of the council to help maintain Yule, it's rare they go against them completely."

Juliet struggled to digest her family's history. She felt like a criminal in this far-away land.

"Anyway, it doesn't matter much now – no one has raised the issue in years. I'm sure the Frosts have forgotten all about Yule at this point." Kevin shrugged, as though her life was merely an issue on the council's agenda. "Are you alright? You look a little green," he added, finally seeming to notice the effect his words had on her.

"Fine. Just sad to think a place like Yule, so welcoming and full of magic, has such a... sad history," Juliet said, wishing she'd never gone into her dad's office.

"It's a pity; I'd never want anyone to lose their family." Kevin shook his head, and she could see that he had a good heart. "We don't have many rules in Yule, but when it comes to safety and secrecy of our village, there is a strict no tolerance policy. For those who find out about Yule later in life, it can sound harsh and hard to understand, but this is our home – our world."

They'd reached the front desk, where Kevin signed out the books he'd chosen.

"Thank you for taking the time to help me." Watching him sign, Juliet was glad she hadn't found a book in the end, or she would've had to come up with a fake name.

"I'm sorry I couldn't be of more help with the finer details." Kevin opened the library door, letting in the cold and the smell of pine trees.

Wrapping her arms around herself, Juliet followed him outside into the evening air misted with snow. More of it decorated every surface and painted shop window. She was about to ask about Eloise Heart, but she didn't get the chance before a red sleigh pulled up at the front steps. Juliet held her breath, terrified she'd been caught.

"Kevin, we've got to get back home. It's nearly four-thirty, and Mum's getting dinner ready for five so we can all eat together before my evening shift starts." A tall blond man stepped out of the sleigh. The weight lifted from Juliet's shoulders when he ignored her. "I told you I'd pick you up twenty minutes ago. I've been circling like a maniac, and I've got to get back to the workshop later."

"Sorry, Juliet, my brother has forgotten his manners." Kevin rolled his eyes as he put his books into the back of the sleigh. Juliet stepped back; the two reindeer were eyeing her. "He gets terribly cranky when he hasn't eaten."

"Sorry – nice to meet you. I just don't like waiting in the snow for twenty minutes," Mason said, glaring at his younger brother. They looked alike, both tall with blond hair and piercing blue eyes. Mason was clearly the older, with his five o'clock shadow and broader build.

"Understandable. I think I've met your fiancée, Lyla? I'm Will's girlfriend," she blurted out, not wanting Kevin to mention her prying into Yule's history. Will could yell at her later for fabricating their relationship.

"Will's girlfriend?" Mason frowned, only for realisation to dawn. "Right! Lyla mentioned you'd met the other day. Welcome to Yule. I've been stuck at the workshop the past few days and haven't had a chance to call him." He offered her his hand and she shook it, hoping that he'd put her trembling down to the cold and not fear. She was standing in front of the man who had the power to banish Will for helping her.

"Will had something to do, so I thought I'd hang out here," she told him, hoping they'd leave her to it so she could find her way back to Will's home somehow.

"You should come back with us to the cabin," Kevin offered eagerly, hopping into the sleigh beside his brother. "Lyla will be there, and we can leave a message on Will's house phone if he doesn't answer. They've been baking for the gingerbread contest all day, and Mum loves any excuse to feed a full table."

Juliet panicked at the kind offer. It felt like walking into the nest of some very welcoming vipers. She hoped to see Lyla again, but didn't want her to have to lie to her fiancé's family. "I don't want to intrude. I'm fine here."

"The library will close in an hour, and Will wouldn't forgive me if I left you out in the cold." Kevin nudged Mason, who nodded.

"I'm sure Lyla would love to see you again, and it'll force Will to come to the cabin. We haven't seen him for ages, and Mum's been begging him to come to dinner."

In spite of their unexpected kindness, she wanted to run,

but given the icy cobblestones, she doubted she'd make it far before falling on her butt.

"C'mon, it's freezing, and I'm sure you're not used to the climate yet," Kevin urged.

To her surprise, the reindeer nudged Juliet's shoulder.

"Dasher likes you," Mason said with a smile.

Juliet stroked Dasher's nose and smiled to herself in disbelief. Just when she thought this place couldn't get any more interesting. She hesitated, praying Will would appear and take her home. When he didn't, she thanked them profusely for their help and pulled herself into the back of the sleigh before she could talk herself out of it. At least this way she could wait for Will out of the cold.

Where the hell is he? Why didn't he use the bell to find me? At this point, being discovered by Diana was far less dangerous than having dinner with the family who'd banished her ancestors and separated her from her mom. Still, she felt she couldn't be mad at them; they were as much to blame for their relatives' actions as she was.

The sleigh shot down a narrow lane, finally making a sharp turn up a hill lined with uncut trees and lampposts to light the way.

"Juliet?" Kevin asked softly, and she realised he'd been talking to her.

"Sorry, what was the question? I was too busy admiring the view."

"How did you meet Will?" Mason put in.

"I'm afraid the story isn't all that exciting. I was reading in a hotel bar when he sent me a drink. Then he showed up at my office the next day, and I haven't been able to get rid of him since." It was a relief not to have to lie for once.

Mason chuckled, glancing at her over his shoulder. "Will has always gone after what he wants."

"How long have you known him?" she asked, moving the topic away from her. She also wanted him to keep his eyes on the steep hill, because as she saw the lights of the town below them, it became clear how close they were to the edge of a steep drop.

"We went to school together."

"They also used to race sleighs together, until Will ended up—" Kevin was cut off with a thump to the arm.

"He's meant to be my best man. If I can ever get him to come home for long enough to ask him! Luckily the wedding isn't for another year, and you've given me the perfect excuse to get him to visit." Mason sounded like he missed his friend a lot. Juliet winced at the idea that Will's actions could ruin their friendship. Swallowing her nerves, she tried to stop herself from wondering what they'd do if they knew who she was.

"I'm sure he'd love to; his work just keeps him busy." *After all this deception, maybe I am a Frost after all.* As much as she wanted to meet her mom, she pledged to herself that she wouldn't come back here again without permission. "The view is beautiful. I can't believe I never knew the village was shaped like a star," she rambled nervously, pulling a blanket from behind her and trying to keep warm under it. "It's so pretty I nearly forgot about the cold."

"Sorry, the higher we are, the colder it gets. We shouldn't be much longer," Mason assured her, and Kevin handed her another blanket. "It took Lyla months to get used to the weather. Make sure to wrap up warm while you're here – I'm surprised Will didn't warn you."

Juliet got the feeling he suspected something, but she decided to focus on the view instead of her paranoia. The less she said, the less she'd have to lie. She didn't want Will to have to betray his friend more than he already had. After what Kevin had said in the library, she couldn't believe how much he'd risked by being close to her.

The sound of the reindeer galloping on the shovelled flagstones through a set of tall gates brought her back to reality. The painted gates were rather chipped, but the golden cursive letters S and K shone brightly. It was very similar in design to the gate to the Frost estate. Juliet guessed her family had tried to replicate the finer details of the home they'd lost after their banishment.

Peering over her shoulder as the gates closed behind them, she felt like she had trapped herself in a nightmare.

Juliet stared at the most elaborate cabin she'd ever seen, wondering if the Frost family had had a place like this once upon a time. Following Mason and Kevin up the porch of their home, she noticed the glass corridors that connected the three logged buildings. Juliet tapped the snow off her shoes as Lyla opened the door to the trio.

"We brought a guest for dinner," Mason started, and Juliet winced, watching Lyla's smile turn to shock. "I believe you two have already met." Mason kissed his fiancée's mop of curls.

Thankfully, Lyla recovered her smile quickly. "Juliet, of course, we met a few days ago. I thought you and Will wouldn't be back for the holidays."

"We didn't intend on returning, but something came up," Juliet said, grateful she hadn't outed her. Now she owed Lyla for saving her twice.

"Sorry – Jones is a bit of an escape artist." Lyla quickly ducked down to pick up a rather chunky ginger cat. "Come in and I'll close the door."

Juliet took a deep breath before stepping into the foyer, where the heat from a grand fireplace beneath the wooden staircase comforted her raw nerves.

"Will should've told me he was bringing her home for the

holidays, we could've had a welcome party," Mason said to Lyla, shrugging off his thick jacket, while Juliet admired the golden tinsel wrapped around the banister and considered doing the same in her own place around her bed frame. She reminded herself to focus less on the Christmas dreamscape and more on the life-altering situation at hand.

"I should've reached out when you ran into him at the coffee shop, but I've been so distracted," Mason said to Lyla. "The workshop is behind on dust production because of a bad snowstorm," he told Juliet, as though she knew what dust was. *Workshop? Like Santa's workshop? Don't workshops make presents? What's dust got to do with anything?* She stopped her nervous laughter from escaping. Luckily, Mason didn't wait for her to respond. "Lyla only got here herself now that her company is on holidays," he explained. Juliet, having no idea who Lyla worked for, gave his fiancée a pleading look, hoping for her intervention before her head exploded.

"I think we shouldn't overwhelm our guest; she hasn't been here long," Lyla said on cue, and Mason zipped his lips, clearly just excited to meet his friend's girlfriend. "Could you make sure Kevin doesn't eat all the gingerbread biscuits while I give Juliet a tour?"

"I can take a hint. I'll let you two talk." Mason disappeared through a tall archway to the kitchen.

With everyone gone, Juliet took the chance to explain to Lyla how she'd ended up here.

"I'm so sorry about coming here. It wasn't planned, and I had no idea how to find my way back to Will's house from the library. The bell separated us when we arrived, and I ran into Kevin. They insisted I came for dinner—" Juliet cut off when she saw the Christmas tree in the sitting room, decorated with beautiful glittering snowflakes. This place wasn't like any cabin she'd been in before; it gave the Frost estate a run for its money when it came to grandeur. Even if the decorations were a little overdone.

"Breathe," Lyla said gently. "I told my share of lies when I first arrived here, and you aren't in any trouble. Though I will be giving out to Will for putting you at risk again."

Juliet was glad to have her on her side, even if it was her snooping that landed her here. She wondered what Lyla had had to lie about, but now wasn't the time to ask.

"How did you get separated?" Lyla asked.

"I don't know. Will used the bell to bring us here, but I ended up in the library and he wasn't with me. I tried to look for him, but I ran into Kevin, and you were the only person I could think to name," she said, wishing she had a better explanation. "Did you know bells can do this?"

Lyla shrugged. "It happens; travel by bell isn't exactly science." It wasn't the concrete comfort she was looking for. However, it was some relief to find that she wasn't the only one who was in the dark about most aspects of Yule's magic.

"There's nothing scientific about this place," she agreed, glad to have someone to confide in.

"Just don't mention anything about the Frosts. Once Will gets here, I'm sure he'll come up with some excuse for you both to leave. We just have to make it to then," Lyla whispered, as Jones, the ginger cat, rubbed himself against Juliet's legs. "Can I ask how long you and Will have been seeing each other? I thought he was helping you with your family, but you called yourself his girlfriend?"

"I'm not – I mean, we aren't really together. I mean we've been together, but not like together together," Juliet stammered, unsure how to explain. She buried her face in her hands. "I'm not making any sense."

Lyla chuckled softly. "Don't sweat it. You aren't the first 'fake' relationship in Yule and probably won't be the last."

Oh God, is Will going to think I'm in love with him? Or that I think we're in a relationship? There was no way Will or Kevin weren't going to mention meeting his 'girlfriend'. She wanted to ask Lyla if they had any duct tape for her mouth so she wouldn't put her foot in it again.

A warm voice interrupted them. "You can't keep her all to yourself, Lyla! Let me get a look at you."

Juliet guessed the white-haired older lady was Mason's mom. Her red apron, which read KISS THE KLAUS, brightened Juliet's mood. Before she could introduce herself, she was wrapped up in a hug which she realised she desperately needed.

"I'm Mrs Klaus, and it's so good to meet you." Mrs Klaus released her, and Juliet recognised the blue eyes she shared with her sons. "Sorry, we're huggers in this family." Mrs Klaus beamed. "Mason told me you're dating Will. He's never brought a woman to us before. He and Mason were inseparable as teens, but now work often takes them away. Although I can't complain – the pair used to eat me out of house and home!"

Juliet smiled. "That doesn't surprise me!" she said, though it only brought home to her how little she knew about Will's life in Yule aside from the fact that he had a sister. The thought made her strangely sad.

"I called Will. He's on the way, and you're both staying for dinner. No argument," Mason said, walking through the archway from the kitchen.

Juliet shot Lyla a panicked look. "I don't want to put you out. This is all rather sudden, and Kevin said you've got a baking competition to prepare for?"

Lyla waved her off. "It's just a holiday tradition, nothing serious. Though I'm determined to win this year."

"If she doesn't burn anything, it'll be win enough." Mason

kissed her curls again, and she elbowed him. He feigned injury, and Lyla rolled her eyes amusedly.

"If she stays conscious, it'll be even better," Kevin called out, eating some dough out of a bowl. Juliet frowned, and Lyla shook her head as though to tell her it was nothing. However, Mason's worried expression as he stood closer to Lyla told her there was more to the story.

"Ignore Kevin. Mason is the judge, and even he doesn't give me any free points." Lyla nudged him. They were so in love it was almost painful to look at.

"Seducing the judge isn't ethical." Mason smirked.

"Regardless of the competition, Juliet, we'd love to have you both for dinner. Please make yourself at home. I'm going to finish making dinner, and Lyla, please give our guest the grand tour!" Mrs Klaus said, not giving Juliet a chance to argue before she headed back to the kitchen.

Lyla didn't hesitate to take Juliet's arm and pull her away for a few moments of peace to gather her thoughts.

AFTER A TOUR of the most luxurious cabin she could have imagined, Juliet and Lyla made it to the dining room. Juliet froze as she saw Will standing with Mason by the set dinner table. He looked relieved while she panicked, wondering if Mason had told him she'd introduced herself as his girlfriend.

"Hi, honey, glad I found you!" He greeted her with a quick kiss, and the humour in his voice nearly knocked her off her feet. Clearly, Mason had quizzed him about their relationship, and Will must have confirmed it. "I heard you had a nice time at the library," he added, taking a seat beside her and squeezing her hand reassuringly under the table.

"Yes, Kevin was kind enough to show me around. I hope you managed to get all your work done," she said carefully.

"You make such a beautiful couple! It's such a nice surprise to have you with us," Mrs Klaus said, adding cuts of turkey and ham to the table. Given that it would be around nine at night back home, the smell of the delicious food only increased her appetite.

"We should be thanking you – this all looks incredible," she said, her stomach grumbling.

Mrs Klaus sat at the head of the table, and Juliet couldn't help but notice the seat at the other end remained empty. She guessed it was for Mason's deceased father; Lyla had told her on the tour that he'd lost his dad just before Christmas last year. As much as she wished to keep her distance from her own family, the sinking feeling in her gut told her she still couldn't think of losing her dad. Maybe because she hoped one day he'd actually become the father she needed.

"I hope you don't mind me asking, but you look awfully familiar," Mrs Klaus said, passing the gravy boat to Mason. "Do you have any relatives in Yule?"

Juliet nearly choked on her roast potato, and Will gently rubbed her back. She tried to dance around the truth. "I only found out about Yule through Will."

"I was going to say the same – when I saw you walking out of the library with Kevin, I couldn't help but think you looked familiar," Mason said, his eyes narrowing across the table at her.

"She only just got here," Will interjected, "unless you have a twin I don't know about?" He nudged Juliet playfully to break the tension.

"No, definitely not." Keeping her words light-hearted had never been such a struggle.

Juliet couldn't meet Mrs Klaus's studious stare; it seemed she had her answer about whether she looked like her mom. *Does she already know who I am? Is this some test to see if I'll lie?* She hoped she wasn't visibly sweating, because she certainly felt like she was.

Lyla picked up a jug to fill her glass with water, and promptly spilled it all over the table. Mason jumped up as the water cascaded onto his lap. "I'll get some towels."

Lyla winked across the table, and Juliet wanted to kiss her for providing the distraction.

"Anyway, it's not important." Mrs Klaus brushed off the line of questioning, and started grilling Kevin about all the time he'd been spending at the library on his new project. Hopefully safe from questioning for the moment, Juliet couldn't help tucking in.

"How did you two meet?" Mrs Klaus asked, handing Kevin the bowl of sprouts.

It was Will's turn to choke on the delicious turkey and stuffing. Looking up from her plate, Juliet found the family staring at her. She swallowed her mouthful and put down her knife and fork.

"Will approached me at a hotel bar, and I haven't been able to get rid of him since," she said, reiterating what she'd already said to Mason in the sleigh.

Will coughed and took a sip of his beer, clearly surprised by her admission.

"She was reading at the bar, and I couldn't stay away," he admitted, squeezing her leg under the table. Juliet gripped his hand to steady her heartbeat, cheeks heating at how easy it was for him to play the part of devoted boyfriend. "We've been together pretty much ever since."

"Cheers to the happy couple." Mason raised his glass, and the table cheered.

Will masterfully swerved the conversation. "Speaking of happy couples, I believe you had a rather important question to ask me? Something about being best man?"

Mason glared at Kevin, and if the others hadn't been there, Juliet would've kissed the life out of Will for getting the spotlight off them.

WHEN EVERYONE WAS STUFFED to the brim, Will and Mason cleared the table while Mrs Klaus insisted the guests stay the night. Will and Juliet tried to refuse, but the gentle woman wouldn't hear it. Juliet worried Beth would be upset about her disappearing so soon after arriving. Diana probably figured she and Will were getting to know each other as her dad wanted, but she hoped she wouldn't be too worried.

Will stayed and talked with Mason while Lyla showed her to a guest bedroom which was thankfully separated from the main house. The dark green wallpaper and plush cream carpet went beautifully with the dark wood of the four-poster bed, and the dark sheets looked like an abyss Juliet couldn't wait to climb into. Given the time difference, and after so much food and anxiety, she wanted to crash. She wanted to ask Lyla some questions; being from the Outside, she had to understand how Juliet was feeling. But as the adrenaline wore off, she didn't have the energy to tackle any more revelations.

Giving her some much-needed space, Lyla assured her everything was going to be fine before disappearing down the hall with Kevin to talk about the new game he was designing.

Juliet wanted to climb under the covers, but she went to the sliding glass door on the far side of the bed and looked up at the bright stars, unfiltered by light pollution. From this height, she could see what Will meant about Yule being protected by the snow-covered mountains. They wrapped around the village like a basin. How they made it invisible to the rest of the world was still a puzzle, but she presumed it was some kind of magic.

The door clicked behind her, and she turned right into Will's chest. Losing any remaining shred of willpower, Juliet rested her forehead against his chest.

His hands sank into her hair as he rested his chin on the top of her head, each letting the other take a minute to breathe. The world had never seemed so quiet or still, and the moment was complete when he dipped his head to kiss her as though his life depended on it. The sweet, minty taste of dessert lingered on his lips, enticing her further.

"I'm sorry for coming here," she breathed as she clung to him. "I didn't know how to get to you."

"Please don't apologise. I should've been more careful," he said between kisses, each taking her breath away. It didn't seem to matter any more who was right or wrong.

Juliet broke away from him, trying to get her thoughts straight. "I talked to Kevin, about what happened to the Frost family and the danger of guardians falling for their charges."

Will sat calmly on the edge of the bed.

"I know you said you owed my mom, but somehow, I think this situation is worse than us just falling for each other. You helped steal the chest and you've lied for me," she said, wishing she had the strength to leave him, go home and never look back to protect him from the consequences of their actions. Then again, they'd come so far. She dropped down beside him and rested her head on his shoulder. "I feel like I'm being torn in two."

"Please stop feeling so guilty." Will took her face in his hands, forcing her to meet his gaze. "I decided to help Eloise. I found you, and I approached you because I wanted to. The guilt in your voice is breaking my heart. None of this is your fault. Regardless of the rules, it's my job to protect and help those who need it."

"But you're breaking the laws of Yule for me," she sniffled.

To her confusion, he smiled. "It wouldn't be the first time I've broken the law, and it won't be the last," he reassured her. "My company on the Outside helps those who leave Yule. We help them settle in and stay out of trouble. We forge documents, find them employment, things like that. I break laws every day for those who need it, so please don't for one second feel guilty about this. Meeting you was worth any consequence I may face."

"I feel like you're leaving something out," Juliet said, thinking about how she'd seen him at the dinner table with the Klauses. "I don't believe you'd risk hurting people you consider family just because you owed my mom a favour." Hoping he would tell the whole truth, she moved to the centre of the bed, waiting for him to speak whenever he was ready.

He turned to face her. "Growing up, my parents spent most of their time in the sleigh's engineering department. My sister was the golden child, and my only talent was getting into trouble."

"How much trouble can one get into here?" Juliet asked, wondering what he counted as 'trouble' in this winter wonderland.

He fidgeted with his watch. Clearly a lot.

"Let's just say it involved reindeer racing and too much ginger beer."

Juliet tried not to laugh. "What, did you get a sugar rush?"

Will grimaced. "In Yule, ginger beer is alcoholic."

"Oh." Whatever reindeer racing was, doing it drunk sounded dangerous.

"I was acting out, and bringing my friends along for the ride. The Klaus family tried to straighten me out, but I couldn't find my place in Yule as easily as others seemed to. After a particularly bad racing accident, Mason and I ended up in Yule's emergency room. Mr Klaus, Mason's dad, managed to get the council to show us leniency; we were only sixteen. Still, my parents wanted me out of the house. They didn't want me to be a bad influence on my sister. Anyway, Eloise, your mum, helped get me into the guardian program. She took a chance on me when everyone else was willing to give up."

"I'm sure she helped you because she wanted to. You should've considered any debt paid by your success alone. You've done so much for her – for me." Juliet inched closer to him, taking his hand in hers. "You could lose your job if they find out who I am, be banished, and what about your family and the Klauses?"

"I love that you're trying to protect me, but I'm not letting you go through this alone," he said, taking her in his arms. "They'll find out in time that everything I did was worth having you in my life."

She tried to pull away from him so that he would take her seriously. "What if I could hear all this from Eloise? She's in Yule; she's right here. I could meet her, and put an end to all this." She should've been annoyed, but she only felt relief when he refused to let her go.

"You will, but we've got to wait a little while longer." Will leaned back against the headboard with her. "Eloise is trying to lift the banishment for you, but she needs to get the council of Yule's approval and Mason's backing. He's far more lenient than previous Klauses. Eloise is trying to convince him that you shouldn't be punished for the mistakes made before you. Lyla is also on our side; I've explained everything to her, and she'll help Mason see reason."

"I hate the idea that my life could affect their relationship. Kevin told me Eloise had to wait for the legacy law, but I wish she had come to me herself."

"She wanted to, but if the council found out she'd have been banished – and unlike me, there's no place for her on the outside."

Juliet didn't like the idea of him sacrificing himself in her mom's place either, but arguing with him when his mind was clearly made up was pointless.

"You don't need to worry about Lyla," he went on, "she's had her own issues with the council, so she's happy to help us."

I wonder if that's related to the lies she mentioned. "I understand that Eloise wants me to have a home here, but couldn't she have settled in the outside with me?" Juliet asked, wondering what her life could have been if her mom hadn't given her up.

"All she's known is Yule. The village is its own isolated world. I might as well ask you to move to Mars. Being banished back then, she would've had no way to provide for you, no assistance from the guardians, and the Frosts would probably have used the Outside's legal system to have you taken away from her."

Juliet wished her father had defended her mom from his family. But she knew how ruthless her grandfather could be.

Her dad probably would have been shunned and blacklisted if he'd tried.

"Why would the council protest me meeting her now? I haven't done anything wrong. What if I talk to the council and convince them I'm not a threat? I can say I found the bell by chance and did all this alone." Was all of this worth hurting so many people?

"Don't even think about it. They'd inform your father about you violating your banishment. If he finds out you've got a bell and the chest in your possession, he'll do anything to get his hands on it."

Juliet nodded, understanding that her father having that power wouldn't be best for anyone.

"Do you mind that I said I was your girlfriend?" she asked quickly, trying not to sound like she was too invested in the answer. She'd avoided the topic out of embarrassment so far, but she did want to know how he felt about it.

"Depends," he said quietly.

"On?"

"Whether you said it because you meant it, or you were just trying to protect us."

"Can both be true?" Juliet whispered.

Will didn't say anything. He pulled her in closer to his chest, and that was answer enough.

They drifted into a quiet moment. The weight of the day had clearly exhausted them both; they found peace in each other's arms in the house of the very people they should be hiding from.

She glanced at Will, realising that their situation wasn't any different from her parents'. "If the council don't approve my return, you could be punished for helping me?"

She wasn't sure how he'd suddenly got so close, or the room so hot.

"You're worth any punishment. Now, can you please stop worrying, just for tonight?" he whispered, brushing his lips against hers.

A soft moan escaped her as he ran his tongue along her lower lip, grabbing her waist to pull her body flush against him, where she felt safe and warm.

"We shouldn't. Someone could hear us," she breathed half-heartedly between kisses, resting her forehead against his.

He sighed. "As much as I love hearing you scream my name, I think there's been enough excitement today for both of us." Closing his eyes, he pulled her close until there wasn't an inch between them. "I missed this."

He was right, and she *was* tired. Trying to put away the other big questions she had, Juliet remembered something else she was curious about it.

"What's dust? Mason mentioned it when he picked me up with Kevin. I thought Santa's workshop made presents?" she asked, running her fingers over his where they rested on her hip.

"You caught that?" Will mumbled, already half-asleep. "Dust is mined from the mountains that protect Yule. The rock has a magical essence that brings hope and luck to those who need it. That's the gift that's brought to the world every year." He yawned.

Juliet studied his dark lashes as they rested on his cheek. She wondered if one day talk of magical rock dust and gifts of hope would seem normal to her. "So... Mason is Santa Claus?"

"A Klaus ensures the production and watches over the distribution of dust over Christmas. Your idea of Santa is more of a myth – I don't think Mason would like to climb down millions of chimneys every year." Will chuckled sleepily, clearly imagining the scene.

Juliet traced his lazy smile with her fingertips. "I suppose magic dust is much more believable than workshops of elves making presents," she teased.

He squeezed her tight. "No more questions. Get some sleep."

Her lips parted to tell him how much he meant to her, for helping her and staying with her through the roughest festive season of her life, but no words came out. She stared at him, already dozing peacefully. *What could our future be?* She was the product of falling in love with a guardian; falling for him was out of the question. More was at stake than just heartbreak for both of them. She might lose him, but he would lose so much more, and she didn't know if she was worth it.

Juliet slept for a few hours, but given the time difference between Yule and home, she woke up early with her head still full of questions. Turning it all over in her head, she came to a sudden decision and slipped out of Will's arms in search of information about her mom's whereabouts. Lyla had shown her the Klaus family office during her tour, and she couldn't stop thinking about the answers it might hold. It didn't help that it was only a few doors down the hall from the guest bedroom. One conversation with Eloise – that was all she needed. And if she could find an address book...

"You're up early," Mrs Klaus said ten minutes later, standing in the doorway of the office.

Juliet froze, caught red-handed with the address book in her hand.

"I just wanted..." She faltered, unable to think of an excuse fast enough, and put down the book, embarrassed and ashamed at her break of trust and privacy. Part of her berated herself. *You need to get better at sneaking around. So far, you suck at it.*

"You were hoping to find out more about your mum. Judging from Lyla's wellies and Will's coat, you were going to try find her?" Mrs Klaus stepped into the room and flicked on the overhead light. Juliet had only dared to turn on the small desk lamp.

Her words cut like an icicle, and Juliet couldn't find a lie fast enough.

"Don't look so frightened. I haven't mentioned who you are to my son. I've known who you were the moment I saw you." There was no anger in Mrs Klaus's wrinkled eyes, only concern.

Juliet's words stuck in her throat.

"Juliet, you don't have to lie. You're the spitting image of your mum at this age." Mrs Klaus offered her a reassuring smile, which slightly lessened her desire to plead for mercy. She didn't know whether to laugh or cry as the weight of discovery lifted from her shoulders.

"I didn't want to lie to you," she blurted out, "but I didn't want Will to lose his job because of me. Please don't tell Will or the others that you know. I just wanted to meet my mom before anyone got in trouble. Will told me to wait, but after the kindness everyone has shown me, the guilt is eating me up." She walked around the desk, leaving the address book behind.

"Juliet, take a breath." Mrs Klaus took her hand. "You aren't in trouble – not right now, anyway. However, we do have some things to work out, and I need to feed the reindeer before they get cranky. I think some fresh air will do you some good." She motioned for Juliet to join her. Unable to say no, Juliet stepped into the hall, but she noticed that Mrs Klaus's gaze lingered on the empty desk across from the one she'd searched. There was a longing in the older woman's gaze she recognised – it was the same she'd felt when she'd looked over the letters in the chest.

"Thank you for not outing me and Will. I really didn't intend to cause trouble. I've been warned about the memory removal thing, and I've got no plans on telling anyone about Yule."

"I have no doubt that none of this is your doing, and don't worry about causing trouble. I've seen plenty over the years, and I can see how much you care about Will. This morning can be our little secret," Mrs Klaus reassured her.

Lyla's wellies were a little big, which made it a struggle to trudge through the fresh layer of morning snow. Thankfully, Will's coat reached her knees, keeping her extra cosy. Juliet followed Mrs Klaus to the stables, relieved to find there wasn't a tribunal or shallow grave waiting for her amongst the stalls.

"I figured you would want to talk away from the others." Mrs Klaus started, walking into the stables. A reindeer with the name tag Dixon bobbed her head over the stable door, surprising Juliet. "I spoke to Eloise about your arrival on the phone last night, and she dropped something off for you this morning."

"What? Why didn't she see me? Why didn't you tell me she was here?" Juliet asked. Dixon nudged her shoulder when she stopped rubbing her nose.

"It's not the right time yet, though she does desperately want to see you. Please don't underestimate how hard this is for her, as I'm sure it is for you," Mrs Klaus said, handing her a red envelope from her bright yellow padded coat.

Juliet stared at the envelope; it was the first one she'd read addressed to her alone. Present tense. Conflicting emotions rushed through her.

"I appreciate you giving me this, but I really wish I could've seen her," she confessed. "I can't ask a letter a question, and being drip-fed information is driving me crazy!" And she'd had enough of envelopes to last a lifetime.

"I can understand that your patience is wearing thin, but Eloise didn't want to overwhelm you by just turning up. She wanted to prepare you first."

Juliet sighed, her breath visible in the air. "She was probably right; I don't know what I've have done if she just appeared in front of everyone. I wouldn't want to put Mason in a bad position with the council." She didn't want Mrs Klaus to think she wasn't grateful for her help – not when she could've sent Eloise away, and turned Juliet and Will in.

"You need to save some of that care and worry for yourself. We all make our own decisions. I spoke to Lyla when you and Will went to bed. Given that you'd already met, I figured she knew more than she was letting on. I told her I knew who you were, and she told me she supports you. As do I." Mrs Klaus calmly moved down the row of sleepy reindeer, giving them their breakfast. "What you decide to do with that letter and the chest is up to you. You can close the door on Yule with no questions asked, as is the choice given to every legacy."

"But those legacies haven't been banished." Juliet followed Mrs Klaus to the stable doors as the sound of crunching carrots echoed behind them.

"If you want Yule to be a part of your future, I'm sure we can help you find a way. No one else's opinion or desires matter – not mine or your mum's or, even if you care for him deeply, Will's. This is your life."

Reaching the front porch, Juliet looked at her name written in her mom's writing for the first time. She didn't even know if her mom had been the one to pick her name. Had it been her dad?

"I'll give you some time. Breakfast will be inside whenever you're ready to come in," Mrs Klaus said, leaving her on the porch swing.

Once the door clicked shut, she tore open the envelope. Taking a deep breath, she unfolded the thick paper.

Juliet,

I'm so sorry. I wish that was enough, but I know it isn't. I'm a coward for not speaking to you in person. To know you're in Yule has brought me so much joy that I dare to selfishly hope we will be reunited soon. I know this must be all a terrible shock to you, but I hope you'll forgive me for putting you through all this. There's nothing more that I want than to come to you right now, but it's not time yet. I wanted you have something from me personally. For you to hear our story from me.

There is one thing especially I want to tell you, so that you know without a shadow of a doubt how much I love you. When I found out I was pregnant with you, I couldn't have been happier. Your father and I were going to go to the council of Yule together and tell them everything.

However, your grandfather found out and reported us to the council before we got the chance. I was escorted back to Yule, and they wouldn't let me talk to your father or leave the village. My family were enraged by what I'd done, the shame I'd brought to our family. You come from a long line of those who have protected Yule and their descendants, and my love for someone from the family who tried to expose our world was the ultimate betrayal.

I was so young, only twenty-one – not that my age is an excuse. Watching over the Frost family was my first assignment, and I fell in love with someone I shouldn't have. That being said, I ~~want~~ need you to know how much it tore me apart to give you up. But I thought you deserved a life away from shame. I feared what it would be like for you to be raised in Yule, given the stigma that comes with the Frost name. I truly believed in my heart that you would be better off.

Once you were born, you were brought to the Frost family. I held you for only three hours before you were taken from my arms. I thought it would kill me, but I hoped and prayed that in time, I would get to see you again.

THE TEAR-STAINED letter told Juliet that it had been as hard for her mom to write as it was for her to read. She couldn't believe the world could be so cruel as to take a newborn from her mother's arms. She rationalised that it had been a different time, but still, an anger she'd never known before gripped her heart.

The council decided that the only way for me to remain in Yule and maintain my position with the guardians was to be stripped of my Outside guardian rank. I wasn't allowed to leave Yule, and forbidden from making any contact with you or the Frost family. I can only hope that the legacy laws will play in our favour and that we can be reunited. Not a day has gone by that I don't regret my decision to give you up. It kills me to know you're so close and I can't see you. Mrs Klaus told me how kind and beautiful you are. I hope you can forgive me. I've enclosed the last letter your father sent me, because I need you to know how much we loved each other and how wanted you were. Are.

Mum x

I hope very much that you will allow me to earn this title in time x

Juliet forced herself to start the next letter before she crumbled completely; she wasn't sure how much longer she had to herself before the rest of the house woke up. Her dad's writing was faded, as though the letter had been read repeatedly.

My love,

There is so much I need to say to you, but no words will describe how my heart aches. I wish you hadn't left us. I promised you that I'd find a way for us to be together, but I fear my father and the council have got to you. Whatever he promised you, or threatened you with, we can figure it out. I know you love me, and I won't accept your last letter. Even if you can leave me for your oath to Yule, I can't believe you can leave our girl. She is so like you, and I swear she scrunches her nose just as you do when you're upset. She won't sleep at night unless I hold her tiny hand, and I've named her Juliet after your favourite play.

I know how much you love her, and I can't imagine how hard it is for you to be without her. To hold her is my greatest joy and sorrow, but even if it's a day, a week, or five years, we will be waiting for you to be a family again.

I don't even know if this letter will reach you. Please come back to us – we can have a new life away from the past. We can forget about oaths, names, fortunes and find our own world to disappear into. Please, Eloise, I beg you to come home and marry me. Let us be a family. I know sacrificing Yule would mean sacrificing your home, your family, but we can build our own. We can start again, just us three. Please. I love you.

I've attached a polaroid of Juliet with her favourite toy. She won't let the pink duck my dad got her out of her sight.

Forever yours,
   J x

Numb, Juliet sat on the porch and set the letters down beside her. She couldn't even feel the cold. If she hadn't recognised the handwriting, she would have believed her father's letter had been written by a perfect stranger. She'd never seen this side of him – never known him to beg for anything or anyone. His heartbreak echoed in his words. How could her mom have read this and held strong?

Maybe this heartbreak is what froze his heart for good. She couldn't remember him ever speaking to Gillian this way, or even telling her he loved her. Then again, she realised her dad had kept his promise; he'd waited those five years. Thinking back, she couldn't remember if she'd been six or seven the first time she'd met Gillian.

Juliet knew Mrs Klaus had passed this letter on to satisfy her curiosity for a time, but it only fuelled her desire to meet Eloise. Resting her head in her hands, she remembered the green Post-It note in her pocket. *Mom's address.* When Mrs Klaus had caught her with the address book, she'd already copied it out.

Over her shoulder, she stared at the front door. She knew she should go back, have breakfast, and hear more embarrassing stories about Will. Or… if she followed those ridiculously cute candy-striped lampposts, they would lead her to a sleigh rank, and she could ask her mom why she'd decided to stay when her father had wanted to build a new life with her.

"Will, have you seen Juliet?" Lyla asked, coming into the kitchen, where Will and Kevin were discussing whether mint or strawberry candy canes were better. Mint, obviously. "I was going to ask her to be my partner for the snowman contest this afternoon. Thought it'd be a good way for her to get used to the village."

Will had quickly realised the plan to leave Yule as soon as possible was going to be an impossibility with this lot. He just hoped Juliet's family weren't too worried about her disappearing act. Then again, Mr Frost would probably be pleased they'd disappeared off together.

"Nice try, but she said last night *we'd* partner up for the snowman-building contest," Kevin said. "You gotta be faster than that."

Lyla swatted him playfully, and Kevin blew her a mocking kiss.

"She wasn't out with you this morning?" Will asked, putting down his coffee cup. "When I woke up, she was already up and gone." There was no way she'd run off again, not after last time – was she trying to give him a heart attack? He tried not to jump to conclusions.

"No, I had breakfast with Lou and dropped her off at the

sleigh workshop," Lyla said, securing her curls with a red ribbon.

Oh God, where the hell is she? Will tried to stay calm, but the look in Lyla's eye told him she was thinking the same as him. If she was caught, they'd all be in trouble.

Mason walked in, all sweaty. "Relax, guys, I saw her on my run. She was following the lamp posts, heading down the back trail to the village. I'm sure she just wanted some air. I tried to call out to her, but she couldn't hear me."

"Out for a run in the snow? You're doing a great impression of Rudolph," Lyla said, kissing her fiancé's red nose, then groaning as he snuggled her in his sweaty arms. "I'm sure you warned Lyla about the wolves in the woods?" she asked Will with a hopeful smile.

Will's eyes widened, and Mason's expression flattened as his arms dropped to his side.

"No, it never occurred to me." Will's stomach sank; cold sweat poured over him.

"She should be fine." Kevin shrugged off the danger.

"If she keeps to the road – but if she takes the trail through the forest, the wolves might get her scent," Lyla said, looking a little green. Mason kept her close, as though she was liable to get gobbled up. Will knew she'd had her own run-in with the wolves who protected Yule.

"Let's not freak him out," Kevin said calmly. "Not everyone likes to wonder off into the woods."

Lyla glared at him.

"Shit. I'm going to go and find her." The chair scraped against the kitchen tiles as Will stood sharply. "Why would she go to the village without telling me? I got up early to cut firewood. I didn't think—" He couldn't move fast enough.

"I'm sure she's fine," Mason called, following Will to the

front door, where he pulled on his boots. "You need to be careful!"

"It's my fault," Mrs Klaus said, catching him off guard. Will frowned as he spotted the old woman sitting on the stairs. He went to grab his coat, but it was gone from the hook by the door. *She must've taken it. At least I know she'll be warm.* He took Mason's.

"Mum, why are you sitting here? You look pale." Mason knelt in front of her on the stairs.

"I gave Juliet something I shouldn't have, but I didn't think it would cause her to go off on her own or upset her," she fretted, fidgeting with her wedding ring.

"Upset her? What did you give her?" Will demanded, in a tone he'd never used with Mrs Klaus before.

Mason glared at his friend. "You're upset, but you won't talk to her that way," he snapped.

Lyla appeared and got between them. "You're wasting time. Now isn't the time to argue!" She turned to Mason. "You didn't act rationally when it was *me* who ran off."

Mason backed off reluctantly, sitting by his mum. Will couldn't blame him for being defensive of her.

Mrs Klaus took her son's hand as she confessed. "Eloise dropped by this morning."

Will felt like he'd been sucker-punched.

"She asked me to give her a letter, and I couldn't refuse."

"Juliet's probably gone to find her. It's what I'd do," Lyla reasoned.

"Eloise? Why was the Chief Guardian here? Have you got yourself in trouble again, Will? But why would Juliet want to find her?" Mason stared at his fiancée. "Lyla, what have you been up to?"

Everyone ignored him.

"Why wouldn't she tell me?" Will muttered, pulling on the navy coat. "Can I have the keys to the sleigh?"

Mason looked at him warily, and Will rolled his eyes. "It's not like I'm planning on racing the damn thing."

"Not until someone tells me what the hell is going on!"

"Now isn't the time. Can I have the keys?" Will barked. To his relief, Mason tossed them over.

Pulling open the front door, he heard Lyla and Mrs Klaus filling Mason in on the situation. At least he didn't have to see his friend's face when he learned how many laws Will had broken.

Secret's out now.

Driving the sleigh recklessly down the narrow slope, he nearly ended up in a snow bank or two. Thankfully, it wasn't long before he found Juliet walking along the tree line with her arms wrapped around herself, each step weighing her down. With a sigh of relief, Will pulled over to the side of the road.

"Where are you going?" he called, settling the reindeer and climbing out of the sleigh.

"To put an end to all this!" Juliet grumbled. Her lips were already blue.

"You only have to wait a little while longer!" he pleaded. "You're going to freeze to death by the time you even reach the village."

She refused to look at him, focusing on the wellies on her feet, which he guessed were Lyla's. "I don't want to read any more letters. I want to face her. My heart is breaking over a woman I've never even met, or spoken to!" She put her hands over her face. "You've no idea the guilt I feel for everyone involved now."

Her words cut him. "I never wanted you to feel this way." He stepped towards her cautiously, afraid she'd bolt. "I should've considered how you would feel about all this before I agreed to get that chest to you." He managed to get in front of her so that she had to stop.

"If you hadn't, then we wouldn't have met, and I don't regret that. I don't regret even learning about Yule." She stared up at him, before resting her forehead against his chest. "I just want all the secrets to end. To know she's so close and yet I can't get to her is driving me crazy." Juliet kicked a pile of snow. "Mrs Klaus shouldn't have given me those letters; I feel like I'm going insane."

"Letters?" Will ran his hands over his face. He took a deep breath then let it out, the long exhalation visible to them both. "Mrs Klaus has been friends with your mum for years. I can understand her desire to help, but I'm sorry you found out she knew so abruptly."

"She scared me when she found me in her office, but none of this is her fault. Her heart was in the right place. We never should've brought this burden to their door."

Will placed his hands on her shoulders, trying to get her to listen to him. "They don't see you as a burden. In fact, Lyla and Kevin are currently debating who should be your partner for the snowman-building contest – they've had to reschedule the gingerbread contest, thanks to the snowfall. Mason's pissed because his missus would rather partner with you than him. Please come back and have some breakfast; I don't want you to lose any fingers or toes out here."

"Really?" she sniffled, and he rubbed her back to try and get her blood flowing.

"Really. They're only worried about you getting eaten by

the wolves. Mrs Klaus is beside herself with worry, blaming herself for giving you the letter."

"That's the last thing I wanted," Juliet mumbled into his chest, and he felt the fight leave her limbs.

"Then let's go back before we freeze to death."

She took his hand, and he tried to conceal his relief as she followed him back to the sleigh, only to come to a sudden halt, tugging on his hand. "Did you say wolves?"

"They protect the outskirts of town from outsiders, but they tend to stick to the forest." Will scolded himself for not telling her about them sooner.

She looked to the edge of the forest lining the side of the road and swallowed. "In the museum, you said you didn't like wolves." Her panic turned to annoyance, and her nose scrunched up. "You're only telling me about this now?!"

"Shh! Do you want them to hear you?" He pulled her close. "It's amazing they haven't smelt you yet. To them, you smell like dinner." He bit his tongue to stop himself from laughing as she paled and curled into him. "Better stay close."

Juliet remained huddled close to him in the sleigh as they made their way back to the house. It was already the 13th, and with only thirteen days until the 26th, when they could petition the council about her legacy case. If the council agreed, then she could meet with Eloise; it felt unfair to Juliet to keep them apart for too much longer. If it didn't go well, he hoped she wouldn't blame him for bringing her back into her mother's life. Seeing the toll his actions had taken on her made him question whether he done the right thing for her. He understood Eloise's desire to meet her daughter, but he'd never stopped to ask what was best for Juliet, and given his feelings for her, he'd made a real mess of her life. Still, he hoped she'd let him spend the rest of his days making it up to her.

"I'm worried about Di and Beth. Is there any way I can contact them?" Juliet asked.

"We can leave now, if you want?"

"But I promised we'd stay for the snowman-building competition," Juliet said, sounding torn. He guessed she didn't want to disappoint her new friends, and he couldn't blame her for wanting to get better acquainted with Yule.

"If you want to stay, how about I get a message to Di and Beth and let them know we're okay?" he suggested. He didn't know why he hadn't thought of it before, but Mr Frost had given him the house phone number, so he should be able to contact them and make up some kind of excuse about where they'd been.

"Really? Thank you, and I'd like to stay," she admitted as they passed through the Klaus gates. "I promised Kevin I would be his partner last night – I was caught off-guard and I didn't know what to say. Or would it be too risky in case I'm seen?"

Will considered it, but he figured they could use some fun. A break from all the stress and worry – if he felt *he* needed it, he was sure it would do Juliet a world of good. Experiencing some of Yule's traditions might also help her feel less like a festive fugitive.

He pulled into the garage, and Juliet hopped down from the sleigh. "There'll be crowds of people participating; you'll hardly be noticed." He decided to leave out the fact that if she was with the Klaus family, no one would assume they were harbouring another Outsider after all that had gone down with Lyla.

"What did you tell the others before you came looking for me?" Juliet asked.

He'd wondered how long it would take for her to ask. He hesitated, unsure of how to break the news that their secret was out and he wasn't sure how Mason would welcome them once they got inside.

"They know?" Juliet froze on the driveway.

Will nodded apologetically. "Mrs Klaus was upset when she realised you'd gone off to find your mum."

"I should be thanking her for helping me, not making her worry." Juliet buried her face in her hands. "Should we just leave? If we leave, then they can just pretend none of this happened and that I was never here."

"I think it's too late for that." Mason opened the door, clearly having overheard their conversation.

Juliet shrank behind Will. He didn't blame her; Mason had one hell of an intimidating aura when he wanted. He stared at them, his resolve unwavering, until Will noticed his eyes soften. It was a relief that he and Lyla had already broken tradition themselves. Will hoped he wouldn't be too mad at him for breaking ranks.

"Come in. Mum and Lyla would never let me hear the end of it if I let you freeze to death." Mason moved aside.

They did as instructed, and Will noticed how Juliet stood shivering by the fireplace.

"I'm not going to pretend that I'm okay with what you've done, Will. You're taking one hell of a risk bringing her here." Mason's gaze fell to Juliet. "However, I don't believe our laws should separate families and those who love each other. I've had my own battles with the council over such beliefs."

Will knew he was talking about Lyla.

"Thank you," Juliet started, and Will gripped her hand as Mason cut her off.

"Don't thank me yet. You've both broken numerous laws. As Klaus I have some sway, but to convince the council, who speak for the village as a whole, will be a different story."

"We know the risks, and we'll be more careful."

"I'll help you petition the council on the 26th December, in keeping with tradition. It'll be easier for them to accept you if I put it forward," Mason said, offering Will a reassuring look.

"I don't know how to thank you." Juliet squeezed Will's hand, and he could feel her elation. He wanted to hug his friend for helping them; Mason's backing gave him greater hope that he wouldn't be separated from her.

"Thank me by promising that until that day comes, you'll be careful. Juliet, please refrain from talking to anyone you don't have to, and you must remain with one of us at all times. I don't want to see either of you banished," Mason warned, very much the leader of the village and not Will's friend.

"You have our word," Juliet said, and Will nodded in agreement. He owed his friend one hell of a Christmas present.

"Good." Mason softened. "Now, I suggest we all get ready. We have a snowman-building competition to prepare for." And to Will's surprise, he embraced him.

"I think my snowman-building days are behind me," Will joked. Being able to share his secrets with his friend eased his own troubles.

"Kevin! Will just told me he wants to help you with your snowman," Juliet called out, removing her wellies and coat. Will scowled at her, and Mason chuckled.

"Why are you smirking?" Will asked him. "If I'm spending the afternoon freezing my ass off, you're going to be standing right beside me."

Mason's smirk disappeared.

Lyla rushed into the foyer and enveloped Juliet in a hug. "Are you okay? We were worried you went into the forest!"

"Sorry to worry all of you – I wanted to get some air.

Finding out about Yule and my family… it's all been rather overwhelming," she admitted. Spotting Mrs Klaus lingering by the stairs, she made her way over to the older woman. "I'm sorry I left without telling you. I never wanted you to feel bad about helping me."

"My motherly instincts kicked in, and when Eloise gave me those letters, I couldn't help but empathise. If you were my daughter, I don't think I could bear to be separated from you for so long, but I should have been more sensitive to how you would receive such news," Mrs Klaus told her.

"Please don't be sorry. I'll never be able to thank you enough for helping me – all of you. I know this is a lot to ask, but I'm so grateful to have your support," Juliet said, and Will could hear how much she meant it.

Mrs Klaus suffocated Juliet in a hug which they clearly both needed. Mason's mum had a heart the size of Yule, and Will was sure she would support Juliet in front of the council. He got the feeling Juliet wasn't used to having a group of supportive people in her life. Hell, he knew she wasn't. Her own family didn't even let her sleep in the main house. If he could give her a family that loved her, blood-related or not, he'd damn well try.

"Enough of the sappy nonsense – we have snowmen to build," Kevin called over the second-floor banister. "Will, you and I are going to get that trophy, so consider your girlfriend your enemy for the next few hours."

Will rolled his eyes. He'd forgotten how competitive the Klaus family could be.

"That means you're free to partner with me." Lyla grinned, taking Juliet's arm. Some fun was desperately needed, and seeing Juliet's smile was well worth the risk of her being seen in town.

After breakfast, Mason informed them that they were to meet in the town square at two, which gave Will and Juliet some time to explore the village. Will bundled Juliet up in a thick winter coat, scarf, and mittens, and refused to let go of her hand as they walked through the streets of Yule. She took in the sights and smells of the home she could've had. She wasn't sure how long it would take for her to get used to it always being so dark. Still, with darkness came the beauty of all the twinkling lights.

"What's that?" she asked, looking at a particularly imposing building.

"The town hall," Will told her. "They're currently decorating it for the end of year ball."

"I think I've had enough of those for a year," Juliet mumbled, thinking of how the last formal event they'd been to had ended. "And that?" She tilted her head, studying the circular building across from the square.

"That would be one of the oldest buildings in Yule – the Hall of Guardians, where I trained and boarded for most of my teens." She noticed how proudly he admired the building.

"You lived there? It looks... intimidating," she commented, looking at the church-like place with a tall spire and star on top.

"Eloise helped me get into the boarding programme when my parents kicked me out. Boarding also helped keep me out of any mischief."

"You still haven't told me what exactly landed you in the guardian programme. Something about sleigh racing?"

Will sighed. "My sister was apprenticing in sleigh engineering with Mason's sister, Lou. They've been best friends for years. Lou was the one getting married in the photo you saw before – she married my cousin, so we're practically family. Anyway, part of their apprenticeship included designing and building a sleigh of their own. A few of us took them for a test drive..." He trailed off.

Juliet stopped walking, tugging him back. "Please tell me no one was hurt?" she gasped.

"No, no! Everyone was fine. My sister's sleigh, not so much. I wasn't aware my sister was working on developing a special engine – faster, quieter – to help take the pressure off the reindeer on the Klaus sleigh. When I hit the accelerator, I went straight into a tree. Thankfully I jumped out before the impact, but I destroyed a few too many gold coins' worth of equipment, and my sister nearly lost her apprenticeship."

Juliet was horrified. "You could've died!"

Will looked as if even he couldn't quite believe how reckless he'd been. "Since I destroyed something precious to Yule, what better way to make amends than to spend my life protecting it? I've got to admit, there might have been one or two other incidents... including freezing the school's pool with liquid nitrogen, and removing all the ornaments from the grand tree before Christmas Day." He squeezed her hand, a little shamefaced.

"I shouldn't have been surprised you broke the rules to help me. Sounds like you're quite the rebel!" Juliet nudged him playfully, before giving him a serious look. "That's the most you've told me about your family. Thank you for letting me in."

He shrugged. "I've got too comfortable keeping secrets." She wanted to know more, but his eyes lingered on the tall building. "Want to see more?" His smile told her he was up to no good. "I'm feeling rebellious."

"Are you insane? We can't go in there!" Juliet hissed as Will hurried them up the stone steps to the outer gates to the Hall of Guardians.

"Kevin told me you were looking for information on people banished from Yule. I can show you. I've got access, and at noon most of the guardians are out on duty. Trainees will already be out helping plough the snow for their physical training. We should only have to worry about Phyllis." He winked and lightly touched the metal gate.

"How did you do that?" she asked, watching the door open as though it knew who Will was and had granted him permission to enter.

"It's—"

She held her hand up, silencing him. "If you say magic—"

"I was going to say enchanted." She glared at him, and he grinned. "Stay behind me, and when I give you the signal, head down the corridor on the left until you reach a gold door."

"A gold door? Sounds completely normal," Juliet said, keeping close to his back.

Inside, the place smelt like cinnamon, and multiple corridors led from the circular room. She nearly bumped into Will, too busy staring at the tall white pillars that held up the domed ceiling. The painting on it was a map of a much smaller Yule. Judging from the cracks in the plaster and paint, it had been done more than a few centuries ago.

"Phyllis! How is the most important woman in my life?" Will called, his arms wide open. Juliet frowned at his words until she saw the grey-haired woman at a tall desk who didn't even bother looking up from her newspaper at them. Her deep wrinkles and tired eyes indicated that Phyllis was old enough to be long retired.

Juliet matched Will's steps, afraid she'd make enough noise to alert the elderly woman to the fact that he wasn't alone. She wondered if she was supposed to stay close to him because Phyllis's eyesight wasn't the best, and felt bad at the idea.

"Will, what's caused you to darken my door so late in the season? You haven't been assigned any charges recently, so either you want someone, or you've done something." Phyllis peered over her semi-circle wire spectacles, seeming to miss Juliet, who was mostly concealed beneath the wooden raised reception desk. Juliet could just about see her at this angle.

"I've missed you too!" Will said, and Juliet resisted the urge to roll her eyes. "I need the key to the banishment archives on the second floor. Doing some research on a legacy, and I figured I might as well get it done before the season really gets crazy."

"I've received no formal request," she informed him, clearly used to his charm.

"Have a heart, Phyllis! It's almost Christmas. It's for a legacy who's worried that a family member might have been banished because they weren't in Yule when they returned."

Juliet wondered if he was talking about a real case. It was one hell of a good lie to think up on the spot.

"You know the rules, Mr Duncan. File a formal report to

the head guardian, and then Ms Heart has to deny or grant your request before I can give you the key."

Juliet's heart skipped a beat as she realised they were talking about her mom.

"Ah, is Eloise in? I'll head to her office right now," Will said. Juliet stared up at him, but he acted as though she wasn't there. Was he going to bring her to her mom? Was it a who, not a what, that he wanted to show her?

"Ms Heart has gone out to train with the boarders, as you'll already be aware," Phyllis said, reading Will like a book.

"And *you* know that this late in the year, she won't give me the key before the season is over. I promise I'll be in and out."

There was a moment's hesitation.

"I'll be sure to return the favour," Will pressed. "Don't you have a daughter on the Outside? I can make sure she's looked after in a manner befitting your service to Yule?" Apparently his manipulation knew no end.

Phyllis looked thoughtful. "She has been trying to get my granddaughter into a good school in England, which is proving difficult, considering her primary education has been in Yule. She has the grades, and I'm only asking for a fair application—"

"Consider it done."

There was another moment of silence, but then Juliet heard the clink of a key.

"You're a gem," Will said. "And, might I add, look far too young to have a grandchild."

"Be gone before I change my mind," Phyllis grumbled, but Juliet heard the smile in her words. She'd put up a good fight, but it seemed that despite Yule's magical and wondrous nature, its citizens were still susceptible to bribes.

The golden lantern on the walls highlighted the gold flecks in the white marble, making the ceiling look like it was twinkling. *Breathtaking.* She'd have settled for just seeing this. Then she saw Will waving a hand behind his back.

Juliet made a run for the corridor, careful to keep low. She barely made it around the corner when she bumped into someone.

"I'm so sorry!" Juliet exclaimed, but the woman, whose dark hair was streaked with grey, just stared at her blankly. "Are you alright? I didn't mean to startle you; I was in a hurry." Juliet fidgeted with the ends of her scarf.

"There's no running in the corridors, and visiting hours are restricted for family members. If you wish to see a boarder, then you must wait until 7pm." The dark-haired middle-aged woman looked down at the file in her hands, continuing with what she was reading while scolding her.

"Right. I must have got the times mixed up." Juliet started to back away the way she'd came.

The woman closed the file and held it behind her back. "You're here now, and since we're so close to the holidays, you can go ahead and wait quietly. The students out training will be back in thirty minutes." In spite of her warning, there was a kindness in her eyes.

"Understood." Juliet nodded.

"Don't stay too long – I don't want the students to be put out by one getting special treatment," the woman reiterated, opening her file once again and heading down the corridor past her.

Shivering at the close call, Juliet hurried on to find the gold door. She only had to wait a few anxious moments before Will appeared.

"I think we should get out of here. I ran into a woman, and she said the students out training will be back soon. She only let me through because she thought I was visiting someone," she fretted.

Will frowned, looking back down the corridor. She wondered if he'd seen the same woman. "Don't worry," he promised, "once we get inside, you won't have to worry about being discovered." Using the gold key he'd obtained from Phyllis, he unlocked the door. Juliet stared into the room, dumbfounded.

Chests. Dozens and dozens of chests lined the walls.

"All of these families were banished?" She swallowed, thinking she'd underestimated just how strict Yule was about rules.

The chests, identical to the one she'd been sent, each had their own section built into the high walls. To get a closer look, she moved around the small individual desks with study lamps that she suspected were for visitors to inspect the contents of the chests.

"No, every family in Yule has an ancestral chest. Only those with the key for their family chest can get in here, and my sister has ours. I can also request any documents the council has on the Frost banishment. I removed most of what was contained in the Frost chest so you only had access to what you needed to see. You didn't need generations of birth certificates and wedding licenses. I'll return them when you're done with it."

Will walked over to the wall, where Juliet saw a metal pneumatic tube. He pulled out a scroll from his pocket, apparently having come prepared; before she could ask what was written on it, the scroll was sucked up the pipe. Next, he turned a brass dial on the wall. One row of chests was pulled back and another was pulled forward until Juliet saw a row with names beginning with F. The Frost name was labelled in gold on an empty wooden shelf.

"These chests are so old that only legacies really come to visit them, which is how we got yours out. No one would know yours was missing unless they went looking for it," Will said.

Juliet placed her hand on the empty shelf to make sure she wasn't dreaming, and a thin layer of freshly settled dust coated her fingertips. "You risked bringing me here to show me an empty shelf?"

Her question was answered when a small dumbwaiter positioned in the middle of the wall binged and flashed green, opening to reveal an object.

"A book?" she asked, looking at the brown leather volume. She was afraid to touch it.

"It's yours."

The Frost signal embossed in the cover told her as much. Juliet picked it up, surprised by how heavy and thick it was. Its uneven pages tried to escape the binding.

"Why wasn't this in the chest?"

"It's an important Yule text, so the council prefers to keep it locked up," Will said. "It's the history of Frosts in Yule, in your family's own words. No one knows who truly founded Yule – whether it was the Klaus family or the Frost family – but the Frosts were always the protectors of dust, responsible for its mining, while the Klaus family oversaw distributing it. They worked together," Will explained, as she walked over to one of the tables and flicked on the study lamp.

She flipped through the pages until Will stopped her on a page of illustrations: miners working, gold dust flowing through their fingers. Their clothes reminded her of the ones from her grandfather's era.

"How could anyone have found this place if it's protected by the mountains?" she wondered aloud. Had it been explorers who'd stumbled across it one day? Kevin had mentioned Yule had been founded in 270AD.

"Your ancestors had an answer for that," he said, pointing to one of the lines of handwritten text.

"The magic seeps out of the mountain rock when it's being mined, generating a type of forcefield." She let the explanation sink in. "So… if they stopped mining dust, then the protections would fail?"

"The Frosts believed so, and your great-grandfather – after generations of peace – planned to test it. If they'd succeeded, they'd have exposed Yule."

Juliet turned to a page illustrated with fighting miners, pickaxes raised high. She guessed those were the only weapons they'd had to use. She couldn't believe her family had committed such violence against their own. "But why would they want to run that risk?"

"Because when your great-grandfather led the Frost family, he believed that if they had the power to expose Yule, no one would be able to stand against them. They could get away with anything, just by threatening to stop mining. But then the desire for power grew, and Yule wasn't enough for them. They wanted the world to know the power they held, and wanted to expose Yule and its magic. Then again, no one can really agree on what your family truly desired, since legend and truth have muddled the history. Some people argue it was a misguided attempt to bring Yule's magic and warmth to the whole world. Others say it was just a grab for power."

"But the Klauses stopped them?"

"Yes, the Klauses and other families gathered to retake the mine when their plans were discovered."

Juliet closed the book on the bloody scene. "Were people killed?"

"No, but many were injured. Our medicine is rather advanced, another secret we protect – all those hurt were able to recover."

"So that's why you couldn't tell me how the protections work? Because no one has actually tested the theory?"

Will nodded.

"The workers in the mine… they wanted to test the theory as well?" Juliet asked, wondering if there was anyone still in Yule who supported her family. She couldn't even imagine what would happen to this place if her dad had such power.

"Yes, a few families were punished for their involvement. However, leniency was shown, as many were just following orders. The threat of banishment was enough to make them see the error of their ways."

"And the banishment of the Frost family made it clear they would make good on that threat." The words escaped her in a breath. Part of her wasn't surprised by her family's hunger for power; she was ashamed to say that not much had changed over the years.

Will nodded again. "Up until the 1800s, Yule was governed by all the founding families. However, after everything happened with the Frosts, the Klauses were put in charge of the council. Our delivery technology wasn't always as advanced as it is now. Sleighs being pulled by reindeer were spotted repeatedly over the years; Outsiders came up with their own myths. The idea of Yule, or Santa Claus living at the North Pole – we think that with the coming and going of those from Yule to and from the Outside, whispers were warped and expanded upon over the years."

Juliet's head started to swim. "Does everyone in Yule know about this?"

He shook his head. "No. Many know that the Frost family tried to expose Yule to make a grab for power, but not how."

"Shouldn't people know the truth? Is that why the council don't want me coming back, so I won't expose the truth of what happened?"

Will shrugged. "I don't know. Maybe they fear the Frost family returning; since Yule's population has expanded greatly over the past generations, they could gain a lot more followers now. Maybe if they tried again, they might not be stopped."

"Shouldn't that be left to the people of Yule to decide?" Juliet couldn't help but think that if the majority wanted the world to know about Yule, maybe they should have a say.

"It's up to the council and Klaus to decide, but I understand what you're saying. One of the reasons I helped you come back here was to show that the past is not to be feared. If everyone in Yule wanted the world to know we exist, I think the council would accept it, but it shouldn't be forced on them either because one family wants power."

Juliet could understand the desire to test the theory about the dust and mining, which also explained why her own family had been in the industrial industry for generations – they had merely changed location. She wondered if the Frosts had ever tried searching for more rock like what was found in Yule. She remembered her grandfather talking of how the company had almost been bankrupted a few times because of his father's explorative mining schemes. Juliet had assumed he was a gold or diamond hunter. *Maybe he was just trying to find his way home.*

"Can we get out of here? I think I've had enough." She shut the book. Now that she had the full story, she didn't know who the victim or the villain was. Her ancestors were wrong for threatening to expose Yule, but she wondered if the crime had truly warranted this generational punishment.

"It's coming up to two anyway. I know this is a lot to digest, but I wanted you to know everything. You don't deserve to be blindsided again like you were this morning," Will said, putting the book back in the dumbwaiter.

The wooden doors shut, and the small lightbulb turned red. When the doors opened again, it was gone as though it had never existed, but Juliet couldn't stop thinking about the illustration of those fighting hand to hand, pickaxe to pickaxe. She didn't condone violence, but she didn't like that the council and the Klaus family had kept the truth buried and turned the story of her family's hunt for the truth about the protections into a tale of warning against those who favoured facts over faith. What if the Frost family had only wanted to test the theory? What if they hadn't been trying to make a claim for power?

There was no way to know, but she needed time to think. She only been in Yule for a matter of days; she couldn't make any snap judgements about a place or people she barely understood. Hell, it wasn't like the outside world was a beacon of honesty and virtue.

She nodded at Will. "Let's go."

L aughter filled the air. Children playfully chased each other around the makeshift courtyard, packed with snow for crafting their masterpieces, by the Christmas tree at the centre of town, leaving a trail of footprints. Hurrying across the square, Juliet saw that Lyla stood out in the crowd that had gathered for the competition, bundled up in a bright purple scarf and matching earmuffs. After a quick grilling from Kevin and Lyla about where they'd been, they gathered in the designated courtyard around their assigned piles of snow.

Mason had left them to it, due to some workshop issue, and the competition began once Mrs Klaus started the clock. Juliet was surprised to see so many teams participating; she couldn't imagine her own family taking time to build a snowman.

Kevin and Will pelting each other with snowballs was a nice distraction from everything Juliet had just learned about her family history. It was hard to believe Will was as happy in the Outside as he was here. He'd seemed so serious that first night at the bar, but the bass of his laughter, the way his shoulders shook as he pushed Kevin over into the snow, only made her heart grow even more tender towards him.

She started rolling a small snowball, packing it tightly

until she needed Lyla's help in growing it with each revolution. They stepped back, admiring their creation. The light from the bright moon cast a silvery glow on the snow-covered landscape.

"That should be big enough for the base! Time for the middle part!" Lyla joined the two parts with some extra snow, giving their snowman an hourglass shape. They began to gather more snow for the head, and Juliet went to the long table set up with accessories for the participants to choose from and picked out a brightly coloured pink and red scarf and matching hat. They adorned the snowman with the accessories, creating a face with rocks for eyes and a big smile made of pebbles.

As they revelled in their snowy accomplishment, Juliet realised she'd almost forgotten about the morning's events. She glanced at Will and Kevin, struggling to put the giant head of their snowman on, and it hit her: Mrs Snow was missing something very important.

"We need a carrot for the nose!" she exclaimed, while Lyla gave Mrs Snow some false lashes.

"You're right!"

Juliet bent over to pick up a carrot, only to hear a plop as her phone dropped out of her pocket and into a puddle of melted snow at their feet. She cursed silently, not likely to find a bag of rice in the sea of snowmen. She dried it as best she could with her gloves and zipped it into her jacket pocket. It wasn't like anyone could reach her, even if they wanted to; she didn't have access to Yule WiFi, if such a thing even existed. She'd be home soon enough – what would another few hours away from the world matter?

WILL, Juliet, Lyla and Kevin sipped their free mulled wine and ate one too many mince pies as the winners were announced. It was an afternoon Juliet wouldn't forget, even if there was no way either of their teams was going to win. Some of the snowmen around them looked like they'd been crafted by experts. She was proven right as an elderly couple were announced as the winners – not a shock, since they'd somehow managed to create a miniature sleigh and driver out of snow.

Juliet snuck them all an extra mince pie from a passing tray while photos of the winners were being taken and trophies handed out. She didn't pay much attention, because the flaky pastry put any she'd had back home to shame. She wished she could get the recipe for Diana.

Mason finally joined them and kissed his fiancée. Lyla grumbled a bit about losing, but Juliet figured it was more to make Mason squirm than out of not winning a silver snowman trophy.

"I have no sway over the judges," Mason told her with a kiss. "There's always next year."

"Fine, but I'm looking forward to you making it up to me," Lyla said, pinching Mason when he rolled his eyes. They might pretend to bicker more than they got on, but the way they looked at each other made Juliet want to blush.

Will caught her by surprise, wrapping his arms around her waist. It was nice to have her own human heat blanket. "I'm surprised you didn't get the trophy. I really like how you added that sparkly nail varnish to the end of your sticks."

"At least we finished," Juliet said, eying the two blobs

beside theirs. "Yours doesn't even have a head because you and Kevin were too busy torturing each other."

He grinned. "Let's get you back home. If you're away too long, I'm afraid Beth or your father will think I've kidnapped you. Though I'm not embarrassed to admit that Margot finding out you disappeared again frightens me more than your dad." Will shivered, and Juliet internally applauded him for his good sense. Margot had connections even she didn't want to know about.

"Don't worry, she knew I was coming home. She's probably distracted by your friend Harvey trying to seduce her into working with him," Juliet reassured him, knowing Margot got tunnel vision when it came to client recruiting. Juliet hated keeping secrets from her, and wondered if she'd ever be able to tell her. If everything went well with Will's friend, Harvey, then perhaps she'd find her way here someday. Margot would die of excitement if she learned about a secret land.

BACK AT THE KLAUS CABIN, Juliet took the longest and hottest shower of her life. She wasn't sure if she had any skin left when she stepped out. Not that it mattered, because she could finally feel her toes again.

"I got your phone working again, though I'm not sure you want to look." Will, sitting on the edge of the bed, handed her a steaming cup of coffee.

Wrapped in a white fluffy towel, Juliet sat by the fire, letting the heat sink into her bones. He remembered exactly how she liked it – black with extra sugar. The sweet, sharp scent revived her further; she couldn't wait to take a sip of the steaming liquid, even though it burnt her tongue. Taking the phone from Will, she found she had missed several calls from dear ol' dad. She didn't even know how he'd got through; her phone showed she had no signal.

"Mr Frost has probably returned to the estate and is wondering where we are," Will said softly, reviving the topic she'd avoided for the last twenty-four hours.

"I wouldn't be too concerned. If he thinks we're together, then he'll consider it a win. Us sleeping together means he has leverage over you," Juliet told him. She knew her dad too well.

"I don't recall us doing much sleeping." Will brushed her hair over her bare shoulder, planting a kiss on her neck. "And this is not exactly how I do business."

"I thought seducing those in your charge was your speciality," she teased, putting down her mug so she could wrap her arms around his neck.

"Only you." His gaze darkened as his hands rested on her waist. "And if you keep talking about my seducing skills, then we won't be getting back any time soon."

"I'm not sure if you're from a fairytale or a nightmare." She kissed him, hoping to soak up some of his cheerful optimism before she ventured into the lion's den back home.

"Can't it be both?" He smirked devilishly, and Juliet lost herself in his hungry kisses, easily forgetting what awaited her back home.

Juliet

"Want me to come in with you?" Will offered, pulling up to the curb outside the barber shop where she was mentally preparing to meet her dad. She figured the unexpected location had been chosen to somehow throw her off-balance.

She wished she'd stayed in Yule with the Klaus family. It had been a sad goodbye, but hopefully it wouldn't be long before she saw them again. At least the bell travel back to the manor to get Will's car hadn't made her nauseous; they couldn't use the bell to drop her at the meeting, in case her father saw them magically appear. She expected he was going to scold her for leaving Beth at the estate – they been in such a hurry that she hadn't had a chance to tell Beth and Diana they were back. Then again, given how Will had disappeared with her, her dad might be preparing for wedding bells. Either way, the lump in her throat was making it rather hard to breathe.

"No, I've got to do this alone. I'll see you tomorrow." She leaned across to kiss him. In that split second, she just wanted to get back into the car and tell Will to drive and never stop until they reached the edge of the world, where their names and past didn't mean a thing. However, as he rested his hand on her cheek, she knew it was time to face reality. "Thank you for dropping me off. Now go have fun with your friends. You need a day or two away from all my drama."

Will rolled his eyes. "I'm to blame for your drama, and if you need me I'm only meeting Harvey. Mason is joining us tomorrow night, since Harvey won't go to Yule. Harvey will probably talk about Margot refusing to work with him, and Mason won't shut up about wedding plans. I'd much rather spend the time with you."

Juliet felt the same, but she didn't know how this meeting would go. It wasn't like her dad to talk about private matters in public, and away from the estate meant he didn't want anyone there to hear them. "One night won't kill us. Hopefully the time will fly by. The next time I see you, we can snuggle up. You still haven't seen The Grinch, which is a sin in my eyes."

"Because it's a little too close to home," Will chuckled. "But I give in. We can watch a movie about a hairy green guy. Whatever gets you going."

Juliet swatted him playfully as he brushed his stubble against her cheek. He hadn't shaved in a few days, and though the Grinch did nothing for her, she liked Will's rugged look.

"Go!" She scampered out of the car before she changed her mind.

He rolled down the window as she closed the door. "I'll have my phone with me; call me if you want me to pick you up. For anything." His tone had turned serious, reminding her of what she was walking into.

"Yes, sir," she mocked, and he pulled away from the curb. Even if she was teasing, she kept her phone tucked in her back pocket in case she wanted a quick getaway.

Heading into the shop and down a long, narrow staircase,

she eyed the dark green wallpaper lined with images of all the prestigious men who'd patronised the business over the years. The photos spanned from black and white to colour, a reminder to those who entered of how long the men's-only establishment had been open. Windsor Barbers reeked of expensive cologne and shampoo, and its interior still looked like it belonged in the 1940s, with its worn brown leather chairs and varnished counters. The waiting area sat empty; it wasn't the type of place patrons were left waiting.

Juliet's father's reflection greeted her in the long mirror as the barber finished wiping away the remaining shaving cream from his cutthroat shave. The rest of the chairs were empty, and she guessed he'd bought out the place for this conversation.

"Prompt as always, chickpea. Please take a seat."

The immaculate barber stepped away from Mr Frost and swivelled the brown leather chair beside him so she could sit facing her dad. She sat down and thanked the elderly barber, who just blanked her.

"I'm surprised you wanted to meet here. I thought there was some kind of emergency." No point in wasting time on small talk.

"I wouldn't say 'emergency', but there is an urgent matter I wish to discuss," he said, looking to the moustached barber in the mirror and dismissing him with a curt nod. Without a word, the man disappeared through a door at the end of the row of chairs.

"First, I want to know about what happened between you and my mom," Juliet said, wanting some answers before he got a chance to distract her.

"Why the sudden interest?" His eyes narrowed, and he crossed his legs. "What exactly do you want to know?"

Juliet didn't know what to say; she'd expected to be shut down. He never spoke about her mom, and asking usually resulted in a punishment. Suspicion crept up the back of her neck. Why was he letting her ask now?

Her father lifted an expresso cup to his lips and took a sip, leaning back in his chair. His calm demeanour made her sweat. "Did you think I'd be surprised by your questions? I thought this might happen, and it brings me back to my own subject. I was going to ask you, have you met her yet?"

Juliet's jaw dropped, and her blood ran cold. She should've known better than to think anything she'd done recently could've escaped his watchful eyes.

"I'll take your silence as a no." He sighed. "Maybe I should've started with an easier question. How was your trip to the North Pole? Yule is lovely this time of year, or so I hear." Smugly, he wiped the last trace of shaving cream from his jaw.

Juliet tried to put aside her anger and focus on getting through to the man who'd written her mom such a beautiful love letter. She sat forward in her chair, trying to bridge the gap between them.

"Dad, why did you keep the truth from me? Why not tell me about you and Mom, about where we're truly from? I would've understood how hard it was for you to lose her, and what Grandfather did to separate you," she said, hoping, wishing they could find some common ground. That the truth might be able to mend their relationship.

Her father sighed. "What your grandfather did was make me see sense. He was right to report us to the Council of Yule. Look at all that I've built – what our family has built in spite of our banishment. If I'd given it all up to be with Eloise, who knows where we would have ended up?"

"You can't mean that." He acted like their relationship had meant nothing to him, but she'd seen his letter. "You loved Mom, and you wanted to be with her, but Grandfather had you separated."

He rolled his eyes. "I should be mad at you for breaking into my safe and going through my personal things. However, like my love affair with your mom, I chalk it up to youthful exuberance. Our love was a mistake. I'm sure she'd say the same. Last I heard, she's Head Guardian."

Juliet didn't know how to respond. Hearing that the love which had brought her into the world was a mistake felt like taking a steak knife to the heart. She didn't know why she'd been expecting another answer. She should've known better.

"I couldn't believe she dared to reach out to my mother in her old age. Your grandmother always had a soft spot for her and our situation, but to smuggle you the Frost chest is a crime far worse than any love affair," Mr Frost went on, shaking his head, and she realised he'd known about the chest all along.

Has he found the chest? And the bell? No, if he had surely he would've used it. "How did you know she reached out to Nana Rose? Did Nana tell you?"

"She didn't say a word, but do you think I'm a fool? Just because our family was cast out doesn't mean I'm clueless. I know about legacy laws. The moment you turned twenty-six, I knew your mom might try and contact you. Even back then, she reached out to your grandfather to steal you away from us. She didn't want me, or to be a family. She only wanted you."

His bitter words turned the knife, but they also clarified his feelings. He was upset because Eloise had left him, but still wanted Juliet. This explained why he'd never cared for her, because her mom's love for her was greater than her love for him. She could see how that could turn to bitterness and anger over the decades, even if he had loved and waited for her at first.

"How could you know about the chest?"

"Just because we were cast out long ago doesn't mean people don't remember our family. The moment Eloise took that chest, I was informed. I knew there was only one person who would get it to you, your grandmother, and I knew the plan was in motion the moment I saw Will at the gala." He smiled. "Your boyfriend should've known better than to wear the Yule sigil on his cufflinks that night. The way he went after you that night when you said you were unwell – God, the man has it bad. I think our family has a talent for attracting tragic love stories."

Juliet's mouth felt like it was full of sand. Her limbs were heavy with anxiety. "You knew my desire for answers would lure me home, and you wanted me to bring you the chest." If he was having this conversation with her, he hadn't found her secret hiding place in the floorboards. "Why do you need it? You already have evidence of its existence in your safe." She raised an eyebrow, and his stoicism wavered at the reminder that the safe's code was related to her mother, a woman he claimed to no longer love.

"I don't need evidence, I just want the Frost bell. We wouldn't have to go through all this if you'd just come to me with the chest in the first place. I didn't expect you to be clever enough not to bring it home – though it does hurt that you picked a stranger over your own father," he sneered, oblivious to the fact that if he'd searched hard enough, he'd have discovered it was right beneath his feet. But how was he to know the secrets of her home?

"Is that why you've wanted to keep me in the fold for past few years? To keep an eye on me in case the chest turned up? In case Nana went through with her promise to my mom?" she demanded, getting up out of her chair. There was no way in hell he was getting his hands on the chest. She had to get it out of the cottage and back to Yule.

"Enough, Juliet!" His bark froze her. "Bring me the bell, and I won't report Will and your mother to the council. I'm sure you don't want to get him in trouble. Beth mentioned how close you've become, and how you both disappeared the past few days."

"Leave Will out of this!" she shot back. "If you try to hurt him in any way, I'll make sure you never get close to Yule, even if I have to turn myself and the chest in. Lying is pointless. I read your letter to Eloise after your relationship was reported. You begged for her to be with you, but you didn't have the guts to stand up to your own father."

They stood face to face, neither backing down.

"I'll protect Will. Unlike you, who failed to protect Eloise." Juliet took his letter out of her pocket and crushed it to his chest. Her father's face fell as he read over the words he'd written twenty-seven years ago. "I wish I could've known the man who wrote this letter. He knew how threats can destroy love and families. He's the father I'd be proud to have, but it's clear he's dead."

His jaw clenched. Juliet turned to walk away, but he grabbed her wrist painfully.

"Get your hands off me!"

"Bring me the bell, Juliet!" he snarled, balling up the letter in his fist. "By Christmas Eve. I'm giving you plenty of time, so don't fail me. Or you'll know exactly how it feels to lose those you love."

She ripped free of his grasp and headed for the stairs.

"Don't be stubborn, because it'll be Will and Eloise who pay," he called after her.

She couldn't climb the stairs fast enough. She had until Christmas Eve – that should be plenty of time to return the chest. There was no way she was letting her father get his hands on that bell.

Juliet

"Beth!" Juliet called out over the Christmas music filling the Frost house. She had to talk to her sister before she left. "Beth!"

Footsteps bounded through the halls, but instead of Beth, Diana appeared in her apron. Juliet realised she must be disturbing her from preparing dinner, which meant her father wouldn't be far behind her. They'd always eaten at seven pm sharp, no excuses or delays.

"Are you alright?" Diana demanded. "Where the hell have you been? I got a call from Will saying you'd gone away together for a few days, and Mr Frost said I shouldn't worry, but I couldn't reach you."

"I'm fine – sorry I left without telling you, but I need to talk to Beth," Juliet panted.

"I'm sorry, Juliet, but Beth has gone to stay with a friend. She was so excited, and I promised her that you'd be okay with it. She tried to call you, but she couldn't reach you."

"It's only a week away from Christmas! What about the Christmas Eve party? We're never allowed to miss it!" Juliet desperately needed to see her sister. She feared her father would try to keep them apart until he got what he wanted.

"Mr Frost agreed that she didn't have to attend, since her

friend's family is staying in the city. With the snow it wouldn't be all that safe to come back, so she's going to return to school after the holidays with her friend," Diana explained as Juliet followed her to the kitchen.

The lasagne smelt amazing, but she couldn't even think of food right now. Christmas Eve? It couldn't be a coincidence. Mr Frost must believe he wouldn't be here then, because if he got his way, he'd have Juliet's bell.

"So she's not coming back at all?" Juliet asked, trying not to fidget. They'd only had a few hours together, and guilt washed over her as she regretted getting so caught up in Yule. She vowed to make it up to her sister.

Diana shook her head. "I'm sorry, but it's been arranged that she'll return to school after New Year's Eve. You can give her a call; she was sad not to say goodbye, but given how busy you've been the last few days, I thought it was best for her not to be alone in this big house."

Juliet ran her hands through her hair and took a deep breath. She knew Diana had been right to let Beth go, but it didn't stop the ache in her chest from missing out on spending more precious time with her. Still, she was leaving herself, and this way she wouldn't have to bear her sister pleading for her to stay. Most importantly, Beth would get to enjoy Christmas with her friends.

"I shouldn't say anything, but I suspect Mr Frost didn't want Beth here when you returned, in case—" Diana couldn't meet Juliet's eye; she rubbed her hands on her snowman apron.

"In case what?" Juliet pressed.

Diana let out a long exhalation. "In case you told her about Yule."

Juliet thought her heart would stop, but her desire to

know how the hell Diana knew about Yule kept her blood pumping.

"Y-you know about Yule?" she stammered.

There were tears in Diana's creased eyes. "Yes. I came to the Outside in my early twenties to be a chef. Your grandfather hired me from a restaurant I was temping at. He recognised my family name, and being around people who knew about Yule made me feel safe. I've worked for the Frost family ever since. I was here the day you appeared, wrapped in a bundle of blankets. Your grandfather asked me to look after you, and I couldn't say no." She tried to take Juliet's hand, but Juliet flinched away. "Please don't hate me! They made me swear never to tell you. Having left Yule myself, even of my own free will, I knew how much it hurt to long for home. I didn't want you to feel that way."

Juliet had to sit before her legs gave out. "You let me believe my mother abandoned me because she didn't want me."

The words visibly stung the only mother figure she'd known. "I'm so sorry, Juliet. It was all so complicated, but I've always loved you as my own!"

Juliet kept distance between them. "You let Beth leave because you were protecting her from me? I wouldn't do anything to hurt Beth, but she deserves the truth. That includes telling her our shameful family secrets – she has a right to know."

"You'd never want to hurt your sister, but this is all still fresh to you. I was trying to protect both of you. Beth is still young. Can you imagine how poorly you'd have handled this at her age? Right now, her biggest concern is getting tickets to the Eras Tour. She shouldn't have to bear this secret!"

"Well, she won't have to worry for long," Juliet told her. "Margot was able to get her tickets from a friend who works for her security company. I was so excited to tell her." She'd seen the notification on her phone as soon as she'd got back to the Outside, and had been looking forward to sharing the news in person. "But you and Dad sent her away to protect her from me, when it's all of you she should be protected from."

"My daughter doesn't need your gifts."

Diana and Juliet turned to see Gillian standing at the kitchen door.

"We wouldn't have needed to do any of this if you'd just handed over the chest when you received it," she went on. "If you'd shown any loyalty to this family, we all could have had a perfectly civil Christmas."

Juliet stared at her. "Does everyone in this house know about Yule but me and Beth?"

Gillian scoffed. "How could I not know? After all the years they spent building up a name for themselves on the Outside, your birth nearly ruined everything. Your grandfather practically begged me to marry his son."

"Wasn't he lucky to find a woman with such a lovely, kind heart," Juliet deadpanned.

Gillian's heels clicked against the wooden floors. "He was, and to my detriment." She pursed her lips. "Now that you know about Yule, you'd better remember not to shame the Frost name."

"The only people who've shamed our name are those who've allowed a child to be separated from her mother," Juliet snapped.

Gillian stepped towards her, eyes ablaze with all she'd apparently longed to say over the years. "Don't let your emotions get the better of you. No point in getting upset about a mother you've never known."

"You're right. Why should I have wished for another

mother when I had *you?*" Juliet clenched her fists, her nails biting into her skin.

Gillian's eyebrows would have risen with shock if it hadn't been for the Botox. "I don't like your tone. I did my best."

Juliet didn't want to waste another breath on her. She stormed out of the kitchen and headed outside to her cottage, but she wasn't getting rid of her stepmother that easily.

"Where do you think you're going?" Gillian said, following her inside. Without the fire lit it was freezing, but Juliet didn't care; she wouldn't be there long.

"To stay with a friend." She didn't mention who or where.

"With Will – a man you barely know? You're going to abandon your family just like that?" Gillian sneered.

"Abandon my family? This is not a family. You don't want me here, and I thought you'd be delighted to see the back of me. I think what you're truly upset about is losing your connection to Yule."

Gillian scoffed and folded her arms across her chest. *Bingo.*

"All that talk about you volunteering at the library – that was just a lame excuse for why you weren't home. You stayed away on purpose, hoping I'd fall for Will, to use him against me. I'm surprised you didn't install cameras to spy on us."

She rolled her eyes. "I certainly didn't expect you to throw yourself at him so quickly. He really is the perfect leverage! I told your father that we shouldn't even need that, though I see now that you've never considered us your family. If you did, you'd have handed over the chest. I never thought you could be so selfish." Gillian surprised Juliet by taking hold of her, her long, manicured nails digging into her wrists. "We raised you and gave you a home!"

Juliet twisted out of her grasp. This was the second time today someone had laid hands on her, and she was getting sick of it. Gillian followed her into the bedroom, where she stuffed clothes into her suitcase. She really needed to get rid of her stepmother in case she stumbled across the chest's hiding place.

"Don't ignore me! Your mother wanted nothing to do with you. You'll break Beth's heart when she learns how you're throwing us all away over a home and a mother you've never even known. Then again, if your mother is anything to go by, abandonment runs in the blood."

Juliet bit her tongue, refusing to rise to the bait. She was sure they'd spin some story to tell Beth that would paint her as the villain, but she couldn't be held hostage by the love she had for her sister. In a few years, she could tell Beth the truth – the whole truth.

"First you try to use Will against me, and now my sister." Juliet laughed, trying not to show how the threat stung. "Love would've earned you my trust and loyalty. But all you and Dad know are threats and manipulation."

Gillian's eyes narrowed as she fought to keep her composure. She wasn't used to losing a fight. "Fine. Since I can't make you see reason, go. I'm just relieved Beth isn't here to see this –though you won't be gone long. You only have until Christmas Eve."

"Relieved that Beth isn't here to see me stand up for myself? Or to learn the truth about Yule and how you're blackmailing me into handing over the only thing that connects me to my mom?" Juliet hissed.

Gillian flinched, and Juliet knew she genuinely feared losing Beth. Still, even if it did bring her a fraction of joy to see her stepmother hurting, she'd never do anything to upset her sister.

After a second of silence, Gillian stormed out of the cottage without another word.

Juliet tucked the chest safely in her suitcase and concealed it with thick jumpers. She'd called the hotel in Hartdale town on her way back from the barber's; thankfully, they had one room left, so she'd be able to hide away from her dad. She didn't want to go back to the apartment, since it was the first place he'd look for her.

"Can you tell Victor I'll call him once I'm settled?" she asked Diana, who'd come out to say goodbye at the side gate. Juliet didn't want to risk leaving by the front door, just in case her father had instructed Gillian to inspect her bags.

Diana sniffled. "Victor will understand. You need to do what's right for you, and Beth will be fine with her friends. I'm so sorry I kept the truth from you," she said again, opening the gate. "Find your own family. Beth will understand in time, and you still have us."

This time, Juliet let her take her hand. Hope shone in Diana's eyes.

"I'm mad at you, but you're my family – always have been." Juliet couldn't ignore the hurt she felt about her part in the lie, but years of Diana being there when others hadn't outweighed the deceit. It would take time, but she couldn't hold any more hurt in her heart. She didn't want to be poisoned like her father had been over the years.

"I know it'll take time for you to trust me again. But please, be safe, and keep Will close. I see the way he looks at you. I haven't seen a man look at anyone that way since I saw Victor walk to the altar with that goofy smile."

"My smile is far from goofy," Victor interrupted, stepping towards them from the other side of the gate. Diana must have called him and asked him to bring the car around.

Juliet looked at him, wanting to ask him why he'd lied,

why he'd sided with her father, but now that she was leaving it all felt pointless. Besides, she knew deep down that they'd had little choice in the matter. If they'd gone against the Frost family, they would've been fired, and she really would have lost the only family she'd known.

"I'm sorry, love, for the part we played." Victor wrapped her in a bear hug. It took all her strength not to crumble, but she had a plan to get through. Now was not the time to fall apart. "We made our choice, and now it's your turn. So long as you'll have us, we will always be in your life. As will Beth, no matter what they tell her. She loves you." He released her and took her suitcase, putting it into the car.

Standing on the gravel path, Juliet wondered if she'd ever come back.

"As much as I wish you'd both told me the truth… thank you for raising me." She gave the aging couple a wobbly smile, swamped with memories of all the kindness they'd shown a sad and lonely kid. "Please look after Beth, and no matter what the others tell her, make sure she knows she'll always have a home with me. That she can come to me whenever she needs or wants to."

"Don't worry about Beth; she has her school and friends. I don't believe for a moment they'll be able to taint her love for you." Diana gave Juliet a quick hug before opening the car door for her. "It's time to look after you – and give Will our love. I've already packed his things. Just have him call Victor, and he can bring them wherever he needs."

"Thank you, but I'll take them now, I'm probably going to see him soon." She was sure that Will wouldn't have brought anything incriminating with him, but better safe than sorry. "Di, I'm sorry for what I said in the kitchen. You've been the best mom I could've asked for."

Diana's eyes filled with tears. "Call me when you get where you're going."

"I will," Juliet promised, and Diana closed the door.

"Ready?" Victor asked in the rear-view mirror.

Juliet nodded, finally able to say goodbye to the house that had never been her home.

ONCE SHE WAS SETTLED into her hotel room overlooking the snow-covered Hartdale, Juliet argued with herself. She wanted to see Will, but she couldn't bring herself to interrupt his night with Harvey. He'd done so much for her; he deserved some time to himself. There was so much to digest, to think through before she could even begin to tell him about her dad's scheme.

I need you.

Juliet sent the text before she had a chance to overthink it.

It didn't take five minutes for Margot to respond.

I can be in Hartdale first thing in the morning.
Just wrapping up with a client xxx

She turned up the following morning as promised.

Juliet had spent most of the night agonising over this decision, but she couldn't stand the taste of another lie on her tongue. Even if it meant breaking yet another of Yule's rules, she couldn't be like her family; she needed to choose truth and trust. Once the small kettle on the desk had boiled and two large cups of coffee were made, she told Margot *everything*.

When Juliet had finished her story and Margot had examined the contents of the chest, her best friend put down the snowman-shaped hotel mug and let out a long sigh. "We're going to need something stronger than coffee."

Will hadn't heard from Juliet since he'd dropped her off outside the barber's yesterday afternoon. Despite having enjoyed his night with Harvey, he couldn't stop himself from stressing about Juliet when he didn't hear from her. He'd tried her phone a couple of times and even stopped by the Frost estate this morning, but Diana had told him she wasn't there. He figured Juliet needed some time and space, and he wanted to give it to her. Thankfully, he had his friends to distract him while he waited for her to reach out.

"Lyla explained everything after you left. You should have been more careful! Though I don't know why I didn't suspect something was going on sooner. After that day when Lyla met Juliet, she kept asking about banishments, and if anyone's punishment had ever been lifted," Mason said, downing a glass of expensive whiskey.

Will wasn't sure if the heating in the country club had been turned up or if it was the pressure of the situation that caused him to pull at his stifling collar. He, Mason and Harvey sat around a poker table. They weren't playing, but the table was far enough down the long lounge that they wouldn't be disturbed by the other members of the old country club and they could speak freely.

"How did you not suspect she was up to something?" Harvey asked Mason.

"Helping Will smuggle someone into Yule wasn't the first thing to come to mind, and she told me that she and Kevin were doing some kind of research for a game. Why didn't you tell me Will was getting wrapped up in this mess?" Mason leaned back in his armchair.

"I like to stay out of Yule-related trouble," Harvey said, waving it off as though trouble was contagious.

"In Harvey's defence, I told him not to tell you, and he did warn me not to get involved," Will admitted as Harvey poured Mason another glass of whiskey. Harvey didn't drink; he was far too much of a control freak.

"There was no convincing him. He's been obsessed with her case for months," he said into his glass of sparkling water.

Will glared at him.

"What? I'm not judging you. You wouldn't be the first man to forsake the rules for a woman." Harvey smirked.

"Low blow – and at least Lyla's my fiancée now," Mason pointed out. He ran his hand through his ash-blonde hair. "Are you telling us that you're planning on marrying Juliet? If you were, that would make life a lot easier. We could petition the council to allow her to stay as an individual instead of a member of a banished family."

Will shook his head, his cheeks burning under their scrutiny. "We've known each other for less than a month; I don't think proposing is the answer. She has enough to think about – I don't think getting down on one knee would help calm the situation. I don't want Juliet to feel pressured into being with me to establish her Yule citizenship. If I ask her to marry me, I want to be sure that she's doing it because she wants to be with me. Anything else wouldn't be fair to either of us." He focused on the glass in his hands, relieved he had them to confide in.

"Does Juliet know it was Eloise who approached you? I can't believe she used her status as Head Guardian to remove a chest! I'm going to have to speak to her about this. I can understand her longing to be reunited with Juliet, but she should've come to me before taking such drastic action," Mason said, shaking his head.

"Yes, Juliet knows about her mum's involvement. Eloise's plan was set in motion after your father and the council refused her last petition. I think it was only a few months before he passed, and you'd only just returned to Yule to take over, so Eloise wasn't sure if you could be trusted to help," Will said cautiously, not wanting to hurt his friend's feelings.

"I suppose I don't blame her. If we weren't friends, your crime would result in banishment," Mason said sternly, clearly not happy about the position he and his family had been put in. Still, even if he was on his third drink, Will felt he was taking the news rather well.

"I'm not asking for any special treatment. I had no intention of getting you or Lyla involved, but things didn't go to plan."

"As much as I don't approve of the secrecy, Lyla and I are the least of your concerns. Actually, I think having Juliet to talk to makes her feel more at ease in Yule. I don't want to banish you or punish Eloise," Mason said.

Will nodded gratefully, feeling more at ease, but the worry in his friend's eyes told him the coming days weren't going to be easy.

"But if the council finds out before we can find a solution, then I might not have a choice. I don't agree with my father's decision to deny Eloise's petition for reunification. However, mine is only one opinion."

"Find a solution?" Harvey interjected, staring between them like they'd lost their minds. "The solution is to stay away from anything to do with the Frost family. He's risking his career and everything he's worked for. Is she really worth all this? I didn't expect you to be encouraging this, Mason."

"I'm not encouraging anything, but they've gone too far to turn back now. It's more of a risk to try and hide all that's happened," Mason reasoned.

Harvey shrugged. To him, self-preservation outweighed anything else.

"I understand your concern," Will admitted, "and Juliet understands what's at risk for all of us. Hell, she worries about us more than herself. I'm the one who got her into all this by agreeing to help Eloise. Bringing her to Yule so soon was my mistake. The first time, when she met Lyla, was an accident. She didn't know that the Frost bell she found in the chest would bring her to Yule."

"Surprising that it still worked after so many years. I thought it was decommissioned when the family was banished," Mason said, frowning. "The bell should've been melted down and returned to the Keepers of the Bells to be recrafted. Well, at least we don't have to worry about Juliet reacting badly when she found all this out. Starting a relationship with a lie doesn't tend to go well."

"Regardless of how Juliet and I feel, I only want to ask you to help me do what's right. I need your help to petition the council. I know you don't agree with Juliet being separated from her family, and if she has a Klaus on her side, I'm sure the council will listen." Will turned to Harvey. "You also have connections to those on the council. If you both work your magic, this could go seamlessly. What if this was Margot?"

"Who's Margot?" Mason grumbled. "Please tell me you haven't got another Outsider involved in all this!"

"Juliet's best friend – she doesn't know anything about Yule," Harvey said, though his hard stare didn't leave Will. "She has nothing to do with this, and my interest in her is purely professional. I want her to come and work for my company."

"Are you trying to convince us, or yourself?" Will quipped, and Mason smirked.

"And you're sure Juliet hasn't told her about any of this?" he asked, reaching for his glass. At this rate he'd return to Lyla drunk.

Will side-eyed Harvey. "Not as far as I know," they said in unison.

Harvey sighed. "If I can't convince you to give Juliet up, then I'll talk to some of the more lenient council members on your behalf. I might be able to make a case for her to be allowed into Yule."

"You mean bribe them?" Mason gave him a suspicious look.

"Do you want my help or not?"

"We do," Will said quickly before Mason could disagree.

"Given how Eloise has helped train the next generation of guardians without incident, the council may lean in her favour," Mason said thoughtfully, "but if they find out she stole Yule ancestral property and risked Yule's safety, all this might be for naught, and Juliet might have her memories of this season wiped from her memory. That would include her relationship with you."

Will set his jaw. "If it comes to that, then I'll have to make her fall for me all over again."

"You might have to decide…" Harvey winced, trailing off.

"It wouldn't be my home without her," Will told him, and Harvey threw up his hands in defeat.

"You love her." Mason sighed. "I know the feeling."

Harvey started to put on his jacket. "Now that we've got a plan to convince the council, I might just make my plane."

"Not so fast – I need you to distract Margot. Juliet might reach out to her," Will said slyly. Perhaps some matchmaking might make his life a little easier.

"I was going to go skiing in Aspen with some clients. A couple of the council members will be there, if you need me to charm them discreetly," Harvey said. Since he didn't return to Yule often, he liked to treat higher-ups in Yules to vacations and lavish gifts to keep his connections fruitful.

"Take Margot with you, but keep her away from the council members," Mason suggested.

"You expect me to keep her busy *and* help you with the council?" Harvey asked. "Do you think I'm a miracle worker?!"

"You'll figure it out," Mason smirked. "Just make sure you keep her away from your bell – they have a habit of fast-tracking relationships."

"Unlike you two, I want to be engaged *before* I bring anyone back to Yule," Harvey drawled.

"Ironic, considering how much you despise the rules," Mason teased him.

"I can't just force her onto a plane without any explanation!" Harvey exclaimed, as if they wanted him to kidnap her.

"What's the big deal? Take her to your ski resort. Tell her it's a seasonal perk if she comes to work for you? Make it about business," Will countered. Harvey had never put this much effort into hiring anyone, so Will was sure that adding her to the company roster was only half of his friend's plan, even if Harvey didn't want to admit to his feelings.

Harvey lifted his hands. "Don't you think she'd be creeped out by a guy she's just met asking her to travel to another country?"

Will didn't get a chance to argue; Harvey's phone buzzed. "Speak of the little devil," he muttered, pulling it from his pocket.

Mason leaned forward as Harvey read the text with a frown. "Lyla wanted me to give you her number for Juliet in case she needs anything. I'll text it to you. She knows how hard it can be to adjust to Yule, and she wants to help in any way she can."

"Thank her for me – Juliet will appreciate it. It's a relief to know she has someone she can call a friend in Yule."

"She has more than just Lyla. Kevin and Mum want to have you both over for Christmas dinner," Mason chuckled, slapping Will on the arm. "Let's just make sure we don't all end up banished first."

Will nodded. "We just have to make it to Christmas. I'm worried about her meeting with her dad; I hope she didn't reveal too much. I doubt he'll look kindly on her mum reaching out after all this time." Frost wasn't the type to be happy for someone else's gain, not if he wasn't getting anything in return. Despite what could be mended between mother and daughter, the banishment for the rest of the Frost family was permanent.

Harvey caught their attention as he sat up straighter. "Margot's with Juliet. She says Juliet saw her dad and it didn't go well. They've gone to a bar, but Margot's worried about her. I think we should head over and check up on them."

"What bar?"

"Alexandria. She doesn't know I own the place. I'll have my staff cut them off, and keep them in the private rooms," Harvey said, already setting his phone to his ear. "It's only twenty minutes from here. We can get there before they leave."

Will pulled on his jacket, apologising to Mason for

cutting their evening short, and hoped his nerves didn't show. Whatever had happened with Mr Frost yesterday, it had been bad enough for Juliet to call on Margot for support and go out drinking. He needed to make sure she was okay. With everything going on, it was a relief to know Margot was with her.

J uliet's one goal for the evening was to get blind drunk and make an absolute fool of herself by singing as loudly and as off-key as humanly possible. Dancing – check. Singing off-key – check. Drunk – not even close. She feared it would be one of those nights when it didn't matter how many overpriced margaritas she had, she'd remain sober as a sailor on land.

"I need water," Margot pleaded, taking her hand as they pushed through the sweaty, crowded club to the front of the bar. Usually, Juliet didn't particularly enjoy the smell of sweat or having drinks sloshed over her every few minutes, but after the last few days, she needed to disappear into a sea of carelessness. The gold tinsel decorating the edge of the bar irritated her skin as she ordered another margarita from a bartender with a skull tattoo on his neck.

Margot chugged her water, swaying to the remixed Christmas music. Skull-Neck blended some ice for Juliet, but another bartender walked over and turned off the blender before turning to approach them, without their drinks.

"Sorry, ladies, but you've had enough for the night," she said, raising a pierced eyebrow.

"It's only my third drink!" Juliet called over the music. She'd never been cut off before. She glanced at the group beside them, clearly much worse for wear, being given a tray of shots.

"Boss's orders." The bartender shrugged. "Though Mr Bryce said you're welcome to head to the private rooms upstairs. There's a private bar, and he feels you'll both be more comfortable there."

"Mr Bryce! Harvey must own this place." Margot side-eyed Juliet, but before either could respond, the bartender moved on to the next customer. Juliet tried to wave down someone else to make the drinks, but the other bartenders in their tight black shirts and slacks pretended they didn't exist.

Defeated, they made their way to an empty table. Most were too busy dancing to sit.

"Why would Harvey cut us off? How did he even know we were here? You aren't even drinking, and it's not like I'm falling over myself," Juliet complained.

To add insult to injury, a sealed bottle of sparkling water and two glasses were dropped off at their table.

"We could try the private bar upstairs. It's getting really crowded down here," Margot grumbled.

"I want to dance, not sit in some stuffy room," Juliet groaned, but Margot was too busy texting to listen.

"Will and Harvey are here?" Her eyes darted to the door.

Juliet didn't have to search the crowd long before spotting them. Margot waved them over. Will looked the same as the night they'd first met in his long black coat over a blue shirt and black trousers. He whispered something to Harvey, who looked more relaxed in a dark red sweater and tan trousers, and his serious gaze cut through the cheerful room as he searched for her. Worried that he would find out she'd told Margot about Yule, Juliet wanted to sink into the leather booth. She also wasn't ready to tell him about her conversation with dear old Dad.

The dance floor was the only way to avoid any conversation about the day she'd had – even if her legs were a little numb from dancing and the generous margaritas.

Margot didn't follow. Instead, she greeted the men with a warm smile and a kiss on the cheek. Juliet hoped they'd sit and talk while she had her fun dancing to more horrible Christmas remixes, but when she spun around Will was towering over her, looking rather amused.

"Can we talk?" he shouted.

"No, I've done enough talking. Dance with me!" Juliet grinned, dancing around him.

Will ran his hand over his face and leaned in, taking hold of her waist to stop her moving so much. "Let me take you home. Talking with your father couldn't have been easy, but this isn't the way to deal with it."

"This is exactly the way to deal with it."

He glared at another man who got a little too close to her, then pulled her flush against him. The stranger took the hint when she chuckled and wrapped her arms around his neck.

"Leave or loosen up," she argued. Will rolled his eyes, but he spun her until she was a little dizzy. "That's more like it!" She laughed, loving this side of him.

Over Will's shoulder, she noticed that Harvey had his arm around Margot's shoulder. Harvey winked as he caught her staring. He raised a glass to her before returning his attention to Margot, who seemed far more at ease now that he'd arrived.

"Wait. How did you find us?" Juliet asked, a sinking feeling in her gut made her wonder if Margot might have had something to do with it. Could it be a coincidence that they'd ended up in a bar Harvey owned?

"Margot texted Harvey while we were with Mason. She told us where you were and that she was worried about you,"

Will confirmed, spinning her around so her back was against his chest. It reminded her of the first night they'd danced together at the gala.

"Mason?" she gasped; her eyes snapped back to Harvey. "Holy shit, Harvey is from Yule?"

"Please keep your voice down! This isn't the place," Will reminded her.

Juliet tried to distract him from her faux pas by running her hands down his chest while she swayed her hips. He gritted his teeth, looking like he wanted to lock her up away from anyone else's eyes.

"I need a drink, and we need to talk," he huffed, clearly distracted. "There's a private bar upstairs."

"I thought we were cut off." Juliet pouted, letting him guide her through the crowd.

"Harvey owns the place. So I've got access to every floor, and I'll be your own private bartender," Will whispered.

However appealing that sounded, Juliet hesitated as they reached the bottom of a long staircase. If she went with him, they'd have to talk about yesterday, and she wasn't ready for that. Not now. She just wanted Will to hold her and help her pretend that all was right in the world.

"Actually, I really want to just keep dancing. Can't you stay with me down here?"

"Is this man bothering you?" The man who'd been leering at her earlier had returned. He was obviously very drunk.

"I'm fine. He's my—" Juliet tried to think of the correct way to finish that sentence. Will's gaze suddenly felt like it weighed a ton.

"She's my girlfriend," he finished for her. "Mind your own business."

She chewed her lip to stop herself from smiling like an idiot.

"Is that true?" the drunk stranger slurred, putting a hand on Juliet's shoulder and making her jump.

"She doesn't want anything you have to offer," Will said, removing the hand a bit too forcefully for her liking.

"The lady can answer for herself." The stranger shoved Will away from her.

Juliet clenched her jaw. All she'd wanted was a nice night. She started to walk away from the dick-measuring contest, but the stranger caught her by the hips. The smell of cheap beer and cigarettes drifted over her.

"What the fuck to I have to do to be left alone?" she barked, shoving the stranger off her. She turned to tell him to go to hell, but he tried to grab her again.

Juliet saw red. Before she could stop herself, her fist connected with the stranger's jaw. His bloodshot eyes widened with shock as he stumbled back into a table and landed hard on the sticky carpeted floor. Suddenly, the dimly lit bar felt very quiet.

"What the fuck was that? You crazy bitch!" the stranger shouted, clambering to his feet. Will got between them, keeping Juliet close to his back, and tried to talk him down while she shook out her hand, pain radiating up her arm. The stranger tried to swing at Will, but he shoved the man back into an approaching bouncer, who caught him.

Before Juliet could blink, Harvey appeared and whispered something to the bouncer. Juliet recalled how Fiona had mentioned back at the gala that he wasn't someone to be messed with when the stranger raised his hands in defeat and left with the bouncer without a word of argument.

Overwhelmed by the shock of her actions and the pain in her hand, she made a bee line for the door, not caring if anyone was following; she had to get out of here. Only a few feet from the club, someone laid a hand on her shoulder.

Terrified that the man she'd hit had come back for revenge, she clenched her already aching fist and whirled to confront him.

"It's me – relax, fighter." Will held up his hands defensively.

Juliet groaned and closed the distance between them to rest her forehead against his chest, not caring about getting make up on his shirt.

"I'm sorry I wasn't there for you yesterday, but I'm here now." Will wrapped his arms around her. "You don't have to handle all this alone. I don't know what happened with your dad, and you don't have to talk about it now," he said into her hair, kissing the side of her head.

The comfort in his touch nearly killed her. Her father's comments about how his love for her mom had been a mistake echoed in her mind.

"We never should've got involved with each other. We're going to end up just like my parents, and I don't think my heart can take it," she said quietly. "I don't want you to grow to hate me."

Will pulled back, forcing her to look at him. "What the hell did your father say to make you think that? We'll never be like them, because I've got no plan of ever leaving you. You're stuck with me, whether you like it or not, and you have been the moment I heard that damn laugh that first night in the bar."

Juliet tried to hold back tears. "Nothing that's worth repeating. I just wish this didn't have to be so hard."

"Everyone worth having comes with its challenges, but I'd give up everything I have just to spend my days with you." Will brought her bruised hand to his lips.

"If you keep saying stuff like that, I'll never be able to give you up," she hiccupped, trying to believe she was worth it.

"That was a hell of a punch. Are you sure nothing is broken?" he asked quietly.

"I don't think so. I've never hit anyone before," she admitted. "Felt good in the moment, but not so much now."

"He deserved it." Will smirked. "He should've known better than to put his hands on you."

She rolled his eyes at his caveman attitude.

"We've got to get some ice on this. You ready to go?" he asked.

"Yeah, that guy killed my buzz," she sighed, wincing as she tried to flex her fingers. "But I can't leave without telling Margot."

When they headed back inside, the table that had been knocked over in the scuffle had been corrected. Will hovered at Juliet's back as though ready to protect her from all angles. Any other night, she'd have brushed him off as being over-bearing; right now, she appreciated it. The crowd felt over-whelming, and she didn't let go of his hand.

Harvey and Margot sat in a quiet booth, both oblivious to their return. Juliet noticed how Harvey stared at Margot like she was the only one in the room. Still… he was from Yule. She wondered how he would react if he knew that she'd told Margot about the winter wonderland hidden in the North Pole. She swallowed her worries down and focused her attention on getting out of the bar without starting another fight.

Will leaned down to tell Harvey they were leaving, and Juliet hugged Margot, letting her know she was okay. They left the couple to enjoy the rest of their night.

Outside the bar, the quiet was all-consuming. Only a few patrons waited for taxis or were heading off to another, less crowded place.

"My car's at my hotel, but I'll get us a taxi to the Frost estate," Will said at the door.

She looked down at her feet. "I'll go with you. It shouldn't take too long, since I'm staying at the Hudson hotel."

"You left the estate?" His surprise was obvious. Thankfully, he was distracted by a passing taxi and held his hand out to hail it.

"I'll explain when we get to the hotel," Juliet said, not wanting to talk about her family troubles on the street. She wrapped her jacket tightly around herself as snow peppered her hair.

"We don't have to talk about it at all. I'll wait for whenever you're ready." Will opened the car door for her and she climbed into the back, grateful to the driver for having the heating on full blast. Resting her head on Will's shoulder, she spent the drive back to the hotel comforted by his embrace and patience.

W ill took Juliet's spare key card to the hotel room and let her head up first. She looked hesitant to leave him, but he assured her he wouldn't be long. At Reception, he asked for room service to send up an ice pack and a hot water bottle. If her hand got any worse, he'd take her to Yule in the morning, where she'd be healed far more quickly than going to any hospital on the Outside.

He found her curled up on the couch in front of the TV, watching old reruns of cartoons. Her heels had been kicked off on the rug under the table by the couch. Will sat down beside her and pulled her into the crook of his arm. He eyed her purple knuckles.

A knock of the door made her jump, and he chuckled. "It's just room service." Heading to the door, he tipped the man before taking the items he'd requested.

"What are you up to?" Juliet called as he went to the bathroom, where he found the sink covered in make-up and skincare products along with a myriad of snacks. This must be the aftermath of her and Margot getting ready. He tidied up a little, so she'd be able to find things more easily, then wrapped the icepack in a facecloth so the cold wouldn't be so biting against her skin.

"It doesn't hurt that much," she protested as he left the

bathroom and revealed the icepack. "I don't think I need that."

It weighed on his chest how much she hid her pain. He sat down again and took her hand, watching her wince as she clenched and released her fist.

"Your face tells me you do," he said, placing the wrapped ice pack across her knuckles. "Luckily, I don't think you've broken anything. Let the ice work, and hopefully the swelling will go down. If not, I'll take you to get it looked at in the morning." He'd had his fair share of bruised knuckles, both before he'd joined the guardians and during training. It didn't help that she had such a tiny fist compared to that man's jaw. He was sure Harvey's men had taught him some respect before barring him for good.

She pouted up at him. "It's cold."

"This will keep you warm." He handed her the hot water bottle from the table. Her smile reached her eyes as she hugged it to her tummy with her good hand.

"Thank you." She beamed.

"Keep the ice on for fifteen minutes, or I'll take you to the hospital," he said sternly.

"So bossy," she muttered, letting him rest her hand on the arm of the couch so the ice pack could balance on her knuckles.

"Bet you wish I'd done the punching now," he mused.

Juliet rolled her eyes, settling deeper into the soft cushions.

"Feel better?" Will asked as her expression relaxed.

"Much," she admitted with a sigh of relief.

"Mrs Klaus used to always give us an ice pack and hot water bottle whenever we got injured getting up to mischief."

"I'll be sure to thank her next time." The comment

lingered in the air; it assumed that she would be returning to Yule. "Thank you," she added quickly.

"Are you okay for a few minutes? Do you mind if I have a quick shower? The arsehole split his drink on me when he took a swing," Will said, unbuttoning his stained white shirt.

"I think I'll survive," Juliet said, snuggling into the pillows. He turned up the volume of the old cartoons while she unashamedly ogled his muscles, then leaned down and kissed her.

"If my hand didn't hurt so much, I'd join you."

He loved how disappointed she looked, though he worried it might be the alcohol talking. "And if I weren't a gentleman, I'd let you. Now rest." He kissed her again, pulling himself away with a groan as she ran her tongue against his lower lip.

In the bathroom he stripped off his shirt, hating the sticky sensation on his skin, washed out the stains as best he could with hand soap, then put it out to dry on the towel heater while he showered. Feeling and smelling a lot less like a sweet alcoholic popsicle, he put back on his boxers and trousers, wanting to make Juliet more comfortable. Going out in nothing but a towel might surprise her, and she'd had enough excitement for one night.

Running his hand through his damp hair, Will tried not to overthink about whatever had caused her to call Margot. The night they'd met, she'd left the party opting for the bar and a book; whatever had driven her to Alexandria and away from the estate where her sister was must have been especially painful. He gripped the sink. He didn't want to assume the worst of Mr Frost, but seeing her so disheartened and worn-out tugged at his heartstrings. *I shouldn't have left her there.* Even if he risked coming across as controlling and possessive, he wished he'd been there when she left the meeting, just to hold her hand. He tried to remind himself that he couldn't control the situation – not when he'd been part of lifting the veil on her life.

A thud outside broke his train of thought. He smiled, wondering what on earth she was up to now.

"How's that hand doing?" he asked, closing the bathroom door behind him so the steam wouldn't escape. He was surprised to find Juliet still sitting on the couch and everything apparently in its place.

"Throbbing, but better." She lifted her head from the back of the couch to look at him. Her tired eyes told him she was sobering up.

Carefully, he removed the ice pack. "The bruising looks normal, and thankfully the swelling isn't getting any worse."

"I'm not going to the hospital, but I'll admit it does hurt more." She winced, trying to extend her fingers.

"I'm not going to toss you over my shoulder and drag you there if you don't want to go," he promised. "As long as you tell me what that sound was."

"Sound?" Juliet diverted her gaze to the TV, confirming she'd been up to mischief while he was indisposed.

"You know, I *am* feeling a caveman urge coming over me." He sighed, resting his hand on her bare thighs. Fuck, if he hadn't noticed how short her little black skirt was before, he had now. Judging by her flushed cheeks as her eyes lingered on his hands, she was on the same wavelength. He swallowed his desire, reminding his lust that now wasn't the time.

"I wanted to get the chest out of the wardrobe," she explained, surprising him.

Will glanced at the wardrobe beside the bed behind them. He waited for her to explain, wondering why it was here and why she'd wanted it at this precise moment.

"I want you to take it back. I want you to put it back in the hall of guardians before anyone knows it's missing."

"Where is this coming from? It's yours."

She wouldn't look at him. Gently, he tipped her chin up so she couldn't hide those beautiful brown eyes. "Is this about the meeting with Mr Frost?"

She swallowed, and her little sigh confirmed his suspicions. "He knows about the chest. He knows about you and the bell. He wants me to give it to him." The fear in her confession was tangible.

"How?" was all Will managed to get out, as the air disappeared from his lungs.

"I don't know, but I do know that we shouldn't underestimate him." Juliet rested her face in her hands as though she couldn't believe it either. "Please just take it. I don't want everyone getting in trouble because of me. He's heartless when it comes to getting what he wants, and he wants the bell most of all. He's given me until Christmas Eve to hand it over, or he's going to report us to the council."

"You're so close – just a few more days. Mason is going to start petitioning the council!"

Juliet shook her head as though she didn't want to hear it. "As much as I want to meet her, to finally have the last piece of this puzzle… there are others I care about." She hesitated. "You."

He pressed his lips together. He'd never thought he'd be one of the factors getting in the way of her reunion with Eloise. As much as he ached to be a part of Juliet's life, their chemistry had become an obstacle in the task he'd been given.

But it was too late to change paths now. He couldn't let her go. Even the thought of being separated from her woke a fear in him he'd never experienced before.

"I don't want to have to pick between the people I care about and someone I've never even had the chance to know – to love. The only thing I can think to do is give the chest back to you and we agree not to see each other again. Maybe one day, we can find another way to meet. For now, the only evidence my dad has is information about the chest being stolen and in my possession. I don't want to put anyone or anything at risk, including my own heart."

The heartbreak in her words told him it was too late for that.

"I'm sorry you had to face your dad alone. He never should've known. And I'm sorry I didn't do more to protect you." Will wrapped his arms around her and held her close.

"It's not your fault," she said, resting her head on his shoulder. "He said there are people who still believe the Frost family deserves a place in Yule. He'll always find a way to get what he wants, but this time I won't let him. I left the estate because it was a miracle he didn't find the chest in the cottage. He had his security search the place while we were in Yule."

"I love how ferociously you want to protect us, but we can sort this out. Trust me and have a little faith." Will brushed the hair from her face and wiped smudged mascara from under her eyes.

"I trust *you* – it's him I don't trust. I doubt he'll even wait until Christmas Eve before he reports us. He won't like that I've left the estate. He even sent Beth off to stay with a friend for the holidays to keep her from me."

Will kissed her hair, kicking himself for underestimating Mr Frost. He'd known letting her keep the chest in the cottage was a risk, but he hadn't known the Frost eyes and ears travelled so far. If the family did have allies in Yule, they were lucky his greed had delayed him from reporting them the minute he found out about Eloise's plan.

"Let's worry about all this tomorrow. Today has been hard enough; you need to get some sleep." He didn't want her to make any rash decisions out of a desire to protect him or her mum.

She sat up abruptly, resting her injured hand on his chest. "No! Please, we can't keep the chest here. I need you to take it back to Yule before he discovers I've checked in here. I used one of Margot's fake IDs at the desk, and paid in cash to buy myself some time. I won't be able to sleep if I know he's searching for it, and me. Once it's back safely with the guardians, then we'll have plausible deniability."

"You want me to go now?" he asked, looking down at himself. His shirt wasn't even dry. "I need clothes…"

She jumped up from the couch and opened the wardrobe by the large double bed. "I already brought them to the hotel. Victor won't tell my dad where I am."

"You've really thought this through?" Will asked, joining her by the bed and helping her put his suitcase on the bed.

"I have. I don't want you to go, but we can't risk delaying. When Dad talks to Gillian… my stepmother and I didn't exactly part on the best of terms. He might realise that I've got no intention of giving in to his demands, and with Beth away for the rest of the holidays he doesn't have much leverage, so we need to use this time to our advantage." Juliet sat on the bed, watching as he took out a thick navy jumper and some jeans.

"Okay, but I'm not leaving you alone. I'll have Harvey bring Margot to the hotel," Will said, loath to leave her. Seeing her so panicked, he had to do what he could to help her. He didn't want her to spend the next week frightened of her father's shadow.

"She's staying in this hotel." Juliet frowned, apparently confused that he didn't know. "She came with Harvey."

"They're staying here? Together?" Will clarified as he got changed. Harvey had left out that small detail; it seemed his friend was keeping secrets of his own. "He didn't say anything to me. I know he's been trying to get her to work for him, but I've never seen him so invested…" That was putting it politely. He'd never seen him answer anyone's texts faster than he had Margot's at the country club.

"I think it's a little complicated. Margot doesn't want to work for him because she doesn't mix business and pleasure, so until they work it out, they're staying in adjoining rooms." Juliet grinned.

"I'm sure Harvey's loving that. He loves a challenge."

Will reached for his phone on the table, remembering how his friend had stared at Margot at the bar. They might have met their match in each other. Harvey answered on the third ring; he and Margot were in the hotel bar downstairs.

"They're on their way up. Harvey and Margot's rooms are close by, just in case you're worried about your dad coming here."

"I don't think he'd go that far, but thank you," Juliet said, fidgeting with the fluffy white throw on the bed.

"You never need to thank me." Will smiled, kneeling in front of her.

Juliet held his face and brought her lips to his. The small touch made his soul ache for more. His hand slipped behind her neck as he peppered her cheeks with kisses until he lost control and claimed her lips as his own. He felt her sharp intake of breath as he pulled her against him. She arched her back, and he dropped his hands to grip her waist, wanting her to remember the weight of his possessive touch while he was gone. He released her, his nose brushing hers.

"Maybe you could go in the morning."

Her hazy words made his stomach tighten. She rested her hands on his shoulders, not moving away from him an inch; her skirt had risen on her legs, testing his willpower. She moaned softly as his hand slid up her thighs – and there was a knock on the door. Will watched her glare at the door over her shoulder.

"Too late. You'll just have to wait." He winked, and she groaned.

"Fine, I'll just have to take care of myself." She shrugged as he stood, still between her thighs. He leaned over her, encompassing her in his shadow.

"Don't test me." It took all his willpower not to ignore the repeated knocking and take her right there, not caring if they heard her moans.

"You should get that," she told him, looking up at him with those siren eyes.

"When I get back, we'll finish this." His words came out more commanding than he'd intended, but her eyes widened, and that small smirk on her lips told him she loved it.

Adjusting himself, Will went to the door to find Margot alone. He wasn't surprised Harvey didn't want to face the grilling about being in adjoining rooms. He'd get to that later.

The girls sat on the bed and talked about what had happened at the bar. "Judging by your right hook, you really didn't need any help," Margot said, miming the punch.

"I never thought I'd hit him!" Juliet said with a laugh. "It happened before I even realised what I was doing." She showed Margot the bruises on her knuckles. "Safe to say we won't be returning any time soon."

"It's fine. Harvey talked it over with the manager and paid for any damages."

Will picked up his suitcase, ready to head back to Yule. Margot eyed it, and he had the feeling she knew exactly what was inside. Having heard Juliet's plan, he'd guessed that she'd already gone over her plans with the one person she trusted more than anyone. He didn't have time to worry about it; given how Harvey wouldn't leave Margot alone, she was going to find out sooner rather than later anyway. If Juliet trusted her, then he had no choice but to put his faith in her too.

In the Hall of Guardians, Will wasn't surprised to find the corridors empty at this hour – the perfect time for sneaking around with suspicious luggage. Many of the boarders would be in bed by now, if they hadn't returned home for the holidays.

Heading to the vault, he opened the door with his key and only turned on one of the lamps; he didn't want anyone to know he was there. When he removed the chest from his suitcase, he opened it to see that Juliet had returned the bell necklace. He wondered if he should leave it there, but just in case, he slipped the velvet box into his pocket. If Juliet needed it, he wanted her to have an escape. He was also troubled by the idea that the Frosts might have eyes in the Hall of Guardians; this way, he could keep it safe.

Cranking the lever, Will placed the chest back in its rightful place. *You'd never even know it'd been missing.* The shelves reshuffled themselves back to their original state, erasing any trace of tampering.

Will turned to leave – and Eloise stepped out of the shadows, nearly frightening the life out of him.

"How'd you know I was here?" he hissed.

"Phyllis told me you came by the other day. I was

finishing up my rounds, checking on the boarders, when I saw you head in this direction," Eloise said, standing by the desk with the lit lamp. Her dark hair was slicked back in her signature low bun, exposing the strands of grey. She eyed the wall behind him. "You were returning the chest?"

"Yes. Juliet wanted me to." He could see that she took it as a rejection. He didn't know how to tell her that the man she'd once loved was threatening her daughter.

"Why? Has she changed her mind?" Eloise's brows creased. "Does she not intend to return? To meet me?" She sat on the study desk as though to steady herself from the blow.

"It's not that she doesn't want to meet you," Will said quickly. "Juliet wanted me to return the chest to protect us and Yule."

"Protect us from what?" Mason walked through the door.

Will groaned internally. He'd thought his night couldn't get worse; now he had to make sure the leader of Yule didn't find out that they were at risk of exposure.

"Eloise called me when you arrived," Mason said before Will could ask why he was here. "Protect us from…?"

"From our own laws," he said carefully. "This might not be the right time, is all."

"I've already started the paperwork for the petition, as we discussed. What could've possibly changed so quickly? Has Juliet had a change of heart?"

"It's nothing like that." Will struggled not to tell his friend about the threat, but he didn't want to put any more weight on his shoulders.

"Juliet's case is important to Yule. It's the perfect example of how we need to evolve from the past and make allowances for those stuck in the crossfire of our strict laws," Mason argued. "I've already talked with the council about the Frost banishment, and they've no interest in lifting the familial ban."

"Even for Juliet?" Eloise asked, her words laced with defeat.

"No, but there is one way around the banishment. However, Juliet will have to drop the Frost name and take yours," Mason told her.

Will grimaced. "Juliet has a sister – Beth. I don't think she'd cut ties completely, even if she wanted to cut her dad out of her life." There was no way she'd give up Beth. Nor should she have to.

Mason shook his head. "She wouldn't have to cut off her sister. Changing her name and filing for citizenship as a legacy of the Heart family would be a show of good faith to the council." He turned to Eloise. "Do you think your family would be willing to accept her as a legacy? They would need to sign the paperwork for it to work."

Will couldn't believe he hadn't thought of the solution before. Then again, it involved the Heart family opening themselves up to gossip and the scars of the past.

"Yes. I'd considered it as an option if you were willing to agree, so I've already spoken with my sister and parents. It took some convincing, but it's understandable, considering they come from an older generation. They're happy to accept Juliet and leave the past behind, so long as everything is legal," Eloise said, looking between them excitedly. Will had never seen his superior so excited before. She looked like she'd lost ten years of stress. "But the decision is down to Juliet. If she wants to wait, then we can't force her."

Will hesitated, thinking it over. There was no way he could make this decision without her. "I'll talk it over with her. If she can still keep in contact with her sister, I don't think she'd have an issue with it, but I don't want to speak for her." He knew how much she hadn't wanted to hand over the chest, but she'd done so to protect Yule and those she'd come to care for. It made sense for someone with such a big heart to bear the name Heart.

"I should be the one to talk it over with her," Eloise interjected. "This all started with me."

"No, it's too risky." Will couldn't bring himself to lie to them any longer – not when Mason had done so much to help. "Frost is blackmailing Juliet into giving him the bell."

Mason ran his hands over his stubbled jaw. "Merry fucking Christmas to us."

"What Frost does shouldn't matter now. He only knew Juliet had the chest, and we've returned it. He has no proof that we broke the law," Will said, not wanting them to lose faith.

"We'll have to figure out another way to get the two of you to meet," Mason said. "I don't want Frost getting wind of this, and if he knows how the chest left the hall… I don't want to go against the council; I still need their support, now more than ever."

"It'll be handled with discretion," Eloise promised him.

"You've my word that we'll lay low for the rest of the season. I won't put you in a position where you have to pick between the council and our friendship," Will told him. He was itching to leave. The last thing they needed was to be overheard, and it felt like the walls themselves might be listening.

Mason let out a long sigh. "Good. I'll get started on the legacy paperwork and get it over to you as soon as I can, Eloise."

"Now that we're all in agreement, I need to get some sleep," she yawned. "The graduation ceremony for this year's guardians still needs organising. We have to continue on as normal."

Will nodded. Once Eloise had the legacy paperwork signed and sealed, Mason would just have to convince the council to approve it. It felt good to have a plan.

Thankfully, Juliet's bruised knuckles healed faster than her emotions over the next couple of days. This morning, she'd managed to FaceTime with Beth while Will went down to the breakfast buffet. They hadn't left the room since he'd returned from Yule, and now she knew the chest was safe, she was sleeping more soundly than she had since learning about it in the first place – that, or it was the multiple orgasms.

Either way, she'd woken up satisfied and ready to face whatever the rest of the season threw at her today. She opened the notes app on her phone, where she'd written everything that she'd learned about Yule to remind herself it was real, and not some festive fever dream. Looking over the details – the gold coins, magic luck-giving dust, and sleigh taxis – she had to admit it all sounded like the great start to a book.

The click of the key card made her close the app and put her phone back on the nightstand. She didn't want Will to know she was writing about Yule, even if it was for her own personal use. It still added to the risk of exposure.

"They were out of the apple Danish, so I went to the bakery next door. One mocha, one shot and extra cream," Will said, his words muffled by the paper bag hanging from his teeth as he balanced their coffees and breakfast. She'd have gone with him, but he'd left before she'd woken up. He was an early riser, and she most certainly wasn't – though she didn't mind being woken up by a hunky overprotective man with her favourite coffee, fruit, and pastries.

Still just in his T-shirt from the previous night, Juliet tossed back the duvet and climbed to the end of the bed, taking the bag from his teeth and the tray of coffees. He stared at her bare legs.

"Suddenly, I'm absolutely ravenous," he said, brushing her hair over her shoulder as she put their breakfast on the desk by the bed. The weight of his hands on her hips was even sweeter than the mocha he'd brought.

"I need food and a shower first." She turned around and rested her hands on his chest. He was insatiable, and even though she ached for him, she needed sustenance.

Will ran his hands from her hips to her waist, lifting the T-shirt so it grazed the top of her thighs. Juliet's heart pounded in her chest, and she wondered if the effect he had on her would ever wear off. Giving in, she closed her eyes, waiting for his kiss.

"I don't know what you're suggesting," he said, and her eyes snapped open as his hand left her skin and reached behind her for a pastry. She flushed with embarrassment, though his wink made her weak in the knees. She slid off the bed, taking her Danish and mocha with her to the bathroom to get ready in peace.

"Did you get through to Beth while I was out?" Will asked when she returned dressed in an oversized hoodie with a red-nosed reindeer she'd taken from his suitcase and some black sweats, since her yoga pants had proved too tempting for him.

"Yep, and before Gillian or Dad got to her. She's happy at

her friends', and I told her about the concert tickets, so at least I got to see her reaction on video chat."

"How did she react when you told her you weren't staying at the estate?"

She climbed back onto the bed. "She wasn't surprised – she isn't oblivious to what's going on. I said we were going to spend the rest of the holidays together so we could have some privacy. I'm not sure if she believed me, but it's the closest I could get to the truth without telling her about Yule and Dad's threats. She doesn't need to feel guilty about leaving, and I know she'll blame herself if she knows I fought with Gillian after she left. I don't even want to think about it. Beth is happy, and the chest is safe and out of my father's reach."

Will brought his lips to hers, kissing away her worries until she forgot her own name. "You've had a rough couple of days," he said, pulling away but staying close enough to play with the ends of her hair. "I thought we should do something to reignite your holiday spirit?"

"Just point in the holly jolly direction. So long as it's not another snowman contest. As fun as it was, I don't think my fingertips can take the cold." Lyla had promised she'd adapt to the weather of Yule, but now she wondered if she'd even get the chance to.

Will hadn't given her any updates after he'd returned from Yule, but she suspected he was waiting for the right moment. To be honest, she needed a break before facing the next challenge.

"No contests; this is just for us to enjoy." He pulled off his cable-knit sweater, and his white shirt rode up just enough to expose his flat stomach. Juliet was paying so much attention to his physique that she only caught the end of his sentence.

"A Christmas tree farm?" she asked, looking up at him.

"You didn't get a chance to go with Beth, and I don't have a tree at my place. I thought we could do it together." His excitement was adorable.

"Last year, Margot and I just went to a church parking lot and found the cheapest one we could get. She was only beginning to book clients, and my salary wasn't enough for anything fancy," Juliet said. It was one of her favourite memories. It had been her first Christmas without Nana Rose, so Margot had wanted to fill the gap as best she could.

"Yule's trees are sold by donation. The money goes to those who are struggling on the Outside during the holidays, but you only pay what you can," Will explained. Juliet loved the idea of the donations going to help people like her, who were adapting to a new world. "Just because you returned your chest, it doesn't mean you can't visit. For a bit."

A harsh rap on the door distracted them both. Juliet's heart stopped; what if her father had found her, or worse, found out that she no longer had the chest? Her paranoia was only dissolved by Margot calling her name. She let out a long exhalation and considered taking a break from caffeine for a while.

"Juliet! Open up! I have news – please tell me you aren't still in bed!" Margot yelled through the door.

Juliet shoved Will off the bed. He landed with a hard thud.

"What the fuck?" he cried, rubbing his elbow. She stifled a laugh as he stared at her in confusion.

"Hide in the bathroom!" She scrambled off the bed and made it as quickly as she could.

"Are you kidding? She knows about us! What's the point in hiding?" Will got to his feet, staring at her as though she'd lost all sense.

"Please! I don't want her to think we're *this* together,"

Juliet insisted, tossing the bag of clothes he'd brought back from Yule into his arms.

"'*This*'?" He copied her gesture pointing for her to him. "I think she knows we have sex!"

Juliet rolled her eyes, trying to shove all six feet of him towards the bathroom.

"Sex is one thing, but we've been staying together and – would you just move it? We don't have time to talk about this." She didn't want him to know that she'd told Margot about Yule, so keeping them apart was the best thing she could think to do. Also, Margot had warned her about getting too close to someone she might not be able to have a future with, and instead of listening to such wise advice she'd spent the last few days in bed with him, ordering room service and watching old sitcom reruns.

"Does this make me your dirty little secret? I don't know whether to be turned on or offended." He grinned as he backed up into the bathroom.

"You can think it over and decide while you're in there," Juliet said, closing the door on him. She checked the room and was satisfied that he'd left no trace behind. She should've been pleased, but a chill went down her spine as she realised how easy it was for him to disappear from her life.

"Sorry for popping in so early, I wasn't sure you'd be up yet." Margot scurried inside when the door was opened, beaming. "I only have a few minutes, but I couldn't leave without telling you."

"Telling me what?" Juliet's stomach dropped; she wasn't sure if she could handle any more sudden news.

"Harvey is taking me skiing," Margot squealed excitedly.

Juliet had never seen her friend so excited about participating in any sport. There had to be more to the story. "You don't know how to ski. And you hate the cold!" she pointed out, praying for anyone who was about to ski with Margot. Her coordination wasn't as good as her coding.

"I don't *need* to ski. Harvey said there's some gathering happening with loads of execs at a resort in Aspen. Since I've refused to work with him, he wants to introduce me to some new clients," Margot said, still smiling as if a hanger was stuck in her mouth.

"So, does this mean you are or aren't going to sleep with him?" Juliet probed. It seemed Harvey had found a loophole in her friend's rule.

"Technically, he's only helping me, so I wouldn't be breaking any of my rules." Margot fidgeted with her nails.

Juliet had to give Harvey props for his smart thinking. Still, she wondered why he was whisking her off now. Had Will put him up to this, to keep Margot out of the way for the rest of the season? Maybe he was afraid that Juliet would tell her about Yule – too late. Still, her getting out of the blast radius was probably a good idea if everything fell apart.

"How did things go with Will?" Margot asked more calmly. "Have you spoken about your dad and the—"

"It's fine!" Juliet cut her off, glancing at the bathroom door. "We talked; everything is cleared up. You should go and have fun."

"Are you sure you're okay? I don't want to leave if you need me." Margot's tone turned serious.

"I'm fine, and you can't give up this opportunity. I think Harvey might kidnap you if you refuse him. I saw the way he was looking at you at Alexandria – you've got him hooked."

Margot folded her arms. "We're friends. We're even staying in separate rooms at his cabin."

"But you'll be in the same cabin?" Juliet teased.

"Shut it." Margot stuck her tongue out at her. "He respects my space." She looked at the breakfast, which Juliet suddenly realised looked far too plentiful for just one person. "Are you going to spend the rest of the season with Will?"

Juliet shimmied to the edge of the bed to hide the tray. "I don't even know what the rest of the day looks like, never mind the next couple of weeks. I haven't even been able to think about starting the new editing job," she admitted. "I'm rambling – stop worrying about me and go! I don't want Harvey coming to get you."

"We won't be back for Christmas. What about presents?" Margot asked, giving her a tight squeeze.

"We can exchange gifts when you get back! Have fun and get out of here," Juliet ordered.

"I'm going," Margot laughed, before hesitating at the front door by the bathroom. She glanced at the grey sweats strewn over the couch. Juliet blushed, wondering how the hell she could've missed them, but Margot just grinned. "Thanks for taking care of Juliet," she called. "It's safe to come out now."

"My pleasure," Will answered through the bathroom door. "Don't make life too easy for Harvey – he's used to getting what he wants."

Margot chuckled, clearly needing no encouragement, and closed the door behind her.

Will emerged, a towel wrapped around his waist. "Speaking of my pleasure…" He backed Juliet up towards the bed. "I decided that I want to be your dirty secret, because right now, you're looking far too clean." His minty breath tickled her cheek, and her stomach flipped. She dropped onto the bed and he rested his hands on either side of her, pinning her to the mattress.

"I thought you were hungry. Breakfast will get cold," she argued, looking at the food. However, he was looking far more appetising.

"That can wait for a few hours," he said, trailing kisses

along her neck. "There's something else I want to taste." His hand slipped under her jumper, and all thought of food, jobs, and life disappeared.

"I thought—" Juliet struggled to find the words as he undid the knot securing her sweatpants and eased them down her thighs. "What about getting the Christmas tree?" she managed to ask, in between kisses that took her breath away.

"We've got all day. Right now, you're all I want to decorate."

Will

That evening, walking down Cane Lane, Will pulled at his collar, regretting that he'd left his coat at home before heading out to pick up dinner. He didn't have any food at home; he hadn't been expecting an impromptu Christmas tree shopping trip. But he'd wanted to give Juliet a day to remember before breaking the news about Mason and Eloise's legacy plan.

He planned on how to talk it through with her once he got home. He'd never expected, when Juliet's file had crossed his desk, that she'd be at his place one day putting as many ornaments on the tree as possible. When he'd left, Meet Me in St Louis was playing in the background and she was surrounded by the boxes of baubles he hadn't taken out of the attic for the past few years. Leaving her was the last thing he wanted, but he'd stepped out to deal with something urgent. Eloise had called to warn him that she had been confronted by Council members Frederick and Una after the guardians' graduation ceremony, having received information about a missing ancestral chest. Thankfully, the Frost chest was exactly where it was meant to be, but she'd wanted to give him a heads-up.

When he walked in the front door, the Christmas tree in the front room by the TV shone brightly.

"Tree looks great!" he called out, walking through to put the Chinese takeaway on the kitchen table. "I got a mix of everything, since I figured you'd be hungry after all the decorating. I was lucky to get in when I did – they're super busy before Christmas Eve. I did find one packet of mince pies left in the shop for dessert, though!"

When she didn't respond, he figured she might be upstairs. He put down the plates he'd taken from the cupboard, listening for movement in the house.

"Juliet?" he shouted up the stairs, but there were no lights on in the house except for the Christmas tree. He searched the house, and there was no sign of her. His heart raced as he considered where she could've gone. Had someone from the council called after he'd left? He slapped his hand against the banister. *She promised not to disappear again.*

She couldn't have gone far. He'd been with Eloise and the council members for about an hour to clear up the chest misunderstanding. In that tense moment, he'd thanked Juliet for her foresight. Even with the Christmas Eve deadline given by Mr Frost, it was likely her disappearing act had prompted her father to report their activities. Without evidence, they were in the clear. For now. Still, they'd come dangerously close to ending up on the Naughty List.

His eyes fell on the small silver dish on the mantlepiece where he'd left her bell. It was empty.

Not again. He sat on the couch by the tree and rested his head in his hands. She'd left her bag here, though, so she must plan on coming back. There were two options: she had either gone to see Lyla or Eloise; he didn't think there was anyone else she would go to right now. Reaching for the house phone, he considered calling Eloise, but as he went to dial, he stopped himself. *If she has gone to see her mum, this is their chance. I can give them some time.*

Instead, he typed in the Klauses' house number.

Juliet

"What the hell was I thinking?" Juliet paced outside a store with a large perfume bottle and several smaller versions scattered around. She hadn't meant to take the bell, but when she'd been decorating the mantle with gold tinsel, the glimmering orb had caught her eye. When the cursive name Frost shone up at her, she couldn't believe that Will had removed it from the chest before returning. Before she'd thought it through, she'd ended up on some random street in Yule. She blamed Judy Garland for making her wish she had a family like in the movie and sparking her desire to see her mom.

She tucked the bell into her pocket and wrapped her arms around herself. She had been expecting to find her mom, but like that day in the library, clearly the bell had a mind of its own. Thankfully, Will had given her one of his oversized fleeces before they'd gone tree shopping so she'd be extra toasty. The cold still nipped at her nose, but it bought her some time. She hadn't got the chance to grab a coat before the bell took her to Rudolph knew where.

A couple of people stumbled out of a crowded pub; the laughter and music was comforting. Juliet considered going inside for a hot chocolate or whiskey to warm up. And, more importantly, to ask if they had the number for Eloise. She opened the door, only to spot Mrs Klaus and a woman in a wheelchair she hadn't met. Juliet guessed she must be Lou, from what Lyla had told her about Mason's elder sister. Now wasn't the right time to run into them, and Juliet turned sharply, not wanting to be caught.

Sneaking away, she made it back to the perfume shop and tried to pick a direction. She didn't get the chance before a woman slammed into her, dropping an armful of wrapped presents.

"I'm sorry, I wasn't paying attention," Juliet exclaimed, crouching in the snow to help her collect the presents before the green and gold wrapping paper was ruined.

"No, please don't apologise. I was the one who crashed into you. I've been running around trying to get some last-minute shopping done before the stores close. I stacked them so high I couldn't see where I was going." The dark-haired woman laughed, taking the presents from Juliet.

With all the presents collected, Juliet dusted the snow from her knees. Face to face, she recognised the woman from the Hall of Guardians, except her dark hair wasn't pulled back so severely. Instead of the deep red pant suit, she looked far more approachable in an oversized cream woolly hat and long puffy pink coat.

"We've met before." The woman smiled, getting there first. Juliet wasn't sure if it was an excited or nervous smile. "You were at the Hall of Guardians the other day. Seems we're destined to run into each other."

There was something in her eyes that Juliet thought she recognised, but she was too embarrassed that she'd nearly toppled the woman twice in one month to focus on it.

"Did you find the boarder were looking for? No one

mentioned having a visitor. But many come and go over the season, so you might have missed them."

"Right, they probably went somewhere for the holidays," Juliet said quickly, breathing into her hands. The cold starting to set into her bones.

The woman's eyes narrowed. "You should really have a coat on. I don't live far – just one street over behind the perfume shop," she said. "You can borrow one of mine."

Juliet hesitated. "I should get back. Is there a sleigh rank around here?" She didn't trust the bell to return her back to Will's, since this was the second time it had sent her on a wild goose chase.

"The night before Christmas Eve? You'll be waiting a while. I could call you one from mine and you can wait out of the snow?" the woman offered, balancing the presents and the bag on her shoulder. Juliet's teeth started to chatter, so she didn't argue. She didn't want to return to Will's a popsicle.

"You can have a seat anywhere, I'll just pop the kettle on and call you a sleigh," the woman said, taking off her coat and hanging it on a hook by the front door. Juliet admired the blush pink couch and bright floral wallpaper.

"I'm sorry to impose. I hope I'm not interrupting your plans," she said. The warmth of the house was greatly appreciated.

"Please don't be silly. I don't think my arms could handle another parcel. I was getting some of my students a few stocking fillers. Some don't go home for the holidays, so I like them to have something on Christmas morning. Thankfully, I ran into you, which stopped me from getting carried away," the woman answered, heading down the corridor to the kitchen. Juliet figured she must be a guardian instructor. *Wait, she must know my mom! Maybe she can tell me where she lives.*

"I'm Juliet, by the way," she called out, looking around the small, cosy sitting room. The tree by the frosted front window was decorated with various shades of pink and rose gold baubles. On the wall above the fireplace were beautiful antique picture frames.

"Is this your daughter?" She picked up one of the frames on the mantle, only for her hand to tremble as she got a better look at the little girl with pigtails. Her mouth went dry as she recognised the pink Barbie birthday cake from her sixth birthday Diana had made for her. She dropped the frame, and the glass cracked over her young, toothy smile.

"Are you alright?"

Juliet heard footsteps nearing and knelt to pick up the photo, unable to even find the words to apologise.

"Leave it! I don't want you to cut yourself," the woman fretted, gently taking the frame from her hands and setting it down on the mantle. She examined Juliet's hand, frowning as she noticed the yellow bruising.

"I punched someone," Juliet found herself saying. "But they deserved it."

The woman looked proud. Juliet took her hand back and stared, recognising herself. The bone structure, her round eyes, and the same shade of pink lips. She couldn't believe she hadn't seen it the first time.

"You're Eloise?" she stammered. "You're my mom?" Her dark hair, despite being flecked with grey, had the same honey highlights as her own. There was no mistaking the resemblance.

"Please don't be angry. I knew it was you when we bumped into each other the first time." Eloise's brows pulled together; the fear in her eyes confirmed Juliet was right. "I didn't know what to say, and I didn't want you to run off. You didn't have a coat on. Not that it's my place to tell you what to do, or how to dress. What am I saying? Yes, I'm your mum. I'm sorry, I didn't want this to go this way." She looked to the mantelpiece. "The pictures… I didn't think. I'm so used to seeing them every day, and I never thought you'd come here. I mean, not never, but once we'd met properly." She covered her face with her hands.

"Now I know where I get my nervous rambling from." Juliet said, giving her a break.

Eloise's expression softened. "I've made a right mess of this. I understand if you want to leave, but please let me get you a coat first."

Silence fell between them, and Juliet tried to digest the situation.

"I was trying to find you. The bell brought me to the perfume shop… I thought it had led me wrong, but you were inside shopping," she said slowly, realising it had brought her to exactly where she needed to be. "I can stay, if you want me to?" The words left her before she thought too much. "I mean, it's the reason why I'm here, why you gave me the chest?"

"Of course I want you to stay!" Eloise pulled her into a tight hug, and Juliet froze, unsure of how to react. Sensing her discomfort, Eloise released her sheepishly. "Sorry."

As odd as it was for Juliet, she couldn't imagine how nervous her mom was after waiting to meet her for so long. Suddenly, she worried that she wouldn't live up to the idea of the daughter her mom had been wishing for all these years.

"What do we do now?" She fidgeted. There was so much to say, and yet she couldn't think of anything.

"I can make us some coffee. We can talk, or watch a movie? Mochas are my favourite, and I'd have chocolate with every meal if I could. Training the new guardians keeps me fit and healthy," Eloise rambled, again.

Juliet didn't know whether to laugh or cry as she saw so much of herself in her mom. She could listen to her all night.

"Your grandmother, Rose, told me you like Miracle on 34th Street? I think I only have the tape, but I can find it." Eloise made for the old box TV, and Juliet didn't know what came over her, but she wrapped her arms around her mother.

Immediately, she began to pull away, not wanting to over-whelm her. Before she could, Eloise engulfed her in an all-encompassing hug. Tears slipped down her cheeks. *Home.*

"I'm so sorry, my darling." Eloise's tearful words broke through any anger or hurt Juliet had held on to for so long. "I'm so sorry. Please forgive me."

Juliet wanted to put a wall between them, make Eloise earn the right to be close to her, but she couldn't. Not when she could hear and feel all the love pouring out of her heart. A love she'd never felt from her father.

"You're so beautiful. You look like my mother; she'll be so happy to see that someone in the family shares the dimple in her chin." Eloise released Juliet, but held her face tenderly. "I'm so proud of you – of how you've handled everything with such grace. I couldn't believe it when you gave the chest back. Those letters belong to you, and you had every right to keep them. I'm so sorry for putting you in this position; I wish there had been a better way. But I have to say that I've never regretted you or trying to have you in my life for a second. I only regret that I couldn't have been there for you every step of the way."

Hearing that she wasn't a mistake was the only thing that mattered. Juliet swallowed the wave of emotions.

"Giving up the chest was the right thing to do," she said firmly. "I didn't want you or Will to get in trouble. You're far more important to me than a magical bell and some letters. Will told me you know about Dad's threats to reveal what you'd done, and I didn't want to bring you or your family any more hurt."

"That should be the last thing on your mind. None of this should have landed on your shoulders," her mom assured her.

"Still, I wanted to protect you. And not only you – the Klaus family have been so kind to me, and I didn't want to involve them in our mess."

"A mess is an understatement," Eloise agreed, taking her hands. "But you're here now, and that's all that matters."

Juliet nodded. "I don't know how long I'll be able to stay, though. I'm worried about Dad—"

"You don't have to worry." Eloise sat her down on the couch. "As much as I don't want to believe that your dad would go so far, that he would try and keep you from me, once the council sign off on your legacy petition then he can't do anything to stop you or us from being in each other's lives."

Even after so many years and so much hurt, there was still a trace of love in her mom's eyes for her dad. It broke Juliet's heart to realise Eloise still had some faith in him.

"The heartbreak killed him, or at least the person you knew," she said, recalling her father's last pleading letter to the woman he loved.

Eloise sighed. "I can't say he was the only one. I loved him with everything I had, but losing you nearly killed me. When I received his letter about being together, I wanted to give in, but we literally came from two different worlds. I worried that over time we would start to resent each other for all we'd given up. I was sure Reginald would never truly leave us in peace; your father was his world. I was young, scared, naïve, and I'd been raised to follow the rules, and when a deal was struck, I did as I was told by those I thought knew best. I don't even want to think about the time we've lost."

"What if Dad reports us when he doesn't get the bell tomorrow night?"

"My family is happy to accept you as a legacy, even if your dad tries to intervene. Once the paperwork is complete, it won't matter. I don't know if Will has mentioned it to you yet, but there's one way the council is most likely to accept your petition. I don't know how you'd feel about it, and it's quite a big change. But I wondered… if you'd consider changing your name from Frost to Heart." Juliet could hear the excitement and nerves threaded in her mom's words.

The thought of being able to stay in Yule, of seeing her mom and Will without the fear of being discovered, without feeling like a criminal, was too good to be true. "But I'm still a Frost."

"By blood, yes. However, the council won't lift the ban on the Frost family, nor you, so long as you bear the name." Getting up off the couch, Eloise went to a small antique writing desk with the same red envelopes Juliet remembered from the chest. "That being said…" Eloise handed her a thick piece of cream paper, similar to the birth certificate she'd seen in her father's study.

"Legacy Citizen of Yule. Juliet Heart," she read aloud, and ran her fingers over the last name. "I don't understand."

"When a legacy wishes to return from the Outside, and they haven't lived in Yule before, they're given a legacy certificate as a way of saying this is their home, and they're gifted their own bell. In your case, if you accept your birthright as a Heart then you can stay in Yule – you can come and go as you please. It'll be your home whenever you need or want it, without question or fear."

"All I have to do is change my name? And sign this piece of paper? Does this mean I can't see any Frosts?" Juliet asked. Her first thought was of Beth. Giving up her sister would be impossible.

Eloise took her hand. "Will mentioned your sister Beth. You can absolutely still have her in your life. As to whether she'll ever be able to come to Yule or even know about it, I don't know. Even issuing you this new certificate is a grey area. My family have signed to say that you are under the guardianship of the Hearts to show the council that they're standing with you."

Juliet saw the hope in her mom's eyes. She stared at the certificate and saw where she had to sign under a long line of Hearts. A whole family waiting for her. One signature, and she'd no longer be a Frost. She'd no longer have to bear the name of those who resented her.

Still, to change it felt like stripping herself of the only identity she'd ever known. To separate herself from her sister and even her grandmother. Yet she knew that they would want her to be happy. To find her home.

"Please don't feel any pressure." Eloise read the uncertainty in her silence. "This is a big decision, and we're asking a lot of you. We've only just met, and I'm asking you to give up your name and to accept a new family of people you've never met. I'm sure you've got mixed feelings, given the past. I'll be the first to admit that my family weren't supportive of your father or my relationship. However, don't for one second think they wanted you to be punished for our choices."

It eased Juliet's mind to know that her extended family wanted to meet her, regardless of the past. They were doing the right thing now. "If I sign, no one will get in trouble? Will and the Klaus family won't be in trouble because of us?"

"My sweet girl, no. But if you decide to become a part of Yule, I want you to want it for yourself, and not just because you're worried about others," Eloise said.

"I want to stay, or at least to have the freedom to come and go without having to worry. It's just a big step, and as hard as my relationship has been with my family, to just let it go…" Juliet wondered if she was clinging to the enemy she knew, rather than risk her heart with a bunch of strangers. But Lyla, Will, and even Mason, who'd risked his own reputation and broken his own laws to help a stranger, told her that as terrifying as it might be, Yule could be her second home. A new chapter.

She stared into the familiar brown eyes of the mother she'd never known. She only had one question.

"Do you have a pen?"

Eloise's hand shot to her mouth as though she couldn't believe it. "A pen, yes. I've got a pen. One second – are you sure? Do you not want some time? Please don't feel any pressure."

"I don't want to dwell on the past any longer. I want us to start anew, and I want to be able to call your home my home. Given all the kindness I've witnessed, and the magic of it all, I don't think I could say goodbye to it or…"

"To Will," Eloise finished for her.

Juliet nodded. "You know about us? You aren't upset that we broke the rules?"

Eloise shook her head. "Mrs Klaus told me after she gave you my letter. She was worried about you and Will. As much as I don't want to share you so soon, he has a kind and loyal heart. I couldn't be happier that you found each other."

"I think he found me is more accurate," Juliet pointed out with a smile.

Her mom flushed. "Sorry about that. I never expected when I sent him to look for you that you'd end up together. Who was I kidding? I should've guessed, considering my own past. Like mother like daughter."

The phrase was music to her ears. This was going to take some getting used to.

"Do you have someone?" Juliet asked, though there was no trace of anyone else in the house. She hoped her mom hadn't been alone all these years.

"I did." Eloise patted her hand, and the happiness in her voice was tinged with sorrow. "I was married for a time, but he passed away some years ago. The trainees at the hall have always been my children. Trust me, they keep me busy, so I don't have time to be lonely. After my husband passed, I felt how short life was and I didn't want to wait another day or spend another season without you. I wish I could've come to you sooner, but I'm ashamed to say that I was terrified of being rejected. It was easier to think of you as a possibility than not be able to live up to the idea of the mother you deserve."

Juliet understood her hesitation. To live up to an idea was impossible. However, she hoped in time that they would learn to love each other as they were.

"To be honest, if you'd turned up on the doorstep talking about magic bells and told me that Santa Klaus was real? I probably would've called the cops," Juliet chuckled, resting her hand over her mom's.

"Enough tears," Eloise said, tipping her head back. "Now, I'll make the drinks and find that tape. We are celebrating." She rose from the couch, leaving Juliet with the certificate.

She looked again at her new name. Of all the emotions swirling inside, she'd never expected such relief to settle in her heart.

Christmas Eve Morning

The smell of coffee woke Juliet up. For a moment, she didn't know where the hell she was, until she recalled all that had happened the night before. *I must've fallen asleep while we were watching the movie.* She pulled the cream blanket off her legs and went to the bathroom to wash up.

She nearly knocked over a tower of books as she opened the bathroom door and winced as one landed on the wooden floor, not wanting to wake up her mom. It seemed both her parents had a love of books.

Abruptly, the kitchen door opened and Eloise, wearing yellow rollers in her hair, popped her head through. "You're up! I just finished brewing a pot of coffee."

"I should call Will. I meant to before I fell asleep," Juliet said, knowing how worried he'd be. Still, she was surprised he hadn't turned up last night. He had to have known where she'd gone.

"Don't worry, I already got through to him." The smell of pastries drifted down the hall. Juliet's stomach rumbled, reminding her she hadn't had dinner last night. "Wash up and come eat. I left some stuff for you in the cupboard under the sink. There's a spare toothbrush, and I hung one of my old wrap dresses on the door with some tights that should fit you. All the woman in the Frost family were blessed with wide hips, so I didn't think my jeans would fit. But I could get a pair for you to try," Eloise said excitedly, already heading for the stairs.

"The dress is fine! Thank you," Juliet said, trying to disperse the nervous energy.

Eloise halted. "Alright. I'll pop upstairs and finish getting ready. You take your time down here."

JULIET, dressed in her mom's floral wrap dress, sipped her sweetened coffee. Having breakfast here felt all too surreal. She wasn't sure if her mom was nervous, but she kept looking to the kitchen door as though she was waiting for something.

Juliet was reaching for another croissant when the doorbell rang.

"That must be Will," Eloise said, getting up from the round table.

Juliet waited for a moment in the kitchen, but the sound of multiple voices told her Will wasn't alone. She put her candy-cane-printed napkin on the table and went to the front door. Over her mom's shoulder, she saw a man and woman in what she estimated to be their late forties, and standing behind them, Will.

"Juliet Frost, you need to come with us," requested the man. From their stony expressions, saying no wasn't an option.

"Juliet, please, come with me," Will echoed, and the pair

separated to let him through. Her brows pulled together at his neutral expression. This wasn't the Will she knew.

"I don't understand. Can we talk first?" Juliet inched closer to Will, wanting to tell him she'd signed the paperwork.

However, his cool expression didn't waver. "The Klaus is waiting with the council at the town hall. All will be explained soon."

His flat tone felt wrong. It was the first time she felt that Yule could be the opposite of how she'd been treated thus far. Juliet looked at her mom, who stared at the two escorts with Will as though she wasn't all that surprised to see them.

"I'm going with her," she said, already grabbing their coats. "Put this on."

"That would be best." Will nodded, gesturing for them both to leave the house.

The two suits walked ahead with Eloise, and she could hear them talking in hushed animated tones, but she couldn't make out what they were saying. Will remained at Juliet's side, silent and distant. She reached for his hand, but he shook his head. *What the hell is going on?*

"Can you tell me what's going on? Did the council find out? Are we in trouble? Did my dad report us?" She pulled the thick collar of her coat tight around her neck as she followed him through the town square.

"You'll find out when we get to the town hall. Maybe you should've thought before you used the Frost bell and left without a word."

He was pissed, no denying it, and she couldn't blame him. She'd been so wrapped up in her reunion with Eloise, she'd never thought to call Will and tell him she was okay, and safe. Her heart sank as she realised how worried he must have been, especially when she'd promised him last time that she wouldn't run off again. She broken her promise the first chance she'd got.

She reached into her pocket and slipped the bell into his hand, not wanting to be caught with it. "I'm so sorry, but I didn't know if I'd ever get the chance again. I didn't mean to worry you; I just got so caught up. I didn't plan this."

Will simply put the bell in his pocket and stared straight ahead.

"I feel like we're being arrested," Juliet muttered as her mom fell back to them.

"Don't worry, I brought the papers with me. We're in this together," Eloise assured her, taking her hand. The gesture felt foreign, but right now she really needed the support. She knew she'd been wrong to take the bell, but surely Will had known that she'd go to her mom's house?

In the early morning, the town was eerily quiet, doing nothing to quell the anxiety twisting her stomach. She wished Will would forgive her, just until they got through whatever the hell this was, but she wouldn't apologise for one of the best nights of her life. Meeting her mom and realising how much she'd always loved Juliet, if even at a distance, after all these years was worth any punishment.

The two escorts halted at the top of the stone steps on either side of tall double doors to the town hall. Waiting for them to open the doors, Juliet clutched her mom's hand, readying herself for whatever she was about to face.

It was the smell that greeted her first. As she focused on the high ceiling and the gathering of people inside, her breath was taken away by the breakfast feast to rival any she'd ever seen on the long table at the centre of the hall.

"WELCOME TO YULE!" The deafening cheer of those in the room made her tear up. Then she saw the banner hanging around the wooden beams.

Welcome home Juliet!

"I told you I'd punish you if you ran off again," Will whispered in her ear, and kissed her cheek.

Juliet glared at him, then swatted him playfully. "I can't believe you did this!" She took a long, deep breath as she realised there was no inquisition or firing squad waiting for her.

"I'm sorry to give you such a shock! I knew they were planning a welcome home breakfast when I called my family to let them know you'd signed the papers, but I didn't know they were going to stop by. They can have a funny sense of humour," Eloise apologised, looking at their escorts, who were looking rather sheepish.

"Sorry, Juliet, we just couldn't wait to meet you. I'm your aunt Debbie, and this is my husband Stuart, we are so happy you're here." Debbie engulfed Juliet in a hug.

"Thank you. It's nice to meet you," Juliet answered, not knowing what else to say as Debbie stared at her like she was some Christmas miracle.

"No need to thank us – we're family." Stuart clapped her on the shoulder.

"I know a surprise party is a little overwhelming, but word spread fast and everyone in the Heart family wanted to meet you, as well as the council members," Will whispered as the others left to join the table. The room clapped as they made their way to the head of the table. Juliet swallowed her nerves, wondering if they'd be so happy to welcome her if they knew what they'd all been up to for the past month. Others greeted Eloise with big hugs, and she guessed they were more of her mom's family. *My family now.*

"You'll catch flies if you don't close your mouth," Will teased, pulling the chair out for her.

"I'm just trying to take it all in. I can't believe you let me think I was in trouble! You frightened the life out of me!"

"Eloise called her family to tell them you'd signed the papers, and we all wanted to do something to welcome you. We thought breakfast would be a good start, and she was going to bring you over herself. She didn't know we'd turn up, but she played along. I figured, given how intimidating they can be in their guardian uniforms, that they'd make the perfect cover for our surprise."

As if they could sense her watching, the couple smiled and waved at Juliet. She waved back shyly, trying to take it all in. She wasn't used to people being so happy to see her.

Mason sat at the head of the long table, which was long enough to fit at least fifty people. There were a few faces she recognised – Lyla and Mrs Klaus included – but most were new. Will took out a chair for her to sit beside Lyla, opposite Eloise and her sister.

"Did you know about this? Why didn't you tell me?" she whispered to Lyla.

"I wasn't going to ruin the surprise!" Lyla said. "Besides, this was all rather rushed, so I didn't have a chance. I didn't know they were going to send guardians to frighten you." She beamed, eager to explain.

"How was this even pulled together so quickly?" Juliet felt a little embarrassed they'd all gone to so much trouble for her.

"Mason and Will called an emergency meeting last night with the council when you were at your mum's. Once your mum got your signature, we had what we needed to make your citizenship official. This morning, there wasn't much to arrange; since the council members and heads of departments and their families, and the Klaus family, always gather on the morning of Christmas eve, we only needed you to make it the perfect welcome party. It's tradition for them to celebrate another successful preparation of the season. It also allows everyone to gather and take a breath before tonight's madness."

Juliet was relieved this hadn't all been done for her; it took some of the pressure off. Still, the welcome made her emotional.

"You weren't in trouble. Will wanted to play a little joke on you, and the Klauses love a good prank, but I'm sorry they scared you," Lyla was saying when the clinking of glasses interrupted them.

Mason rose from his seat, and the hall drifted into silence. Juliet saw for herself the power he held, and she wasn't surprised he'd been able to get her citizenship approved so last-minute. She guessed the rush was to prevent her dad from having any chance to make some trouble. She relaxed into her chair, grateful for his and everyone at the table's support. There was no other way she wanted to spend the holidays.

"I want to thank you all for coming this morning," Mason said. "Another year of bringing hope to the world wouldn't be possible without everyone at this table, and this town. This is only my second year in my father's seat, and I want to thank you all for your trust and wisdom. I won't prattle on for too long, because I'm sure you all want to tuck into this fantastic breakfast. As you might have noticed, we have a new addition to our Yule family. I hope everyone will raise a glass and help me welcome Juliet Heart to the table. This season is all about bringing people together, and I'm delighted that she has found her way home."

Hearing the last name Heart instead of Frost felt like a new skin that would take some time to get used to. But as everyone toasted her, Juliet couldn't help but feel like she was at home. Will handed her his napkin for her teary eyes and placed a steadying hand on her thigh.

"I thought this might be too much, but Mason really wanted to give you a big welcome. I think he's trying to make up for Lyla's welcome, which wasn't so pretty. We can go if this is too much," he said thoughtfully.

Juliet shook her head. "I can't believe you arranged all this for me." She wanted to squeeze the life out of him, in a good way. Maybe not in public, though.

"You shouldn't have to hide, not when Yule is your home." As he looked to Eloise talking with her sister, he added, kissing her hair, "This is your family now."

"To Juliet!" Mason concluded, bringing their attention back to the table.

There was a loud cheer, and Eloise winked at her before everyone clinked the champagne flutes filled with orange juice. "Welcome home," she said across the table.

That did it. "I'm such a blubbering mess," Juliet croaked. Thankfully, the rest of the guests were too busy digging into their breakfast to pay her any mind.

Will kissed away the tears. "It's a lot to take in, and just wait until the rest of the village hears there's a new legacy in town. You'll be drowned in baked goods, knitwear, and suitors."

"I can't get enough layers," she said, thinking she'd never adapt to the cold. "Dessert? Say no more. Suitors... hmm. Might be good to have options." She sipped her juice.

In revenge, Will's hand drifted to her upper thigh, and she squirmed, not wanting Lyla to see what he was doing.

"Fine. I'll just have to tell them that the position of suitor has been filled," she conceded, putting down her glass.

Will pulled her chair closer to him. "I'd prefer to show them." He planted a kiss on her lips, and she giggled like a lovesick teenager as she tasted orange juice on his lips. They were interrupted by the sound of hoots at the public display of affection. She felt herself redden.

In spite of the embarrassment, everything felt perfect. The only weight on Juliet's heart was that her Nana Rose, the woman who'd kept her connection to her mother alive all these years, couldn't be here to see how much love and trust she'd been greeted with. Nana had always tried to make her feel like she had a home and a family, and even after passing she made that wish a reality.

"Thank you for everything," she said, resting her head on Will's shoulder.

"You never need to thank me. I was yours the moment I walked into that bar. The moment your eyes met mine, I knew I'd break every rule and tradition to bring you home," he told her, and the weight of his words captured her heart.

She took his hand from her thigh and threaded her fingers through his. "You've got me here now, and I'm not going anywhere."

Christmas Day

Juliet spent Christmas morning with Lyla and Mrs Klaus, preparing dinner and eating one too many mince pies. She'd spent the day before with Eloise and the rest of the Heart family while Will had some time with his own, but Mrs Klaus had been quick to call dibs on Christmas Day. Juliet didn't want to admit it, but she needed a little break from her new family to adjust. As kind as they were, it took an emotional toll to meet everyone, and the Klaus family with Will and Lyla provided the perfect buffer for her tender emotions. They'd agreed to spend New Year's Eve with both the Hearts and Duncans and have one big party. It was still early in their relationship for meeting the parents, but given everything they'd been through, a party felt like a good way to break the ice.

Mason finally got up from the couch, having fallen asleep after his long trip around the world, with some not-so-subtle nudging from Kevin. Eloise and Will were the last to arrive at the table, since they'd been attending the graduation party for this year's guardians.

Juliet hadn't thought it was possible for so much to happen in one day; she'd even managed to get some

Christmas shopping done, with the help of Lyla and a loan of some gold coins. She still hadn't quite figured out how their currency worked, but all she cared about was having a little something for everyone who'd helped her come home. They'd shown a stranger such trust and kindness that she wanted to repay them in some small way.

While they ate, she listened intently to some embarrassing stories about Will, courtesy of Mason and her mom. There were no veiled threats or constant reminders of how she should take care to restrict her calories in January. Instead, extra helpings were added to her plate, and no one batted an eyelid when she reached for a big scoop of cream to top the spiced pudding Lyla had only burnt a little.

Juliet wasn't sure she'd be able to stand once the dishes were cleared, but fortunately the men tidied up the kitchen, since the women had cooked. As the evening wore on, she found herself missing Diana and Victor, and couldn't help but wonder if they missed her. She'd picked up a special bottle of brandy for Victor and a set of new knives for Diana for when she got back. If she'd never received the chest, right now she would be in the manor, hiding in the library away from the annual Frost Christmas party. Instead she was sitting by a glorious fire pit, wrapped in a snuggly blanket, staring up at the stars. Some fresh air was mandatory after such a feast.

Popping inside to grab an extra layer, she found Lyla taking out some small plates from the cupboard.

"Please let me help," Juliet said, taking some out of her hands.

"Thank you," Lyla said, removing the coverings from two baking trays. "I'll bring the brownies and ice cream, since Kevin and Mason will wolf down the mince pies in minutes."

They hadn't had a chance to talk properly yet, and the

night was disappearing fast, so Juliet jumped at the chance while the others were outside. "I wanted to say thank you for being the first person in Yule to welcome me, and for supporting me unwaveringly along the way."

"You don't have to thank me! I'm so happy that you got to find your way home. There's so much for you to discovery and explore. Also, it's nice having another newbie around. Lou, Mason's sister, has really helped me settle in. You'll meet her at the wedding. She'll be devastated to have missed all the drama," Lyla said enthusiastically.

It was the perfect end to an emotional day. Juliet didn't know whether to cry or laugh; her heart was a twist of relief, joy, and uncertainty. As she peeked out the glass door, she watched the family huddled in their blankets around the fire with their marshmallows, bickering about whether Die Hard was a Christmas movie. It all felt so surreal, in a good way.

In the kitchen, Eloise was helping Mrs Klaus dish out the mince pies while trying to keep Jones, Lyla's cat, from having a taste of the brandy whipped cream.

"I don't think I could eat another thing for the next week," Juliet confessed. "It was touch and go whether I could even get up from the table!"

"The feasts are never-ending; you should see how they celebrate Easter. I couldn't look at chocolate for a month afterwards," Lyla said.

"What are you scheming about in here? I hope next year you can all stay on the Nice List," Mason said, leaning over his fiancée's shoulder and stealing two brownies from the tray. He passed one to Will, who was behind him.

"We would never scheme! We were getting more treats for you beasts." Lyla slapped his hand away as he went back for another brownie. Mason kissed her shoulder, and she gave in and let him take it. Juliet chewed her smile, watching the smitten couple.

"You aren't the one I'm worried about." Mason nodded to Will.

"What are you accusing me of now, Klaus?" Will sighed, handing Juliet the napkins.

"He was reminding us to stay on the Nice list?" Juliet frowned, looking between them.

"We can't make any promises." Will hugged her close to him.

"It's not like a naughty or nice list actually exists, though, right?" Juliet said, looking to Will to confirm it. Lyla's sudden laughter and Mason nudging her to silence confirmed that she was very much wrong in her assumption.

"Pretend I didn't ask!" Juliet held her hands up, having had enough surprises for one season. Mason and Will took the desserts, and Juliet doubted there would be any left by the time they made it outside.

Lyla shrugged and grabbed a pitcher of eggnog. "Don't worry, you can be as naughty as you like. You already escaped having your memory wiped once, and you have us to support you."

"I'd have hated to forget all this," Juliet said as they carried everything outside. "The Klaus family made me feel like I'd found a new home. Now I can't even remember how it felt not to know them. Which reminds me – I heard a rumour that Mason kidnapped you and brought you here…?" She was desperate to know the full story.

"You were speaking to Kevin." Lyla rolled her eyes. "Technically, he blackmailed me into pretending to be his fiancée. It's not as bad as it sounds, and it all worked out in the end. Kevin likes to be dramatic."

"And I thought Will stalking me was a red flag," Juliet chuckled.

"I think Yule men just like to act like cavemen." Lyla smirked.

"Not that we're complaining," Juliet quipped, and Lyla nearly choked.

"I'll cheers to that." They broke into whiskey-induced giggles.

"Mason, I think you're right. They seem to be in cahoots with each other," Will said as they reached the fire pit.

Juliet sat down, snuggling under his arm for comfort, and Lyla did the same with Mason on the opposite side of the cushioned snow bench.

"We're merely discussing how lucky we feel to be here." Juliet winked at Lyla.

"Safe to say I speak for both of us when I say *we* are the lucky ones." Will kissed the side of her head.

Under the stars, Juliet glanced at her mom, sitting with Mrs Klaus. She'd never felt more blessed. With the man she was falling in love with, new friends, a warm fire, and a full tummy, she couldn't have asked for a better Christmas present.

Acknowledgements

Thank you so much for taking another trip to Yule! I have to start by saying I never expected my little Village of Yule to be so beloved by you. My dear friend and fabulous editor, Emma deserves an award for the work she does helping shape these stories. Writing and publishing wouldn't be half as fun without her. Readers, you have my heart and soul and always will. Thank you so much for all the love and encouragement you've shown Juliet and Will. I wouldn't be able to do what I love without the love you give my stories. Every share, comment, review, fabulous video or photo brightens my world. Thank you for letting me live my dream! I hope you have a fabulous festive season.

The Naughty or Nice Clause

VILLAGE OF YULE

KATE CALLAGHAN

When Lyla's father retired as CEO of the toy company which has been in their family for generations, she was meant to receive his shares. Instead, she discovers the company is bankrupt and her father has given her shares to Mason Klaus, an investor known in the corporate world for his cold and callous nature. Much to Lyla's frustration, her only option is to run the company with him, despite their evident loathing for one another.

When Mason cancels the annual Christmas party, Lyla throws it anyway – only for the event of the season to result in a terrible fire. With the offices and Lyla's credibility ruined, Mason offers her a deal: he'll forget her part in the disaster, but she must join his family for the twelve days of their Christmas holidays.

Taken to a fantastical winter wonderland, Lyla hopes that she might discover some of the secrets Mr Klaus is hiding, and maybe even a way to get her company back. However, when Mason introduces her to the secret village as his fiancée, she is horrified to realise she has no choice but to go along with the pretence – because the cost of bringing an outsider to their magical land is far too high.

Can Lyla resist the devilishly handsome Mr Klaus and the enchanting village to win back her company, or will she give into temptation?

Read Me

KATE CALLAGHAN

A VILLAGE OF YULE NOVELLA

SNOW, MISTLETOE, AND MIDNIGHT KISSES AWAIT...

Mia Mulrooney has everything she could ever want: her thriving bakery, her cosy village, and a peaceful life free of August, the brooding guitarist who ghosted her two years ago on New Year's Eve.

But August is back in town for a New Year's wedding, and a fierce snowstorm traps them together for the weekend in Yule's oldest castle. As the storm rages outside, their undeniable chemistry ignites. Amid stolen kisses beneath twinkling mistletoe and whispered confessions in the dead of night, Mia's frozen heart begins to thaw. Yet, as midnight approaches, she must confront her feelings: can she forgive him and find the courage to let love back into her life?

Join The Mailing List

Receive your **FREE** copy of Autumn and Elijah's story, Ms Perfectly Fine, by joining my mailing list.

If you love:

Grumpy (her) x Sunshine (him)

He falls first (and harder)

Hates Everyone But You

Forced Proximity

Slow-burn Enemies to Lovers

Romance with Suspense

Healing & Chronic Pain Rep

Be The First To Hear About:
- Advanced Release Copies
- Cover Reveals
- Teasers & More

About the Author

Kate Callaghan is an Irish author who writes adult fantasy, romantic suspense, and feel-good Christmas romance. She's the creator of the Hellish Fairytale series, blending dark magic and intrigue, as well as festive romcoms like The Naughty or Nice Clause. Whether she's spinning tales of dangerous love or cosy holiday magic, you'll find her in a Dublin café with an iced coffee, plotting her next twist.

www.katecallaghanauthor.com

instagram.com/katecallaghanwriter
bookbub.com/profile/kate-callaghan
tiktok.com/@katecallaghanwriter

www.ingramcontent.com/pod-product-compliance
Lightning Source LLC
Chambersburg PA
CBHW051239210726
48287CB00002B/314